WITHIN

J.M.
WALKER

ISBN: 9798564919500

From Within

Updated in 2020

DEDICATION

For everyone that got their second chance, this story is for you.

AUTHOR NOTE:

I wrote this book just over five years ago and what a journey it has been ever since!
This book was my very first attempt at a dark romance and while it does have some sweeter scenes, it is quite intense. I've only re-read this book a handful of times but each and every time, it hurts. It hurts so good. So please be warned, this is not a light read in the least.

WARNING:
Not intended for a younger reading audience. Book contains adult situations, substance abuse, coarse language and raw gritty emotion.
Tissues may be needed. Hearts may hurt. But know in the end, everything happens for a reason.

ONE

Xander

MY LUNGS BURNED AS I tried to force the air into my body. In through the nose, down into my chest. The lack of oxygen rambled deep beyond anything I had ever felt before.

The pain, the sharp shooting agony pierced my muscles was enough to leave me comatose. The need for sustenance threatened to take over when all I could think about was getting high. A drug I craved. Whatever the shit may be, I would inject it. Snort it. Smoke it. Calling on it to coat my nightmares, I allowed it the control I knew I didn't have.

My body bowed off the floor. My back arched as the impending panic attack forced me to submit. To surrender. To give up the control. Become a slave to the nightmare that was my existence. It threatened to ruin me. The chains of my terror consumed me.

As much as I didn't want to give in, I needed to. To be controlled. Possessed. Owned.

I allowed the warmth of pure submission to wash over my skin, heating my body from the inside out.

Breathing in a deep amount of fresh air, my muscles quaked and trembled, vibrating under my skin. Mumbled words left my dry parched lips. The sounds travelled around me, not making any sense. Gibberish. They reminded me of a man gone insane, haunted by the dreams possessing him.

Ice cold fear shot down the length of my spine, swimming in the recesses of my soul.

From the moment I gave in, I fell victim to the afterthought of true terror of hell itself.

The darkness inside, twisting and turning, swirling like a billowing pile of ash. I couldn't control it, and a part of me didn't want to.

Whatever this want, this need that was deep in my soul, it would ruin me in time, taking control from within.

"Xander."

The deep melodic vibrato travelled through me, bouncing off the cartilage of my bones. So smooth and compassionate, but the voice oozed power.

"Xander, come back to me." A strong hand caressed my jaw. So gentle. Meaningful. Bordering on possessive. The touch eased the racing nerves roaring through my body but I couldn't fight the urge to fall inside myself.

"Zee. Please."

Caiden. Best friend. My savior in ways I couldn't repay him. "Caiden," I whispered.

"Yes. Come back to me, big guy."

My eyes fluttered open, landing on a pair of the bluest orbs I had ever seen. "Caiden." Swallowing a couple of times, I winced, my throat burning. Forcing myself to a sitting position, I leaned against the couch, letting my head fall back on the cushion. My muscles jumped, aching and protesting at the movement. I fought against the need to dive into the white powdery substance lining a plate on our coffee table. "How long was I out?" I asked instead, my voice hoarse.

"Not sure." Caiden sat beside me, resting his thick scarred tattooed arms on his bent knees. Having been caught in a house fire as a child, sixty-five percent of his body was covered in scars. The guy was quiet and refused to talk to anyone about it, except for me.

My best friend and roommate, Caiden Yeo, handed me a bottle of water. "Drink."

An unexpected tingle shot through my body at the soft but firm demand and I did as I was told. The cool liquid eased my aching throat but my muscles still jumped and twitched with every move I made.

After a couple minutes of silence, Caiden nudged me in the shoulder. "You look like shit."

I scoffed and took another swig of the refreshing water. "I feel like it too."

"What happened?" He took the empty bottle from me and placed it on the glass table in front of us. His gaze glanced at the drugs lining the top before he sat back, his brows narrowing.

"Not sure. Woke up this way," I mumbled, scrubbing a hand down my face. Scratching the two-day old scruff on my jaw, I let out a deep sigh. My skin vibrated, my blood flowing through my veins. I itched for a taste. A hit. A warm body.

"You're lying."

I turned towards him. "Am I? And you know this how?"

Caiden stared straight ahead, his face impassive. His scarred lips pressed into a thin line, showing no hint of emotion, at all. "I know you. Better than anyone. You do this shit all the time."

My back stiffened. "You don't know shit."

"Zee."

"I wanted a high." I waved a hand in front of me. "You knew this about me when you let me live here."

"It's bad, man." His shoulders drooped.

Guilt ate at my gut but I refused to give in. Rising to my feet, I headed into the kitchen. My muscles and bones protested with each step but I forced myself to walk it off. "Whatever."

"Xander," Caiden barked, coming up behind me.

"What, Caid?" I snapped. "What do you want me to say?"

The corners of his lips tugged, his sapphire eyes softening. Brushing a hand through his short black hair, he waited, keeping his gaze locked with mine. "Tell me you miss her."

My jaw clenched, tightening to the point of painful. It was so strong, it shot a sharp sting down the back of my neck.

"Tell me," he demanded.

"Fuck. You," I said through clenched teeth.

Caiden closed the distance between us and placed his large hands on my shoulders. His calloused fingers slipped to my nape, the pad of his thumb rubbing back and forth over my pulse point.

My heart picked up speed when he leaned into me, his mouth mere inches from mine. Although my brain screamed for me to push him away, my body and my

4

heart told me I needed this. This power. This ultimate domination.

The scent of mint and musky aftershave wafted into my nostrils. From this close proximity, I could see the swirls of violet in the depths of his eyes. And then I saw it. A reflection of myself. Pain. So much pain.

Caiden glanced at my mouth before meeting my gaze. His lips tugged at the corners, the light pink scars reaching from his jaw to his left ear.

"Caiden," I whispered.

"Whatever happens, will be because you want it. Because you need it. I won't push you into doing anything you don't feel comfortable doing. Everything will be consensual. If you want to stop, tell me." He released me and left the kitchen, leaving me alone and confused as hell.

I frowned at the cold shiver travelling down my spine over his hands no longer being on me. He was my best friend. My brother.

Submit.

My gut twisted.

Caiden had always been a ladies' man but I knew he also had a thing for men. He had told me once that gender didn't matter, the heart is what drew him in. I accepted his reasoning. Although I preferred females, I didn't judge.

This little moment that passed between us was nothing. He saved me once again from losing myself. Nothing more. Nothing less.

I let out a deep sigh and grabbed a beer before making my way onto the balcony of our two-bedroom apartment. The clouds in the late afternoon sky darkened, opening up. The rain fell in sheets to the ground, the cool drops hitting my face. It soaked my clothes until they clung to my body.

Tilting my head back, I looked up at the sky, letting the cold water run over me. The tiny droplets hit my skin like shards of ice. Goosebumps spread on my skin, mixing with a twinge of pain the sky assaulted me with.

Panic attacks were the norm in my part of the world. I should be accustomed to them with how many I had experienced. But I wasn't. Your soul gets ripped apart, tearing free from the torment of your mind.

Although the drops of rain bit into my skin, my body was on fire. Tight with a need for release.

It had been so long since I felt the warmth of a woman's body. Yeah, I fucked. But those loose holes were nothing compared to her. Hope Charming. Childhood best friend. High school sweetheart. The fucking love of my life. And then her parents decided to move her across the damn country. Now, here we were, ten years later and I fucked through anything and everything, trying to fill a void. A piece of me she took with her. I drank, snorted, injected shit into my body in hopes to erase the memories of her. Her touch. Her smell. The supple swell of her breasts while they rose and fell. Her full lips parting with each bated breath, riding out the pleasure I gave her.

My dick lengthened, pitching a tent in my sweats.

Fuck, I missed her. So damn much but I would never admit that to her or Caiden. Or anyone else.

A light knock sounded on the patio door, jarring me from my moment of self-pity.

Gripping the railing of the balcony, I squeezed until my knuckles turned white. And I waited.

"Xander?" came a female voice.

"What do you want, Embree?" I ground out through clenched teeth. Embree Young had been a welcomed distraction back in the day but now I couldn't get rid of her and every time she wanted something, she was over. What could I say? I was damn near irresistible. I bit back a scoff.

"It's raining."

I gasped, feigning shock and clutched my chest. "No. Is it?"

She smacked me across the shoulder. "Don't be a dick."

The rain lessened, turning into soft drops. The cool air travelled over my skin, igniting a layer of goosebumps to spread on my body.

"The rain smells nice," I blurted.

"It's water. It doesn't smell like anything."

I frowned. "Yes it does. It smells light. Uplifting."

"You're acting strange." Embree shivered beside me and wrapped her fingers around my forearm.

I inhaled, scenting the air. I didn't care what Embree thought. The rain did smell. Fresh. Crisp. Inviting. I knew of one person who would acknowledge that fact. Thank you, Caiden, for forcing memories of her into my mind.

"Did Caiden call you?" "Yeah. He did."

"Did he say why?" I stepped out of her grip and headed back into the apartment.

"No. I'm assuming it's so we can fuck."

7

My back stiffened at the candid use of the curse word. Why I cared what came out of her mouth was beyond me. Hope would never swear as much. Such a good girl. God, no wonder her parents took her from me. I would have done the same shit.

A classy woman swore in the bedroom or if she was pissed off. Embree swore more than I did, the words pouring out of her gloss-injected lips. For some reason and I couldn't figure out why, it sickened me.

"I'm not in the mood," I grumbled, slumping down on the couch. Grabbing my pack of smokes, I tapped it against the palm of my hand.

"Come on, handsome. I need you and I know you need me. Let me make you feel better." She knelt between my legs and brushed her hands up my thighs. "Please. I can make you feel good."

My body reacted first when her fingers reached the bulge in my pants. Her hand squeezed me, wrapping around the fabric covering my length. Hardening under her touch, I couldn't control the urge to push her face first onto the drug infested coffee table and fuck the shit out of her well used body.

A grin spread on her face, her thumb brushing over my tip. "Please."

I grabbed her hand, tightening my hold until I felt the bones rub together under her soft skin.

She let out a whimper, trying to tug her wrist free from my grasp but my hold only hardened. "Xander."

"I said, no." I pushed her back and lit up my smoke, ignoring her pout and her braless nipples poking through her hot pink t-shirt. She was the reason for a fix. For an hour of pleasure. She was so loose, I would need to grow a couple inches around for me to get any friction from it.

"You've never turned me down before. What gives? Are you fucking someone else? You have a girlfriend? Tell me."

I laughed at the incessant badgering. Yeah, like someone would want to date me. Inhaling the sweet familiar smoke I had become addicted to over the years, I leaned back against the couch, adjusting my pants.

"You're hard. Why don't you—"

"Because I'm not feeling it tonight. I don't need to explain myself to you, Embree," I growled. It was all the explanation she was going to get. Embree was the same as the crack I smoked. I hated it. Hated what it did to my body. But I couldn't control the urge to pick up the pipe again and again. I chuckled to myself. What would Hope think of me now? Little Xander Brant growing up to become a junkie.

My gut clenched, guilt swimming through the recesses of my soul, eating me from within.

"Xander."

"Shit, Embree," I snapped. "I don't want you. I'm done. Get that through your fucking head."

"Fuck you, Xander." She pushed to her feet. "I hope you choke."

I chuckled harder, taking another drag. The burning amber glowed in the dim lighting. A shiver ran down my spine reminding me I was still in my soaked clothes. Shit. I was losing my ever loving mind.

"What's going on?" Caiden demanded, coming down the hall.

"You called me but he turned me down."

Embree's whine irritated the fuck out of me. It was like nails on a chalkboard mixed with the sounds of a dying cat.

"Xander," Caiden said, his voice firm.

That same unexpected flutter travelled through me at the deep tone but I of course, ignored it.

Butting out my smoke, I headed to my bedroom. "She's all yours, my man. Have at it."

Embree huffed, blowing a bleach blond curl out of her eyes and placed her hands on her hips. "I'm not a toy to be tossed around."

"You're a whore. You want to be treated like a lady, start acting like one." I pushed past them, insults flying at my head from Embree. Again. So fucking classy.

"Chill the fuck out, Em," Caiden barked and walked up to me. He placed a hand on my shoulder. "Xander, what the hell, man?"

I shrugged. "Not interested in it tonight."

Caiden's dark blue eyes searched my face. "You good?"

I brushed a hand over my head a couple of times before responding. "Yeah. I'm good."

"You sure?" he questioned, his brows narrowing in the center.

"Yup. Perfect. Everything is fine in the world of Xander Brant," I rambled.

"Zee-Man."

I frowned at the nickname he had given me years ago. "You haven't called me that since we were kids," I pointed out.

His eyes twinkled, his scarred lips turning up at the corners. "Anything you need, I am here. You know that, right?"

"Yes," I mumbled. "I know. Go have fun before that shit gets old."

Caiden popped the collar of his black dress shirt and winked at me. "Embree, get your ass over here."

She huffed. "Listen, asshole. I am not—"

"If you want to get fucked, you will shut up and do as you're told." Caiden headed into his bedroom before turning back to me.

Embree glared, walking past me and lifted her chin in a defiant way.

Caiden glanced at me one more time before closing the door. His eyes had softened, no doubt apologizing for fucking Embree. I didn't care what he did. As long as he protected himself. Who knew where she had been hours before.

She slid through both of us like liquid cocaine, burning down our throats before settling into the pits of our stomachs. Embree was a fix I couldn't kick until a moment ago. That thought threw me off.

My body trembled, my world tilting on its axis. I didn't know what was going on. I didn't know how to fix it, whatever it was, but I knew I wanted…something.

Anything. I found myself having a new addiction. Hope Charming. The thought of her had me on my knees, ready and willing for her to give me what I knew she could. What she wanted.

Ignoring the sounds of muffled whimpers and moans, I grabbed my running shoes. Sticking the ear buds of my phone in my ears, I stretched my arms above my head. My body cracked, shooting a sharp pain up the length of my spine. Fuck, that felt good. Not as mind blowing as sex but it was something. I would use Embree later, when I became desperate. Caiden would make sure of it. She was like a disease and I wouldn't be cured of her until I found that one.

Hope.

Shit. No way. Hope was nowhere to be found. Not in my little world anyways.

Heading down the stairs of our three-story walk-up, I pounded my feet into the ground. The fast bass of the heavy metal seared its way into my soul. The boom of the deep music kept in time with the thump of my heart, as if they were in sync. The music flowed through me, connecting with every fiber of my being.

Stumbling over my feet, I caught myself before falling face first onto the sidewalk. "Shit," I mumbled.

I caught my bearings and took a deep breath. Even thoughts of Hope would put me on my ass.

Placing my hands on my burning thighs, I wiped my sweaty palms on my pants before rising back to my full height.

The city was quiet in the mid-afternoon. A crack of thunder erupted in the distance, sending a shiver over my body.

The moment I hit a block into my run, I rounded a corner and was hit full force with a scent. It was so strong, merely an inch in front of my face. My head whipped around, my eyes dancing back and forth. No one out of the ordinary stood out before me. But I couldn't shake the feeling of being watched. The back of my neck tingled, the hairs standing on end. An ice cold sheen of sweat covered my skin and that was when I recognized the smell. Peaches and cream.

Hope.

TWO

SITTING ON THE EDGE of the bed, I lit up a cigarette and dropped my head in my hands. Letting the acrid smoke fill my lungs, I sucked on the end of that stick like it was my lifeline. Like I needed it to live even though eventually it would kill me. I bit back a scoff.

"Hey, Caiden." Slender arms wrapped around my shoulders. A soft mouth placed light pecks on my neck. "I'm ready to go again if you are."

"Not going to happen." I had already fucked the shit out of Embree once. That was enough for me.

"Baby, please—"

"I said no," I snapped, pulling her roughly off of me.

She huffed, pouted and rose from the bed. "You know, I expect Xander to be an asshole. It's what he's good at. But you, Caiden? It doesn't suit you." She left my bedroom, slamming the door shut behind her.

I sighed, running my hands through my short black hair and took another drag of the cancer stick. A laugh escaped me. Cancer stick. Who the fuck came up with these names?

After Xander turned Embree down, I knew something was wrong. He always gave in to her. But today, something was different. Something was off. With him. With me. With life. God, I was beginning to depress myself.

Slumping back on the bed, I took the last drag before butting out the smoke on my tongue. A slight sting burned through my mouth, sending a shiver down my spine.

"Mama. Daddy. Where are you?" I coughed, my eyes searing from the billowing black smoke. "Alec," I called out.

The raging flames erupted around me, engulfing the living room in an angry inferno.

Skin burned. Flesh bubbled. Hair sizzled. The multiple scents wafted into my nose making me gag.

I did this.

It was my fault. All my fault.

I gasped a breath, my lungs constricting at the memory I had tried so long ago to forget. But it felt just like yesterday. So many years ago I had set that fire in our fireplace. One small spark and the house and my family were destroyed. Because of me.

Tears pricked at my eyes. Sitting up, my gaze slid to the floor length mirror in the corner of my bedroom. My dark eyes took on a sadness. A look I had never been able to let go of until I met her. But she wasn't enough. No one ever would be. Enough.

My phone chimed, letting me know that it was almost time.

Stretching out my aching muscles, I couldn't help but stare at the person standing in the mirror. Scars marred my body. Pink with jagged flesh, sometimes sensitive to the touch. I had tried getting them covered up by tattoos of all shapes and sizes but it didn't work. I could still see the scars. An outsider looking in might not see them. They might only see the black ink covering my body, but I knew the burns were there. I could feel them. Every time I moved, they became tight.

Closing the distance between me and my reflection, I grazed a finger down the mirror.

It's all your fault. They would still be alive if it wasn't for you. You should have died in that fire. Not them. Your fault. All your—

Before I could comprehend what I was doing, my fist landed hard against the glass of the mirror. Pain shot up the length of my forearm. Glass shattered to the floor, cracking in front of me. My face was now distorted in the reflection much like in real life. If only I could fix what had been done so many years ago.

My phone chimed again, this time letting me know that she was here.

THREE

Hope

WATCHING XANDER BRANT FROM afar killed me. It tore at my insides, ripping out my heart and soul. I wanted to go to him. I wanted to be with him but I couldn't. Not yet. Not until Caiden gave me permission. Not that I had to listen to him but after everything we had been through, I needed some solace in my life. Some way to move on past the hurt and pain that was inflicted on me. By myself.

I stood off in the shadows, watching Xander, my ex-boyfriend, pound his feet into the ground. His face, hard and determined, like he had wished the earth would swallow him up. He still looked like the boy I once loved but the air around him was thick with possessive desire. For whom, I wasn't sure but I prayed he was thinking about me. Selfish as it may be, I wanted him to remember me forever. I knew he could have moved on, maybe he did already, but I also knew when I came back, his world would stop.

My phone rang, vibrating in my hand and I took a

breath when I saw it was Caiden. "Yeah." "Well hello to you too, Hope."

"Sorry." I sighed. "I didn't mean to come off bitchy."

"It's fine. I live with Xander remember? I'm used to it."

I winced, a cold flood of energy twisting in my gut. I was jealous. I would always be jealous of the relationship Caiden had with Xander. My bond with my ex would never be what they had. No matter how hard I had tried, I couldn't become close with him.

"Hope?"

I cleared my throat. "Sorry. What's up?"

"Where are you?" Caiden's deep voice dripped with concern.

"In an alleyway," I muttered, leaning against the brick wall.

"Has he seen you?"

"No. It's a big city, Caid—"

"But you saw him, didn't you?"

I let out a huff of frustration. "I swear you're psychic."

He chuckled. "Xander tells me that all of the time." "Please. Please stop talking about him," I whispered, sliding down the wall. "It hurts too much."

"You have to come see him. It's only a matter of time before he figures out we've kept in touch. He's going to destroy himself and no one else but you can make him see reason."

I scoffed. "You are the one he listens to. Not me." "Hope," he said, his deep voice gentle. "You know what

I think about him. You've always known but he will never return those feelings."

"You can't be so sure, Caiden. He could come around." It would hurt but I would step aside for him. If it made Xander happy, that was all I cared about. He had been through too much for me to be the one to steal that happiness from him. I did it once. I refused to do it again.

"I am sure. I am positive he will never feel the same way about me."

"You don't know that, Caiden," I insisted.

"Yes, I do."

"How? Caid—"

"He loves you, Hope. He's always loved you. He still loves you. He pines after you and worships the ground you fucking walk on but when you come back, he will treat you like shit because that's how he is. You hurt him, so he wants to hurt you back."

Tears threatened to burn my eyes. "I had no choice." "You always have a choice. Remember my warning, Hope." Caiden let out a heavy sigh. "I love you but Xander will always be my best friend first."

"I know." I understood what he said. He would always put Xander's feelings before mine. He would always have his back before mine. Bro's before Ho's and shit. I didn't like it but I understood. "I wish I had what you two have."

He laughed. "No you don't." "Caiden…" I frowned.

"It hurts. Our bond is fucking strong but it doesn't make up for the fact he's an ass and needs to learn to take care of himself."

19

"I know. But this is why we love him, isn't it?" I said, trying to lighten the mood.

"Yeah. I guess." A couple seconds of silence passed between us before Caiden continued. "Know that when the timing is right, you will reveal yourself to him. It will be when he needs you most. And Hope?"

"Yes?"

"Don't let him push you away. Whatever you do. Please. Promise me."

"I promise."

FOUR

Xander

WHAT. THE. FUCK?

Tripping over my feet, I landed hard on the ground, the bite of the concrete ripping into my palms. The pain shot up my arms, spreading over my skin like a second layer, heating me from the inside.

"Holy crap. Are you okay?"

I winced, sitting back on my haunches and pulled the ear buds off of me that were now dangling around my neck. "Yeah," I ground out and looked up, being met with the darkest eyes I had ever seen.

The eyes warmed, full lips curving upwards. "Are you sure? You fell pretty hard," the girl said.

I nodded. "I'm fine. Just distracted."

"That happens. I get distracted all the time. My mama says I have ADHD when really, I just get bored."

I couldn't help the lightness in my limbs as her words came out fast. All of her sentences rolled into one as she bounced lightly in place.

"So what's your name? I'm Shana Chase. I started grade nine and it fucking sucks."

I choked, rising to my feet. "That's some candid language for someone your age."

She shrugged, blowing a loose strand of black hair off her pale face. "Life is too short. People get so worked up over swear words when there's worse shit to worry about than that."

I stared at her long and hard before responding. "Who are you?"

She frowned. "Did you fall hard? I already told you who I am."

I shook my head. "You said your name, not who you are."

"Uh…isn't that the same thing?"

Shit. Maybe I did fall harder than I thought. "You…how old are you?"

"Fourteen. I'll be fifteen in a month. I wish I was turning eighteen or something because than I would leave this stupid city."

"Why? What's wrong with it?" I walked back towards my apartment building, needing a scalding hot shower to ease my aching bones.

"I would like to live someplace I've never been before."

"Aren't you going to tell me your name?" Shana followed alongside me, grilling me about my lack of manners.

I sighed, wanting to be alone and not play babysitter to a kid. "Why would I do that?"

"Because it's proper etiquette. I tell you my name, you tell me yours."

"And we become lifelong friends?"

"Wow. You sure are a bitter one, aren't you?"

Mentally counting to ten, I let out a sigh. "My name is Xander Brant."

"There you go." She clapped her hands together. "That wasn't so hard, was it?"

"Wow. You sure are something else," I stated, relaxing. It was refreshing, seeing the world through her eyes.

"Yeah. That's what my mama says. But I'm not sure if that's a good thing or not," she mumbled.

A laugh escaped my lips and for a moment, it shocked even me. I cleared my throat, composing myself. "Well, Shana, this is me," I said, nodding towards my apartment building, not even realizing we had walked all that way already.

"It was nice to meet you, Xander, even though you are a bitter one."

Rolling my eyes, I grumbled out a "thanks" and headed into the building.

Her laughter rang out, setting my nerves at ease. I didn't know much about her but I enjoyed the bubbly in-your-face personality. I found myself wanting to see her again. She'd be like the little sister I was never given. Never allowed as my parents were ripped out of my life faster than a fucking tornado destroying a city.

Caiden opened the door before I had a chance to. "Hey, Zee. You good?"

Not knowing how he knew I was there, I trudged my way into the apartment. "Embree still here?" I ignored his question, not in the mood to talk about myself and my feelings. No need for that kumbaya shit when I'd rather wallow in my self-pity.

"No. She left about a half an hour ago," he said, shutting the door behind me.

I raised an eyebrow, grabbing a bottle of water from the fridge and took a swig before turning back to him. "How long was I gone for?"

Caiden's eyes narrowed. He leaned against the wall opposite me and kept his eyes trained on mine. "You were gone for a couple of hours."

"Huh. Didn't feel that long." I shrugged it off and headed down the hall when Caiden's smooth voice stopped me.

"We need to talk."

"About what?" I pulled off my shirt and that was when I felt the sting in my palms. Remembering my fall, heat radiated through my chest. Shana Chase was something else alright.

"About earlier."

"Caiden, I know I'm fucking irresistible but I don't swing that way," I joked, ignoring the twinge of guilt in my gut.

"I'm being serious, Xander," he said, crossing his arms under his broad chest. The tattoos on his thick arms, protruded with the movement.

I met his gaze. "Caid, I..."

Heat swirled in his eyes before he looked away. "I know the way you swing but I also want you to know I am willing to do anything to help you through your demons."

"My demons are fine," I snapped. I didn't need any help and I sure as hell had no idea what he was talking about.

"Listen, I—"

"I don't know what you're referring to. I love you, man, but you are not making any sense."

He nodded once. "Fine. Enjoy your shower."

Anxiety tingled over my skin. Something changed between us while we continued our stare down. I didn't know what it was. Did I even want to know? He was my best friend and I didn't want anything changing that. "Caid, we good? I don't—"

"Yeah. We're fine." He quietly shut the door behind him, leaving me alone with my thoughts.

My demons. I had none. Or the ones I did have, were quiet. Dormant. Whatever this shit that was going on between Caiden and I was not weird. Not weird at all.

***

(Caiden)

I tried breathing through the smoke. The searing putrid scent that wafted into my nostrils. It was a smell so strong that it stuck.

Pain beyond anything I had ever felt erupted through my being but all I could focus on was trying to find my family. "Mama," I wheezed.

Shielding my eyes, I headed down the hall, holding onto the wall for support.

Sirens sounded in the distance but I knew, God, I knew with everything in me that they were too late. Even before I called 911, I knew.

My fault.

My. Fucking. Fault.

I took a breath, digging my fingers into the palms of my hands as I eased my racing heart. The memories had

25

been coming on fast lately. My body knew. My mind knew. It was almost time.

"Caiden."

The soft voice sent a wave of desire spreading through me. It eased the impending panic attack. It helped me past my nightmare.

I turned to the woman standing behind me, remembering the first words I had ever said to her. "This isn't a relationship. I need someone to control. You need to submit. It's a win win for both of us."

She glanced up at me through her light eyelashes and
nodded once. "Yes. Please."

Erica Tenki had shown up to our apartment that first night after much encouragement from me. Texting back and forth was no longer cutting it as we had been doing it for months.

It became a fast routine between us. She didn't stay long. Erica never stayed long. She came and went as she pleased and it was how I wanted things between us. She was an addiction and I used her whenever I needed that fix. It wasn't fair to her but she knew right away how things would be.

I want you to come over. Wear a trench coat and nothing else. I need you tonight.

I had texted her after Embree left, demanding for Erica to see me.

She complied rather quickly, doing as I said.

I washed Embree off of me, needing to replace her with Erica's warmth and waited in my bedroom for her.

There were rules that we followed for her and for me. I spoke. She answered. Nothing more. Nothing less.

Ten minutes later, the door opened.

My breath caught in my chest at the sight before me.

Erica was beautiful. But not in your typical way. Her nose was crooked from having it broken when she was a child by a baseball. She was curvy, freckles adorning her body but she was mine. I just didn't know how to claim her as such.

"Caiden?" She knelt at my feet, waiting, like she always did.

But this time, something was off. The world had tilted on its axis or some shit because I had no idea what the fuck was wrong. I pinched her chin, tilting her head to meet my mouth.

She sighed against me, returning the small kiss.

"Take off your coat and lay on the bed. Present yourself to me, beautiful girl."

Her eyes darkened and she did as she was told. "Did you sleep with Embree?"

It was the same question every time she came over. "Yes."

"Then use me. Let me erase her."

Our eyes locked.

And *him*, went unsaid.

FIVE

Xander

"DUDE, DID YOU SEE that fine piece of ass checking you out?" Lee Swift asked Caiden. Our mutual friend stared at him in awe like Caiden was a fucking God or some shit. "It's the scars. It has to be. Chicks love them."

"So do some men," Caiden added, winking and took a swig of his beer.

I grunted. "Yeah. You should see the people falling all over themselves to get Caiden to notice them when we go out." I laughed, a sigh of relief washing over me. It had been a couple of weeks since our...moment...or whatever the hell it was. I didn't want to lose Caiden in any way and everything felt normal. Back to the way it was before he mentioned my stupid fucking demons. I had none.

"God, it's been so long since I've been out. Caid, care to be my wingman Friday night? I need to get fucking laid." Lee's bright green eyes twinkled with hope as he waited for a response from Caiden.

"You going to come with?" Caiden asked me. He handed me another beer, sitting beside me on the couch.

"Sure." I shrugged. Maybe I could find some pussy that didn't belong to Embree. She had taken up residence in my bed the past couple of days and I didn't have the energy to kick her out. Call me an asshole, but she was only there to cure my boredom. She knew it. I knew it. Sometimes Caiden and I even shared her. God, I was such a dick.

"Still thinking about Embree?" Caiden asked me, lighting up a smoke.

"What, are you reading my mind now?" I took the cigarette from him and inhaled the sweet addiction.

"No. I know you."

"Embree is a disease I can't cure." My heart felt lighter at saying those words out loud. It was true. I couldn't get rid of her. She was worse than a fucking disease. She would be the death of me. I knew I'd fuck her again. It was only a matter of time but I needed something else. Something to appease this unhealthy craving I had of the female form.

"I'll drink to that," Lee stated, lifting his beer.

We all had her. I never knew what swirled through a woman's mind to think she had to sleep around to get attention. If you wanted me to notice you, just talk to me.

"Well fuckers, I'm heading out." Lee rose to his feet. "Friday night," he said, stretching.

"You're leaving already?" Rolling a joint, I licked the end of the small white square and slid my thumb along the spliff with my thumb.

"Yeah. I have some shit to do." He looked away, brushing a hand through his shoulder length brown hair.

"What gives? You never leave early." Caiden grabbed the joint from me and lit it, keeping his gaze locked with mine.

Since I had the panic attack a couple of weeks ago, something had shifted between us. I liked to think everything was normal but hell if I knew what was going on. I wasn't sure what was different. If anything at all. I was so fucking confused.

"I...I need to go." Lee hightailed it out of there before we could ask anything else.

"Well that was fucking odd," I mumbled.

"I'm going to a club." Caiden inhaled his smoke, letting it out in small puffs shaped like circles. "Wanna come?"

"What club?" I repeated his movement, the spicy scent of the intoxicating weed flowing through my lungs. My body buzzed. It invaded my mind, sending my heart racing. Every time I embraced the high, it was a new experience.

No high was like the one before. Always getting the good shit, the substance was pure. Uncut. Clean. I took another toke when I realized Caiden never answered my question. "Caid?"

He looked down, ripping the label off of his beer bottle. "It's a club that could help you get control of your demons."

He always called them my demons. Like they belonged to me. Well I didn't fucking want them. "My demons are fine."

His dark sapphire eyes saddened. "Until you come to terms with the fact that you do have demons, I can't help you."

"So we're back to this shit again? "I never asked for your help."

He nodded once.

Laying on the couch, I continued indulging in the high invading my body. My eyes fluttered, allowing the weed to take over.

When I opened my eyes, I was alone. Several different emotions travelled through me. Guilt for not listening to Caiden. Anxiety over this new switch in our friendship. I had no idea what the hell was going on. He was a good guy and he deserved a friend who didn't hold him back. God, what the hell was wrong with me?

"Shit," I yelled out, the hot amber burning my fingers.

Not knowing if I fell asleep or not, I rose to a sitting position. My body cracked in the process. Rubbing the grit out of my eyes, I sighed, butting out the roach.

"What are you doing to yourself, Xander?"

My eyes shot up at the smooth feminine voice. Hope floated towards me, her gaze sad.

"Hope," I croaked out. "What…" I shook my head. "Am I dreaming?"

"You are." She sat beside me on the couch and placed her fingers in mine. Her hand fit in the size of my large palm, her thumb rubbing back and forth across my skin. She was pale and smooth, where I was rough and hard. I remembered her being soft in all of the right places. It was perfect the way her body fit against mine.

"I miss you," I blurted. "So damn much."

The dream image of her my mind had made up kept her at the age from the last time I had seen her. Ten years. Ten fucking years.

"Come find me, baby." Her words whispered over me like a gentle caress.

"How?" I asked, shoving to my feet. "Ask Caiden."

The moment I opened my mouth to reply, my skin heated, burning to the point of agonizing. It had felt like someone was ripping off the layer of my flesh.

"Xander."

I frowned at the soft firm use of my name, the voice somewhere off in the distance.

"Xander?" Hope reached out for me.

"Please. I'm losing myself. I need you," I cried, falling to my knees.

"Xander." That voice again.

"Stop," I yelled. Gripping my head, I rocked back and forth.

"Come find me." Hope's body started fading. "Find me," she pleaded.

"No!" I screamed when a sudden force had me on my back. It was so strong, it knocked the breath out of me.

"Xander!"

An unexpected ounce of agony seared its way into my lungs, forcing my eyes to pop open.

"Zee. Fuck man."

The remnants of my dream faded around me when my gaze landed on the dark blue depths of Caiden.

"Caiden." My voice was hoarse, like I had gargled with a cup of broken glass.

Smoke billowed around us making my eyes water.

Caiden looked down at me with pity in his gaze but an underlining hint of anger swam in the pits of his stare.

"Let's get you out of here." He coughed, helping me to my feet.

The room spun around me and I wavered, holding onto Caid's large body for support.

He hooked an arm around my middle, guiding me out of the small apartment that was now erupting into smoke and flames.

Fire. Oh shit.

What the hell did I do?

SIX

Hope

"MY NAME IS HOPE Charming."

"Hi, Hope," the crowd of people sitting before me, said in unison.

"Today marks the fifth anniversary of my sobriety." I let out a heavy sigh, a moment of relief being lifted off my shoulders. I did it. If I would have been alone, I would have fist-pumped the air.

My eyes scanned the small crowd before me. Each of them had their own story to tell. Reasons for why they drank, smoked up, let themselves go. Whatever the situation may be, we were all there to support each other. "We all have something to say. Maybe our anniversary date. Maybe we have a new job. Or maybe we became legal residents of America." I glanced at a Hispanic woman from Mexico who received her legal papers after years of fighting for freedom her home country couldn't give her.

Her dark brown eyes filled with tears, a grin spreading on her tanned face. Thank you, she mouthed.

I nodded and continued my speech. "I've been told I don't need these meetings anymore. That I'm strong. I haven't touched a drink in five years but I've thought of it.

Every damn day." My mouth watered at the mere thought of having a beer or a shot glass of the hard liquor I would always crave. "But I know I need these meetings. I also know I wouldn't be here if it wasn't for Embree Young."

My friend, Embree, waved at me, her back straightening a little more. Although she never had a drug problem or was an alcoholic, her addiction took it to a whole other level. Sex. She fucked through most of the men in this room faster than I could blink. Almost being banned from the meetings, she smooth talked her way out of it.

Even as I thought this, she was sliding a hand up the man's inner thigh who sat beside her. But unfortunately for her, he was married and happy. I shook my head at her antics and carried on with what I had to say. "I remember walking into a bar one day, it was so long ago I don't even remember the name. I drank myself into a stupor, almost going home with some random guy even though I was shit faced and was left alone in an alley. Embree found me and we've been friends ever since." I could never repay her for what she did for me. Yes, at times we fought like any friends would but she was still that. My friend. My thoughts travelled to Caiden and Xander. I would never have the bond with anyone like they had with each other. Even with Embree, it wasn't the same. Maybe it was a guy thing.

Maybe girls didn't have that kind of friendship. A bromance bordering on being gay at times. I wanted that. I wanted a friend I would drop anything for. Who I would do anything for. God, I wanted Xander. "Thank you," I bit out and left the stage, in need of some self-control over my actions. My heart raced, my blood pounding in my head.

"Hope?" Embree called after me.

In a quick move, I made my way to the bathroom, ignoring Embree who was now following me. Pushing into a stall, I hunched over a toilet and threw up the contents of my already empty stomach. The acidic bile burned my throat. I dry-heaved a couple more times, tears now streaming down my face.

"Let it out," Embree coaxed, rubbing soothing circles over my back.

After a couple of minutes of torture on my belly, I wiped my mouth and sat back. "Shit."

"What's going on?" she asked, leaning against the stall wall.

I shook my head. "I have no idea. I was thinking of my ex and then…" I waved a hand in front of me, motioning towards the toilet.

"That bad, huh?" Her brows furrowed.

"I don't know what's going on. I saw him yesterday but I didn't speak to him. I wanted to. God, did I ever want to." My eyes burned with unshed tears, threatening to escape and roll down my cheeks like drops of pain.

"You should call him," she suggested, shrugging.

I scoffed and rose to my feet, flushing the toilet behind me. "No. I don't think that will do anything." If I was going to talk to him, it would be in person and like

Caiden had said, not until it was time. I knew he would let me know when to show up. Caiden was an expert at reading Xander's reactions. He had also told me Xander had fallen into the pits of a bottle a time or two. Looks like I wasn't the only one who was messed up.

Splashing some water on my face, I gripped the edge of the counter, taking several deep cleansing breaths.

"I'm here for you. We've been friends for five years, Hope."

I met her gaze in the mirror. "Yeah. We have." But I still couldn't trust her completely. I didn't know why. Was it me? Was there something wrong with me that I couldn't open myself up enough to allow a person in? To love someone as a whole before destroying the happiness I had with them?

Oh Xander. If I would have known things would turn out this way. I never would have left you. I never would have hurt you.

I still loved him. I thought I always would. But was love enough? Would it help? After what Caiden had told me, if I came back and told Xander I loved him, he would probably laugh in my face.

"I'm heading to the club tonight," Embree said, fluffing her hair. She pursed her lips, smacking them a couple of times.

"Are you sure it's a good idea?" I asked, wondering why she came to my AA meetings with me in the first place. I always thought she wanted to get help but apparently, all she did was pick up men.

"Maybe it is, maybe it isn't." She winked at me. "I need to go out. These meetings always make me depressed."

"Didn't you have a good time with a guy yesterday?" I pointed out.

"Yeah." Embree's cheeks reddened. "He was good." She looked away, fiddling around for something in her purse.

"Are you sure?" I prodded, grabbing her arm.

"He was. But he wasn't who I wanted." Her cheeks turned pinker before she clapped her hands together and grinned. "But enough about that shit. Men suck. I should turn into a lesbian."

I rolled my eyes. "Women can be just as bad. Doesn't matter the gender."

"True." She frowned. "Well…I'll have to get drunk and then I won't remember the person anyways."

My chest tightened and I grabbed my bag. "Have fun." "Hope. Shit. I'm so sorry." She pulled me in for a hug, stopping me from running away. "Please forgive me."

"I don't know why but I will." I sighed, hugging her back.

She laughed and kissed my cheek. "Here's the keys. Don't wait up for me." She whistled a tune to herself and left the bathroom, leaving me alone.

Lord, give me strength. Embree and I had moved in together a year after she started bringing me to the meetings. She was a friend but she wasn't enough. She wasn't what I needed. The walls closed around me, squeezing me in a vice like grip. If only I could figure out how to push them away, or how I could stop them from suffocating me.

Xander.

SEVEN

Xander

"XANDER BRANT, YOU AREbeing charged with the possession of an illegal substance which almost burnt down an apartment building."

"It wasn't that bad," I wheezed, lifting the oxygen mask off of my face.

The officer met my gaze, raised an eyebrow at my remark and continued. "The owner of the building threatened to sue when your friend stepped in."

I glanced at Caiden before looking down at my feet.

Guilt and shame swam through the pits of my gut, no doubt eating away at my soul. Utter despair shook me to the core over the fact I burnt our home. Caiden's home. He had lived there before me, taking me in when my parents passed away. I had told him I was fine on my own but the fucker knew me better than I knew myself. I told myself I had moved in to make rent cheaper for both of us but I knew that wasn't true. I didn't want to be alone. Not ever.

Who knew when the apartment would be repaired. Not like the building manager would have me living there anytime soon.

The police officer talked on and on about morals and drugs, giving me a speech about how they're bad, not for me but for everyone around me. Blah. Blah. Blah.

"Do you have a place to go?" the cop asked when I hopped off the back of the ambulance.

"He does," Caiden answered for me. My head whipped around. "I do?"

"Good." The officer nodded. "We'll be in touch. And Xander?"

My gaze slid from Caid's to the cop.

"You have a good friend there. I'd remember that the next time you take another hit."

The nerves in my body jumped but I mumbled a "yup" before I started walking towards Caiden's car.

"Bags are in the back seat," he said, clicking the key fob. The alarm chimed on his black SUV, the sound of the locks clicking free, jarring through my thoughts.

"Thank you for—"

"I don't want to hear it, Xander. Get in the car."

My chest ached at the bite in Caiden's tone and as much as I wanted to beg for him to forgive me, I couldn't. It wasn't how I was wired. Since losing my parents to a freak accident so many years before, I lost a part of myself along with them. I should have died in that car crash. I should have been the one to go, not them. They were so much better than me. Better people. Caring. Loving. They worshipped the ground the other walked on. I thought I had that with Hope. She was my savior while I mourned the loss of both my mom and dad. But when her parents took her away from me, I blamed her.

"Xander, I'm moving."

"Moving? Where?" I asked, brushing my thumb along the heart shaped lips of Hope's mouth.

"To Seattle." She sat up, ringing her hands in her lap. "Seattle? That's miles away," I cried. "I'll never see you."

"I know." She took a breath. "That's why I'm breaking up with you."

"What!" I turned her towards me. "Please tell me you're kidding."

She shook her head but wouldn't meet my gaze. "I'm not."

"Hope, please. You can't leave me. After my parents—"

"Do not guilt trip me." She rose from my bed, pacing back and forth in front of me.

Something was off. She wasn't heartbroken over this. No dark bags were under her eyes like she had lost sleep. No tears. Nothing. "You want to move, don't you?" I asked, realization punching me in the face.

She stopped in her tracks and took a breath before turning back to me. "Yes."

And that was the last time I saw her. She up and left, taking my heart and soul with her. I tried hating her. I fucked through woman after woman, trying to forget her but I couldn't. She was engrained in my heart where she would always be. I had loved her with every inch of me. Every piece of me. She tried calling, even tried visiting me when she was in town. But I was always busy. She hurt me more than she would ever know. More than she would ever care. And I was an asshole who would let her know it.

"Xander."

My thoughts drifted back to the present as Caiden drove us to his... "Where are we going?" I asked, trying to forget what I had done.

"Get some rest. We have about an hour's drive ahead of us." He kept his gaze straight ahead, his grip tightening on the steering wheel.

"Tell me where we are going," I pressed, curiosity killing me.

His jaw clenched but he didn't answer.

I let out a huff of frustration and slumped back in my seat. I had no idea what was going on. I tried apologizing for the shit I did but if Caiden didn't want my apology, then there was fuck-all I could do about it.

"I'm sorry," I whispered, my eyes getting heavy.

"Words can only do so much. They only go so far," Caiden said softly, a moment later. "Actions are what will help you through this. Help you forget. Help you forgive."

My chest clenched, feeling like it would implode in on itself. "I have no one to forgive." "Yourself would be a start."

I frowned. "I have no idea what you're talking about." "You fucking burnt our apartment," Caiden snapped, raising his voice. "You could have brought the whole building down. Do you even know how lucky you are that you didn't go to jail?"

"I never asked for your help," I bit out through clenched teeth.

Caiden chuckled. "Of course you didn't. Why would you? I've been your fucking friend for years. Since we've been kids. Why on earth would you ask me for help? It wouldn't make any sense at all."

Frowning, I slowly turned my head towards him.

"Where is this coming from? I appreciate your help. I do. I love you, man. You're like a fucking brother to me."

"Brother," Caiden scoffed.

"I'm serious. After Hope left—"

"I'm done. Get some rest."

"Caid."

"Get. Some. Rest," he demanded, his voice firm. He lit up a smoke, his dark eyes staring straight ahead.

I opened my mouth to argue. To beg for him to talk to me. We needed to sort this shit out. Or fight it out. Either way, we needed to finish this but a part of me told me to quit while I was ahead.

I wanted to change the subject, go back to the way things were less than twelve hours before but my eyes grew heavy. My body drifted, falling into slumber that most would call their safe place. Dreams of happiness, fantasies but mine were filled with darkness. Demons, as Caiden called them. A pure black reign of terror tore at my soul, eventually weighing out any happiness at all.

"Xander."

My eyes popped open but all I could make out was smoke.

"Xander."

A shiver travelled up my spine. "Hope?" Her voice. God, her voice.

"What have you done?" she said softly from far off in the distance. "He loves you."

I spun around in circles but I still couldn't see her. "Hope, please. I need your help."

A billowy image of her materialized in front of me, forcing me to take a step back. "You need to help yourself."

I swallowed hard at the sunken pits where her eyes should have been. "Hope, baby. What's going on?"

A maniacal laugh escaped her cracked lips, her dark hair fanning out and around her. "You are worthless. No wonder my parents took me from you. You don't deserve me. You don't deserve happiness. You should have died in that car crash. Not your parents."

My heart jumped, my palms becoming sweaty. "No, you don't mean that. I'm dreaming. This is all a fucked up nightmare."

Hope's form glided around me, hovering to the point where it was inhuman. "A dream you will never forget." Suddenly she was in front of me. Cupping my cheeks, she opened her mouth wide and screamed.

My eyes popped open, my body covered in a cold sweat. "Xander?"

I jumped at the deep voice coming from beside me and was met with Caiden's concerned stare.

"Another nightmare?" he asked softly.

I nodded, rubbing my shaky hands along my thighs.

"This yours?" I asked, nodding towards a large house while we pulled onto a long driveway. My voice was hoarse and I cleared my throat a couple of times, swallowing past the slight burn.

"Yes. It's in the middle of being built but it's livable." Which also meant for me not to burn it down or else I would get my ass kicked.

"Why didn't you tell me?" A twinge of pain tingled through me.

"Because I wasn't sure what I was going to do with it after it's done," Caiden said, turning off the car.

"What do you mean?"

"Forget it. There's clothes here you can wear. Fridge is stocked with food and beer." He looked at me. "There is nothing for you to get high off of that could damage your mind or body."

My blood vibrated through me. "Shit, Caid. I—"

"You want to put shit inside of you…you even think about it…work it out." He stepped out of the vehicle and made his way to the front door.

"Caiden, I can't stop cold like this. You know that. Please," I pleaded. Bile rose to my throat, my vision blurring as spots danced before my eyes. "Please." I pushed open the door and forced my aching body out of the car.

"Caiden." My voice was raspy but I still attempted to inhale as many deep breaths as I could. The moment he told me there would be no drugs, no nothing for me to put in my body was the moment I lost it. It was like I was on a trigger affect. I never noticed I wouldn't be able to do drugs until he said something.

"Shit."

I fell to my knees, the gravel digging into my knees through the cotton of my sweatpants. "I can't stop. I can't quit."

"Yes, you can and you will."

I shook my head. "I don't want to."

He cupped my cheeks, forcing me to look up at him. "I can't help you if you don't want to help yourself. I need you here with me. These drugs will fucking kill you."

I shoved my head out of his grip but not before I saw the flash of pain in his dark gaze mixed with a hint of something more. My skin tingled at the loss of his hands no longer being on me and if I didn't know any better, I would say I enjoyed it. But I didn't. I couldn't.

Rocking back and forth, I leaned on my knuckles, pushing them into the ground. The sharp bite of the small stones tearing at my skin sent an unexpected heat over my skin.

"Not like this. Please," I pleaded.

A heavy hand cupped the back of my neck. "You are strong. You'll get through this. But I can't help you unless you ask for it," he whispered in my ear.

I swallowed several times, taking a deep breath before looking up at him. My best friend. My brother. The only family I had since my parents died.

Caiden's eyes darkened, the deep violet swirling in the depths.

"I don't need your help," I blurted. Inhaling a deep breath, I held it. My lungs burned at the lack of air.

His face hardened. "No. You don't want it. Big difference." His thumb grazed back and forth over my pulse point, easing my racing heart. "Breath, Zee. Please let me help you."

"How?" I bit out, sitting back on my haunches.

He gave my nape a light squeeze and rose to his feet. "Come with me."

Before I could argue, I was following behind him. The front yard was clean and well kept, the brush surprisingly crisp and neat. "How long have you been building this place?" I asked, needing the sounds of our voices over the unwelcomed silence.

"Couple of months," Caiden said, unlocking the large wooden front door. "I'm in no rush to move," he added a moment later.

"Why here? You'd be in the middle of nowhere." I looked out onto the yard in front of us. The house was surrounded by trees and wildlife. The only thing that stood between me and getting out of there, was Caiden. And something told me he wouldn't let me go quietly.

"I like the peace and tranquility," he said softly. He stepped into the house, throwing his keys on a table by the wall.

"I'd rather the noise of the city," I mumbled, taking one last look around me before following Caiden.

Once I stepped over the threshold, my stomach tumbled. Something told me this would be a new beginning. Things were changing. I couldn't place exactly what those things were though.

"Kitchen is this way. There's a bathroom in the basement in the first bedroom on the right. Bathrooms are also on the main floor and second floor, with an additional one being off the master suite. There are four bedrooms. Two in the basement and two are upstairs. Take your pick." He made his way into the kitchen and came back a moment later with a bottle of water. He handed it to me and waited.

I took a swig, the ice cold water easing my parched throat.

"Where did you want to sleep?"

I frowned. "It's early still isn't it?"

"Xander, you had a panic attack outside because you found out you can't get your fix here. You need all the strength you can get while you go through withdrawal." His brows narrowed. "Now, which bedroom did you want to stay in?"

"One downstairs is fine." So then you can't hear me scream.

"Fine. Follow me." He led the way down to the basement and stopped at the first door on the right. Not bothering to give me a tour of the house, he glanced at me. "Try and sleep well, Zee." He clapped a hand on my shoulder before walking past me and up the stairs.

Taking a breath, I twisted the doorknob and headed into what I had assumed would be a small bedroom. When I saw a four poster bed sitting against a wall at the back of the room, I realized I was wrong.

My eyes burned and I stifled a yawn. Not caring in the least the details of the room, I needed a shower. Making my way towards the bathroom, I pulled off my shirt and muddy pants. My feet padded along the soft burgundy carpet and when I reached the en-suite bathroom, I stared in awe at the display before me. Everything was black. The shower stall. The toilet. Even the sink. The walls were a deep burgundy much like the carpet in the adjoining room. It was breathtaking. Caiden must have taken his time in planning out the development of the house. Me? Give me a pillow and blanket and I was happy as a pig in shit. I didn't need fancy appliances or maids or any of that crap. I was easy to please, so to speak.

Turning on the shower, I stepped under the spray, the water washing over my body like a velvet glove. The liquid turned hot and I sighed, the droplets running down my torso and dripping off my chin.

Hope.

My length twitched. Well this was new. It had been so long since I touched myself to thoughts of her. At one point I thought I had forgotten about her. But the way my cock grew at the mere thought of her name, I was fucked.

"God, Hope," I breathed out, wrapping my hand around the base. I squeezed it hard, bringing tears to my eyes. With rough smooth strokes, I jacked off to thoughts of my ex-girlfriend. Her touch. Her pale skin. Her rosy cheeks as they reddened with orgasm after orgasm. The sounds of her screaming my name.

I swelled under my touch, my balls pushing up into my body as a tingle shot from my toes to my head.

A light knock sounded on the door, jarring me from my thoughts. I jumped but kept a firm grip on my hardened dick.

"Xander? You alright?" Caiden called from the other
side of the door.

"Yeah," I groaned, emptying my release onto the tiled floor of the shower stall.

"Are you sure?" The deep vibrato of his voice reigned through me.

Loosening my hold on my body, I sighed and cleaned myself off. "No."

EIGHT

"CAIDEN."

I glanced up at the deep sound of Xander's voice. My heart skipped a beat at the sight of him. So young. Broken. But perfect. For Hope.

Finally admitting to myself that I was in love with my best friend, didn't bode well on my confidence. "Are you sure you want to do this?"

I nodded, pulling off my shirt.

The buzzing sound of a tattoo gun neared me. "We won't be able to cover them completely. Some of your skin is too thin."

"Cover it all. As much as you can. I need..." I needed to not be reminded every time I looked in a mirror at what I had done so many years ago.

"This will hurt, my man." The tattoo artist snapped on a pair of latex gloves.

I embraced the pain as the sting of the tattoo gun drew over my skin. Marking me. Covering my scars. But it wasn't enough. It would never be enough. If only I could see my family again and apologize. Tell them that

I'm sorry for not watching the fireplace. For not getting to them in time.

Scars on the skin was one thing but scars on your soul could never be mended.

"What have you told him?"

"Nothing," I mumbled, kissing Erica's shoulder as she snuggled up against me. I squeezed the bridge of my nose, trying to forget. Trying to ease the anxiety that had crept along my bones, bringing forth the agony from within.

"So he doesn't even know about me?" she asked, cupping my cheek, her brows narrowing.

"No. Now stop asking so many questions." I wrapped myself around her, holding her tight. It was late into the night and I couldn't sleep after the multiple nightmares that kept invading my dreams. Remnants from them vibrated through me.

Erica and I usually only met up once a month but not this time. She had been over every single day for the past week. I could see the questions in her gaze but I had no answer for them. I didn't know what was wrong. I didn't know how to fix this issue. I knew I just needed her.

"How long are you going to keep me from him?"

I sighed, scrubbing a hand down my face and rolled onto my back. "Erica, I have no fucking idea. I told you how I felt about him. I can't do anymore right now."

"Seriously?" she raised an eyebrow. "What did you tell me when we started this relationship?"

"I will spank you," I growled in warning and cupped her chin but that never stopped her. She challenged me and I loved it.

"I want you happy. That's all." She pushed out of my hold. "Now tell me what you said," she insisted.

I rose from the bed and walked towards my closet. "I told you that I was in love with someone else. That I was using you because I couldn't have him. And you were fine with that." I glanced at her over my shoulder. "Why?"

She shrugged. "My ex mentally abused me and you stepped in like a white knight. My prince charming. You were so kind and gentle and then the first time we had sex, I felt your alpha male." Her cheeks reddened.

"That's the part of me you like the most?" I questioned, running my fingers over the edging of a mirror hanging on the wall.

She smiled softly. "I like all parts of you. I don't know. I guess even though I can't have your heart, I can at least have the rest of you. I'll take what I can get."

My stomach clenched, my heart twisting and turning, thumping hard. I was an asshole for making Erica stay. Just like Xander, I hated being alone. But unlike him, I knew my demons were too loud. My nightmares were too fucking scary that I sometimes woke screaming. "I want to give you all of me. I just don't know how," I whispered, grazing my hand down a leather whip that was hung against the wall of my closet.

"You will. In time."

"How can you know this?" I snapped, spinning on her.

Her eyes widened, her hands gripping the white sheets and pulled them up to her chin.

I took a deep breath, easing the rage growing inside of me. Falling to my knees, I rocked back and forth. "I love him. So damn much. I know it's wrong of me but I can't control it. I can't. I fucking hate this."

Warm arms wrapped around me, holding me against a soft body. "You can't control what your heart wants."

Enveloping Erica in a tight embrace, I pulled her onto my lap and grazed my hands down her naked back. "I am so fucking confused. I don't deserve you. I don't deserve to be happy. I'm a monster."

"No," she cupped my cheeks, tilting my head. "You are not a monster. Do you understand me?"

I narrowed my eyes, gripping the back of her neck. "Remember who you're speaking to, little girl."

Her lips parted but then she cleared her throat, ridding herself from the dirty thoughts I enjoyed pushing into her mind. "I enjoy what we have. You control me. I give in. I knew right away that your heart belonged to someone else."

"How could you possibly know that?" "I could see it in your eyes."

I leaned my forehead against her chest, letting out a heavy sigh. "I need to talk to him. I need to tell him how I feel before…before it's too late."

"Then talk to him but know that whatever happens," she brushed her fingers through my hair. "I am here. For you. Always for you."

NINE

I NEEDED OUT. I needed away. Away from my nightmares. Away from the thoughts I tried so hard to ignore. Hurt. Pain. Agony. All of those feelings I inflicted on Xander. My ex. A man I once loved. That I still loved.

How many times did one have to ask for forgiveness?

Not that I had a chance to ask Xander for his yet.

"Hope, stop stewing. I love you, girl, but you're going to get wrinkles and drive me to drink," Embree had told me the night before. "Or have sex. Crazy mind-blowing panty- melting sex." She waggled her eye brows, laughing at her own joke.

Drink. All night I had craved an ounce, even a drop. Of something. Beer. Whiskey. Tequila. Even wine would have worked. But I knew. I knew one drop would destroy me. It would set me back to the beginning or worse. Kill me.

Alcohol was the worst killer of them all. War. Famine. Sickness. Alcohol caused the most accidents in the world. So why did I crave it? Why did I need it more than anything? And how could I let myself get addicted to it?

My phone rang making me jump and I turned on the Bluetooth in my car before checking to see who was calling me. "Hello?"

"Hope, where are you?"

I winced at the harsh tone of my mother's voice. It was worse than nails scratching down a chalk board. "I'm on my way to Caiden's." No point lying to her. She would end up calling Caiden anyways and badgering him with questions.

"Why? Are you seeing him? I thought he was gay."

Taking a deep breath, I mentally counted to ten before I answered. "I'm heading over there because he keeps me sane. No, I'm not seeing him. If I was, I wouldn't tell you. And no, he is not gay."

"You know. Ever since you moved out, you've become so ungrateful. Your father misses you terribly."

I rolled my eyes. "Right," I said slowly. "Like you miss me too?" I smirked when she didn't say anything.

"Is that Xander boy going to be there?" she asked, accusation filling her tone with contempt.

"I have no idea," I cried. "I haven't seen him in years and he's no longer a boy, mother. He's a man." And a fucking hot one from what I saw the other day.

"I don't want you hanging out with him—"

"I am almost thirty," I snapped. "You or dad can't control me anymore." I inhaled sharply, trying to control the racing nerves coursing through my body. "Listen, I don't know why you're calling, mother, but I have to go."

"Your dad's in the hospital," her voice cracked. "He had a heart attack."

Gripping the steering wheel tight, I cursed under my breath. "Is he alright?"

"He's asking for you," she whispered. I could picture her gripping her chest, flailing her hand against her forehead dramatically.

"Fine." When I pulled into Caiden's driveway a minute later, I reached for a pen. I frowned when my hand started shaking. Ignoring it, I grabbed a piece of paper from my purse. "Give me the details." I wrote down what hospital he was at, his room number and how long he would be there for, promising to show up tomorrow. My mother tried guilt tripping me into going over right away but with my dad being in recovery and doing well, I didn't see the point.

I loved my parents. I honestly truly did. But I loved them more when I was a child. Until I grew up and saw them for what they were. My fantasy of the perfect parents popped before my eyes. It could have been worse. I knew that. But my parents were both religious and controlling. As I got older, I no longer had the patience for them and moved out.

Caiden emerged in the doorway, making his way out onto the porch. Watching me.

Stepping out of the car, I stared in awe at the large expanse before me. "I'm still amazed you are building this house and no one knew."

Caiden nodded once.

I closed the distance between us, gave him a hug and allowed him to lead me into his home.

His dark hair shone in the early morning light streaming in from the patio window. "I needed out of the city."

"Is that the real reason?" I asked, my chest tightening.

He didn't meet my gaze and continued to walk into the kitchen. He grabbed a cup of coffee off the table and took a sip before finally meeting my gaze. "Everything alright?"

"Is Xander sleeping?" I asked, ignoring Caiden's scrutiny. I could sense a pull tugging me towards Xander. Even though he was several feet away, I knew he was close. I had to do everything in my power not to go to him and slip into his bed. Wanting to hold him, I knew it wouldn't go over well.

"He is." Caiden dumped the rest of his coffee in the sink. "What's going on?"

I sighed. "My mother called me. I swear that woman is worse than the alcohol I drink."

"She loves you," was all Caiden said.

"She sure as shit has a funny way of showing it," I mumbled.

"I want you to meet someone. In time. With Xander," Caiden said, changing the subject.

I frowned. "Okay. Who?"

"That's not important right now. But what is, is your training. We have to continue, Hope." He headed to the stairs leading to the basement. "Xander will probably be up in an hour."

"I'm ready. For anything," I insisted, following him down the stairs. When Caiden had called me months before, offering to help me, I jumped at the chance. Knowing it would benefit Xander as well, I couldn't resist.

"I know." He stopped once we reached the bottom of the stairs. "How are the meetings going?"

"They help," was all I said. What more could I possibly tell him about my AA meetings? How wonderful they were? How much I loved them even though I had to spill my guts every single week, telling strangers about how tempted I was to pick up a drink.

"You sound like you don't want them to," he said gently, turning on the hallway light.

I shrugged. "I would like once to be able to have a social drink and not lose control. To take one sip without it pushing me over the edge..."

"If Xander only knew," Caiden said softly which I thought was probably more to himself than to me.

Not asking anymore questions about Xander, I decided to quickly change the subject. "How are you doing?"

Caiden turned back to me when we reached a set of double doors at the end of the hallway. "If you think you're going to get any answers from me, think again, Hope."

"Why do you feel the need to demand information but you won't tell us jack shit?" I snapped, my voice a little harsher than what I had intended.

Caiden smirked and made his way into the room.

"Because I can," he said finally.

I huffed, crossing my arms under my chest and leaned against the wall. "I don't know how this is going to help Xander. He doesn't even know I'm here yet."

"But he will." Caiden handed me a coiled up rope. "Remember what you do with this when I tell you."

Taking the rope from him, I remembered exactly what he had told me not too long ago. Even though it had been weeks since my first lesson, I could hear Caiden's words like he said them a minute before.

"Let him trust you. Don't force him into anything he doesn't want to do. He will need a safeword."

Giving Xander a safeword reminded me of those novels that were strictly all about bondage and sex. Or that was what I had thought before I read some books in that genre that were different. Much more.

Trust. Commitment. Communication. It was all key to a healthy relationship no matter what you were into.

But Caiden taught me what he did, what he practiced and how it was different. It was more. Much much more.

And I couldn't wait to have Xander at my mercy, begging me at the touch of my hands. If only he could love me just the same.

TEN

Xander

I HATED SCHOOL. I hated everything about it. We were like caged rats, waiting for judgment day, getting picked off one by one.

The notes from today's class stared up at me but I couldn't make out what they said. My stomach twisted, an ache settling deep inside of my chest.

Something was wrong.

My gaze slid to my right, locking eyes with Caiden.

He raised an eyebrow. "You okay?" he whispered.

I could hear the words leaving his lips but I couldn't form an answer.

The door to the classroom slowly creaked open, a tall redheaded girl making her way into the room. She handed the teacher a piece of paper before heading back out into the hall.

Mr. Puglisi glanced at me. "Xander, can you come with me please?"

At that point I knew. It was the middle of winter and the roads were horrible. My parents were supposed to be going on a trip. Leaving me with Caiden for a couple of days, they trusted that I could take care of myself.

I stood up before I noticed what I was doing. A zombie- like state took over, forcing me to the head of the class.

Mr. Puglisi was talking to me but I couldn't make out any of his words. Maybe I was going deaf. Maybe I was still sleeping and I would wake up and find my parents sitting at the kitchen table drinking their morning coffees. Maybe I wouldn't have had that fight with my dad the night before. Or yell at my mom, telling her she always took his side.

Maybe they would still be alive and I wouldn't be a drug addict. Maybe then I wouldn't surrender to the liquid I craved. And I would be with Hope. And that part, that dark sinful part of me wouldn't want Caiden to kiss me.

I woke with a panic, the tiny hairs on my body tingling and twitching with unease. Remnants of the nightmare pounded its way against the walls of my mind.

My lips tingled and I reached up to touch them.

Whatever Caiden wanted from me, it wouldn't be enough. I couldn't give him what he needed. I just wasn't sure if he knew that.

If only I could shut off my thoughts. Even to ignore the constant badgering my consciousness gave me. But I couldn't. At times, my thoughts were so loud, I had to drink myself into a stupor to quiet them. My mouth watered. Fuck. I needed something. Anything to hide from myself.

Pulling on my pants, I padded across the room before quietly opening the door. I needed a fucking drink.

Something. Anything.

Once I left the comfort of the room, a nagging feeling poked me in the gut. I frowned, glancing at a set of double doors at the end of the hallway. Soft music seeped from under the doorway. It wasn't the usual music Caiden listened to. Although he was born in America, he was raised in the Japanese culture. His mother being Irish and his dad being born in Japan, he had the best of both worlds. He always liked to drive his dad insane by the heavy metal music. It went against the typical stereotype that if you're pretty, dressed nice and are well mannered, you don't listen to heavy metal. Well Caiden was all of those things, minus the pretty part. He did not look like a guy that loved to listen to screaming and someone banging on drums.

"You're up."

I spun on my heel, finding Caiden standing at the top of the stairs, staring down at me. Thoughts of my nightmare came back to me. Clearing my throat, I looked away and rubbed a hand over the back of my neck.

"Follow me," he said, making his way down the steps.

My feet moved of their own accord, following him as if they needed to.

"Although the rest of the house isn't finished yet, the basement is." He wore black drawstring pants and no shirt. Japanese symbols ran down the spine of his broad back, moving and flexing under his muscles.

"Why?" I asked, taking another look where the music was coming from.

Caiden winked. "Because there are items down here I needed first and foremost before anything else."

"Like what?" I asked as we headed towards the set of double doors.

He pushed them open and frowned when the music became louder. "Wait here a moment." He disappeared down the stairs, the soft melody shutting off a minute later. "Ready?" he asked, coming back up the steps. He turned around and I followed him.

The deeper into the ground we walked, the cooler and damper the air became, reminding me of a dungeon.

"What's down here?" I brushed my fingers along the wall, noting the scent of spices in the air.

"A gym and other things." His answer was vague and it was enough to drive me insane.

The only sounds following were of our feet shuffling along the concrete floor. "Caiden, what is this place?"

He didn't respond until we came to another set of double doors at the end of the hall way. "This is the gym. Everything you need to work out is in here. Punching bags, weights, skipping ropes, everything."

I nodded. "Okay."

Caiden moved past me and unlocked the door.

I turned and headed in after him, frowning when I stepped into what was the home gym. "I thought the other room was the gym."

"It is in a way but no, this is the gym you will use."

Curiosity got the better of me and I couldn't help but wonder what was in the other room. "Caiden."

"It's nothing you have to worry about. Yet," he said, his voice final.

"Alright. Fine. What do you do in there anyway? Fuck the ladies?" I laughed, trying to lighten the mood. Even though darkness surrounded us, I needed things back to the way they were. I also still needed that damn drink.

"I will show you that room when you are ready but right now, you are not," was all he said.

"Okay, Yoda." I huffed and glanced back at those double doors. Anticipation washed over me, igniting an unexpected heat to spread over my body.

"Close the door and come here, Xander."

My stomach gave a flip at the firm demand and I did as I was told.

"When I'm upset, angry or even feeling off, I work out." He pressed a button on a stereo system across the room, the sound of heavy bass pumping through speakers following soon after.

The beat vibrated under my skin, rattling the skeleton of my bones.

"I know you work out. You go for runs but you can use this room as well, whenever you want to hit something."

"Does it provide alcohol?" I muttered under my breath. "No. It does not," Caiden said, his voice harsh.

"Listen. There is nothing wrong with me having a drink—"

"Yes there fucking is," Caiden snapped. "When you can't control how much you drink? That is a huge fucking problem."

"You are not my dad. I don't get to have one of those anymore remember, asshole? Now give me a fucking beer or I'm out."

He raised an eyebrow. "Is that so? One thing goes wrong and you're done?"

"Caiden," I growled.

"What? Work it out. Hit something. Hit me but don't you dare abuse your body." He looked at me over his shoulder, waiting. "Would you rather run outside?" he asked, changing the subject.

"Yes," I said without hesitation. Although I was pissed, he knew how to distract me. Fucker.

Running outside was my favorite thing to do. The bite of the crisp air against my skin. My heart beating so hard against my rib cage, it threatened to explode. It helped me be free. Whole. Safe.

"You can run later. Right now, you need to hit something." His eyes glittered and if I didn't know any better, I swore he was challenging me to hit him.

Leaning my head from side to side, the tendons in my neck cracked under the pressure. The sharp sting travelled down the length of my spine, sending a flush of heat over my skin. It was a good pain. Like when you work out for hours knowing the final result is a healthy body. Of course in my case, the shit I consumed contradicted with me getting healthy. A huff escaped my lips and I walked up to the large punching bag. "You enjoy pissing me off, don't you?"

"No." Caiden grabbed the other side of the bag, holding it still. "I know you need to get your head out of your ass. Someone has to set you straight."

Puh-lease. As if that would ever happen.

"I'm more of a loner when it comes to working out," Caiden said, breaking the unnerving silence. "But either way, hitting something or running...lifting the shit out of those weights...whatthefuckever...to the point of burning is..."

I looked at him when his voice trailed off.

His dark blue eyes heated. "Delicious."

I coughed. "Well that's one way of putting it," I mumbled.

"What do you like to do? Besides getting under my skin."

"Fuck that noise." I rolled my eyes. "I think it's the other way around, dude."

"Tell me."

"Excuse me?" I frowned.

"What's your favorite workout? What do you like to do to get your blood pumping? Your muscles burning." He brushed his fingers down the side of the bag.

I watched as he caressed the heavy weight like a lover's touch. "Becoming one with the punching bag?" I teased.

"Tell me what gets your heart racing," he demanded, grabbing a staff attached to the wall by a gold clip.

"Uh…sex?" I blurted.

He raised an eyebrow. "You asking me or telling me?" "Telling you."

"Good."

Before I could process what was happening, I landed flat on my back with an oof.

Caiden knelt at my head, holding the staff with two hands and pressed it against my throat.

My eyes widened. I gasped for breath, my lungs constricting at the lack of air. "Caid," I rasped.

No emotion showed on his scarred face. "Self-defense is an excellent workout," he said, releasing me.

I coughed, choking on the air I tried so desperately to inhale. "What the hell?" I demanded, gripping my throat. I rose to my feet, glaring at him.

Caiden swiped the stick against the back of my ankles, knocking me on my ass for the second time in a matter of minutes. His eyes twinkled, glittering with an accomplishment.

The breath left my lungs on a gasp, my muscles protesting at the unexpected abuse.

He laughed and held out a hand. "Self-defense can also work against internal demons."

I growled, slapping my hand in his and allowed him to pull me to my feet. "Fucker."

He handed me a staff, holding his upright and slammed it hard against the mat. "Fight your demons," he demanded. In a quick move, he kicked my feet out from under me.

Landing hard on my back again, I gasped as the wind was knocked out of me for the third time in a matter of minutes. My lungs burned, my throat tightening. "Shit, Caiden."

He showed up in front of me, hovering over me like a predator. "Give up?"

I barked a laugh and rose to my feet. "Not on your fucking life."

Caiden chuckled. "Try and hit me then."

Moving back and forth from one foot to the other, I watched him. Our eyes locked, the air in the room thickening with Dominance and possession. I would knock him on his ass, eventually, but probably earning some bruises in the process.

"Hit me," he growled through clenched teeth.

Our staffs hit, the sounds of wood on wood banging around the large gym.

"Keep going," he ordered, circling me.

The sticks clanked, vibrating through my fingertips up into my arms and up my shoulders. Sweat coated my brow, my muscles burning and twitching from the overuse.

"Shit. You're fast," I said between breaths.

A wicked grin spread on his scarred lips and before I knew it, I was flat on my back once again, landing hard with an oomph.

"Well that...was...fun," I wheezed between breaths.

He laughed. "And here I was going easy on you."

I shook my head and sat up, stretching my legs out in front of me. "Thank you," I blurted.

He shrugged, taking the staff from me. "You're my best friend. You hurt. I hurt. I want to help you in any way I can but I can't if you don't let me."

Scrubbing a hand down my face, I scratched the scruff on my jaw. "I don't know how to ask for help."

"I know and I'm going to help you with that."

"How?" My brows narrowed and I rubbed my hands up and down my thighs. My muscles jumped under the skin, rippling at the excessive use.

"By teaching you to control your demons," he said nonchalantly.

"I have no demons I need to control," I repeated for what felt like the hundredth time that day.

Caiden laughed. And I mean a full belly laugh rumbling from his chest. He continued chuckling and rose to his feet.

"You know, laughing at me is not going to help me with whatever issue you think I have," I mumbled.

He looked at me over his shoulder, the laughing ceasing. "Stand," he demanded, his eyes going cold.

"If you're going to kick my ass again, I'd rather stay seated."

"Stand. The. Fuck. Up," he said through clenched teeth.

Crossing my arms under my chest, I leaned back against the wall. Scratching my jaw, I raised an eyebrow. "Or else what?" I challenged.

A wicked grin slowly spread on his face. "I can't force you to do anything you don't want to do…"

"But I can."

My eyes snapped up at the female voice coming from the woman stepping around Caiden.

Hope.

ELEVEN

Hope

I GAVE XANDER A smile as I stood beside Caiden. "Hi, Xander."

"Hope," was all he said.

His deep voice washed over me and I couldn't help but soak it in. His dark eyes roamed down the length of me, heating when they locked with mine. I clasped my hands in front of me, my chest rising and falling with each breath. He glanced at my hair, a slight flush spreading up his neck. I remembered a time where he had loved my curly auburn hair. It was so long ago but I bet he was thinking about wrapping the curls around his fingers and giving them a gentle tug as I moaned out his name. A tingle of pleasure raced down my spine and I cleared my throat.

He caught my look, a dark glint passing over his eyes.

"What are you doing here?" he asked finally, rising to his feet.

"Caiden called me." I glanced between them before looking down. The little voice in my head screamed for me to look at him. To see him like I had done when we were kids. Ten years. Ten fucking years since I last saw the gorgeous man standing before me. My body fought back the urge to run to him. To fall at his feet, begging for him to forgive me. Ten years. And I still loved him.

"Xander," Caiden said, his deep rich voice soft but firm.

"Why are you here?" Xander asked me, ignoring him. "Well I..." I chewed my bottom lip. "I was in town." "So Caiden ran into you," he finished for me.

"He invited me over," I added quickly, my heart racing against my ribcage.

Xander glanced at Caiden.

His eyes were dark, filled with a challenging stare when I caught Xander's eye. He had that look I knew so well. It was that run before shit rolled downhill look. He was freaking out internally and I had no idea what to do to help him. I wanted to go to him. To talk to him about why I had left. About the choice I never had but I knew he wouldn't understand. I knew it wouldn't be easy. Stupid naïve me thought if I showed up, everything would be fine. He would love me and I would love him. But I was wrong.

Xander took a step towards us when we blocked his path. He couldn't push me but he sure as hell could make me move. And he knew it too. "Get out of my way."

"No," Caiden and I both said in unison.

Xander threw his hands up. "What? Is this some sort of fucking intervention?" He glared at me. "I haven't seen you in years. You fucking disappeared from my life without so much as a look back in my direction. And you expect me to listen to you now?"

"I want to help," I whispered.

"With what?" he yelled. "I'm fine. I'm fucking fine! I don't need either of you acting like my parents. They're dead. I don't want new ones." He shoved past us and quickly left the room, slamming the door shut behind him.

And that was when I broke. Falling to my knees, I allowed the cries to take over. The sobs to wrack through my body as the one and only man I loved hated me more than ever.

"Shhh..." Caiden knelt beside me, wrapping his arms around my trembling shoulders. "He'll come around."

Shaking my head, I rocked back and forth. Bile threatened to burn its way up my throat and I had to force it back. I couldn't allow another panic attack to set in. What was I thinking coming back here? "I can't do this," I sobbed.

"You can." Caiden cupped my cheeks, forcing me to look up at him. "And you will. He loves you. He's hurt and he may be mean but he wants answers. You can't expect him to be fucking giddy and happy now that you're back. What did I tell you?"

"He'll want to hurt me like I hurt him," I mumbled, dropping my head in my hands.

Caiden sighed, rubbing his hand in circles over my back. "He will."

"I want to talk to him. I don't want any more fighting. I want...him," I cried. "And I feel so damn guilty over that."

"Why?" Caiden asked, frowning.

75

I rose to my feet, brushing off my knees. "I know you're in love with him. You've loved him all of these years, Caiden, but you never did anything about it."

"He doesn't love me back," he said softly. "You should still tell him."

"You want me to tell Xander, the man you are in love with that I also love him?" Caiden stared up at me, sitting back on his haunches.

"Yes. That's what I want." Although it hurt, knowing at any moment, Caiden could steal Xander right out from under me, I couldn't go through life being the reason for them not to be together.

"What did I ever do to deserve a friend like you?"

I stepped up to the punching bag, hitting it gently. "You let us both in." Wiping the tears from under my eyes, I gave the bag a couple more hits. A sharp pain shot up my forearm.

"You're not hitting it right." Caiden came up beside me and grabbed my hand. Tucking my thumb to the side, he curled my hand in a tight fist. "Always keep your thumb behind your knuckles or else you will break your hand." He held onto the bag. "Now hit the bag. Work out your frustrations."

"Why? I'm fine." I walked away when Caiden gently grabbed my arm.

"Trust me. None of us are fine. We all have our own shit to deal with. Some may be worse than others but working out, fighting through those demons can help."

"Is that what you're trying to teach Xander?" I asked, shaking out my hands.

"Yeah, but he's so damn stubborn, he thinks he's fine."

He huffed.

"So tell me about this person you want us to meet," I said, punching the bag.

"Her brother is friends with Lee. Do you remember him?" Caiden asked, holding the bag while I continued to punch it.

I thought good and hard when realization set in. "Was he that guy that kept slapping my ass every time he saw me? The one Xander ended up punching?"

Caiden chuckled. "That's the one."

"Don't tell me. Xander and him are friends now, aren't they?"

"They are."

I rolled my eyes. "Of course they are."

"Anyways," Caiden smirked. "This girl…"

I met his gaze when his voice trailed off. "Caid?"

He cleared his throat and stepped back from the bag. "You know my feelings for Xander. Those will never change. But she is also aware and she gives me something no one ever has. She sees something in me that…" He scrubbed a hand through his dark hair.

"She sounds wonderful," I said gently, placing my hand on his arm.

"I want you to remain in touch with her…after…if…" His voice wavered.

I nodded and wrapped my arms around his middle. "Of course. What's yours is mine," I whispered.

He returned the embrace and we stood like that for what felt like hours even though it was probably only minutes.

Being friends with Xander and Caiden all through our school years, we had a bond. Xander's parents called us the Three Musketeers. I shook my head, remembering how he hated the nickname but after his parents died in that horrible crash, I bet he would give anything to hear them say it again.

Guilt settled deep inside of me, making up permanent residence like I had been born with it. What I did, leaving Xander after his parents passed away…I would never forgive myself. It was not intentional. Things came about where I had no choice but to leave. If only I could explain that to him. I needed to make him understand. I needed to make him see I never meant to hurt him.

"I need a moment," Caiden said, ending the heavy silence.

"Okay." I released him and watched him walk to the door.

"He'll be back in a little bit. He tends to run it out, listening to whatever music is on his phone." He turned back to me. "Please be patient with him. I know it's hard, but he needs that from you as much as you need it from him."

"I'll try," I said softly.

He nodded and opened the door, slowly shutting it behind him.

Taking a breath, I lowered to the mat. "Please, God, help him forgive me. Help us both have patience." But I knew when the time came, it would turn into a fight. And who knew what else?

Rising to my feet, I turned on the music, the heavy metal blasting through the speakers. Gearing up my hands, I started punching the shit out of the bag. Picturing it was all of my frustrations, all of the mistakes

I had made, I hit the bag full force. If only it were that simple. If only I could actually punch my wrong doings away. Maybe then Xander would forgive me. Maybe then it would be easier and I could forgive him as well. He blamed me for everything. I knew that. But he wasn't easy to get along with. He was blind to the fact that he was indeed an asshole. I prayed the shit he was consuming, didn't destroy him like the alcohol threatened to ruin me.

***

(Xander)

"I swear you three are stuck together like glue to paper." My mom laughed. "No, better yet. You're The Three Musketeers." Her smiled widened. "Perfect."

I shook my head, wrapping an arm around my best friends' shoulders.

Caiden only chuckled, while Hope kissed my cheek.

"Together. Inseparable. Forever," she said.

A flutter ran through me. I just hoped she was right.

Heading up the stairs, I pulled the earbuds out of my pocket, roughly shoving them in my ears. Inseparable.

Forever. Please.

Why? Why after all of this time? Hope and Caiden were close. They always had been. The three of us were inseparable at times. But they had a bond I could never understand. Did I share the same bond with Caiden? With Hope? I had no idea.

You are worthless. We don't want you in our lives. Grow up and move on.

I swallowed past my dry throat, my vision clouding over at the words pounding on the doors of my mind.

Pressing play on my phone, the nerves tortured my body, the thoughts trying to destroy me every damn day, eased as the deep melody of the music soared into my skull. The hairs on my neck tingled. I could feel Caiden and Hope staring at me. They were probably talking to me too. But I refused to look. I refused to give in to their badgering and self-help bullshit.

Heading outside, I ran down the steps and down the length of the graveled driveway. I had no idea where we were but I didn't care. If I got lost, I knew Caiden would find me from the GPS built into my phone. Fucking fancy technology. Give me the old flip phones any day over this touch screen shit.

Running down to the end of the driveway, I realized we were in the middle of nowhere. I had nowhere to go. I couldn't run back to the city but I could run from my problems. From everyone. Or try to.

From the moment I stepped out onto the road, I picked up my pace. I felt free. Alive. Whole. It was the only time I ever truly felt normal.

Tears burned my eyes at the sense of loss I had felt deep inside of my chest since my parents died so many years before. Eleven years. And then Hope leaving me after didn't help. Did I change? Was it my fault she left? She never told me and that was what drove me mad.

It didn't take long for my muscles to tighten. My legs to burn and my heart to race. Air left my lungs in quick bursts, escaping the confines of my chest.

Hope.

My feet stumbled and I had to catch my footing before I fell flat on my face like a dumbass.

God, she was back. In my life. For who knew how long. A part of me felt guilty for leaving. I should have talked to her. I should have done something but instead I ran out of there like a pansy-assed pussy. I couldn't deal. But holy fuck, she was more beautiful now than I last remembered. Age did her justice.

My cock lengthened in my pants, hardening to the point of painful. I slowed to a stop, adjusted my pants, not caring in the least if anyone saw me. Not like anyone would. I was in the middle of butt-fuck Idaho. The houses were spread miles apart on what looked like a long winding road.

The music in my ears switched to a new song, forcing me to run harder. I wanted to switch it. Wishing I could change lives as fast as I could change the song but my fists pumping at my sides wouldn't allow me. This song. The words were from an Indie band, not known to many. I had found them one day on the internet while waiting for Hope to get ready. I remembered that night like it had only happened the day before. We were going to a party. As always. And it was the first night we had made love. I scoffed. Please. Make love. That was what she liked to call it but in fact, I fucked her stupid.

The sultry voice of the female lead singer sang not to me but to my soul. She said what I felt. What I could never say in words to Hope. I should have let her listen to the song years before. If only. But a part of me needed to keep it a secret, like I thought she would laugh in my face for being such a girl. The deep boom of the bass vibrated through me. The whir of the guitar eased my aching body. And the thump of the drums beat their way into my existence.

If only I played. To create this music to help someone else with whatever they were going through, whatever shit life threw at them. It would be an honor. If only I could tell the singer. Thank her for giving me an out. A reason. To move on. But I never did, did I? I should be happy that Hope was back. Elated I could finally tell her how I felt. But those words wouldn't leave my lips. Not yet. If ever.

The cool mid-afternoon air whipped around me, floating through the thin layer of my clothes and kissing my skin like a lover.

Embree never touched me like Hope had. Of course I never allowed her to. As much as I tried to forget, to move on, it was damn near impossible.

There was a break in the music where the guitar sped up, following the beat of the bass. The singer purred, sending a shiver down my spine.

I am addicted to you.

Your love. Your touch. Your being. Everything about you draws me in. I am captivated by you.

The heat in your gaze. The beat of your heart. I am addicted to you.

The song ended a minute later and I pressed replay, needing to hear the sound of the love pouring into my ears. The singer clearly felt something deep for someone. So deep, the passion was strong through the words she sang.

From the moment we touch, I crave you.

Your kiss. Your breath on my skin. The warmth of your embrace.

I am bound by the ropes of your love. Restrained by your powerful passion.

Your caress. Your hold on my body. The possession that seeps from your soul.

I am addicted to you.

I replayed the song over and over, the words engraining themselves beneath my skin. My muscles burned, my chest constricting, my heart beating so fast, I thought it would explode.

Hope.

"Shit." I slowed to an abrupt stop and ripped the ear buds out of my ears. Sitting down, I laid back on the cool grass that spread over a field. It was surrounded by trees in the far off distance. The evening air whipped over me, sending a layer of goose bumps spreading over my skin. My sweat soaked clothes clung to my aching body but all I did was lay there. For how long, I wasn't sure. I watched as the sun set, the moon taking its place in the sky.

"You trying to kill yourself?"

My head turned towards the female voice and I saw a girl approach me.

She adjusted her red baseball cap and crossed her arms

under her chest. "You don't remember me, do you?"

I sat up and scrubbed a hand down my face. "I remember you," I muttered. Something about the girl who I had run into the last time I ran in the city, nagged at me. I couldn't figure out what it was but the possessive side of me felt the need to protect her.

"So, are you still bitter?" she asked, sitting down beside me.

I chuckled. That was why I liked her. "Yeah."
"Why?"

"Because," I sighed. "Because my ex is back."

"This is a bad thing?" she asked, pulling some grass out of the ground.

I looked down at her. "Shana right?"

She nodded. "You remembered. So you're not as dumb as you look."

"Gee, thanks," I scoffed.

She giggled and pulled off her baseball cap. "So tell me about this ex."

"We were high school sweethearts. I wasn't the greatest student or role model for her so her parents took her away from me." I mirrored her actions and pulled a couple slivers of grass out of the ground, twisting them between my fingers.

"You're lying. They took her away?" she asked, her eyes widening.

I slumped back down on the grass and let out a heavy sigh. "It was the summer after we graduated from high school. We were hanging out and that was when she told me she was moving." I didn't know why I felt the need to explain things to Shana. She was a teenager, probably naïve and shit, too. But I couldn't stop the words from leaving my lips.

"And it's been ten years since you've seen her?"
"Yeah."

"Where did she move to?" Shana asked, ripping more grass from the ground.

"Not sure exactly. She said Seattle but I blew up and didn't ask for more information," I mumbled, my chest tightening.

"React first, ask questions later, huh?"

"Yeah. Something like that. So, do you live around here?" I asked, needing to change the subject and push it away from myself.

Shana shook her head. "I'm staying with my grandparents for a little bit. They live down the road but I live in the city with my aunt."

Something told me not to ask but I couldn't stop myself. "How about your parents?"

Her back stiffened. "They travel for a month during the summer, so I stay with my aunt."

I searched her face when she looked away.

She distracted herself by continuing to pick at the grass. She was lying but her humming stopped me from asking more.

"Do you sing?"

Her cheeks reddened. "Yeah. A little bit." Her eyes lit up. "Oh! I have a recital you should come to. I don't want to go but my grandparents are making me. You should come."

I frowned, my mouth opening and closing. "Are you sure?"

She nodded quickly. "I'm sure I'll run into you again, so I'll have the details with me next time."

"Okay," I said slowly. Why she would want me there was beyond me.

"How about your parents? Do you live with them?"
"No. They died a while ago in a car accident." A twinge of pain poked me in the gut and I had to force down the urge to run away.

Shana's face fell. "Oh. I'm sorry. I figured as much."
"Why would you figure they died?" I asked, finally sitting up.

"Because." She rose to her feet. "You can only be bitter for a couple of reasons. You're dressed in name brand workout clothes and running shoes, so clearly you don't live on the street. You can't be bitter over having no home."

Yeah well, it didn't matter what clothes I had when I almost burnt down my home. "I don't live on the street. Go on," I coerced, interested in what else she could predict about me.

A slow grin spread on her face, her eyes sparkling. She knelt in front of me. "Your ex left you but by the way you talk, you still love her."

Love was an understatement.

She continued before I even had a chance to respond. "I think you beat yourself up over what happened to your parents and for your ex being taken away from you," Shana said, standing up. She started pacing back and forth, deep in thought and tapped her chin. "I also think your best friend has something to do with this mood you're in but I can't figure out why yet."

I pulled a dandelion from the ground and shrugged. "He called my ex. Her name is Hope. My best friend, Caiden, and I were working out. I was struggling…"

She stopped pacing. "With what?"

"I'm not sure." I shrugged. I couldn't tell her something had changed between Caiden and I. I was probably delusional. I loved him. Like a brother. Nothing more. Nothing less.

"Well if you figure it out, let me know."

I met her gaze and nodded slowly. "I will." And that was the God's honest truth. For some reason I couldn't help but tell her. "I should get back."

"Okay. You staying around here?"

"Caiden has a house down the road." I glanced towards the home surrounded by trees. A part of me was still pissed he never told me about it but the selfish side of me wondered where I would eventually go.

"You good?"

"Yeah." I frowned. "Why wouldn't you tell me?" I whispered.

"Tell you what?"

My back stiffened. "Nothing. Gotta go. Catch you later, Chase." I stuck the earbud in my ear.

"Last names now?" she asked, raising an eyebrow.

"Yup." Turning on the music, I stuck the second bud in my ear. "It means we're friends," I yelled over the loud music in my ears.

She shook her head, making her way back to her grandparents' place.

Talking to Shana was enlightening. I found myself taking a liking to the girl. A part of me wanted to spend more time with her. Hang out, play video games. Do whatever fourteen year olds did. I could only imagine she was a tomboy. I didn't think she was into that boy band shit. I found that I didn't know much about her except for that she sang. Making a mental note that I would go to her recital, I found that I actually couldn't wait.

By the time I listened to three songs, I was back at Caiden's home. He was sitting with Hope on the front step, talking quietly amongst themselves. Hope looked up, meeting my gaze. "How was your run?"

"Enlightening," I said, stretching my arms above my head. My bones cracked, sending a delicious tremor rippling down the length of my back.

"How so?" Caiden asked, raising an eyebrow.

"What were you guys talking about?" I ignored his question, wanting to keep Shana to myself for the moment. She was my breath of fresh air and I didn't want to share her yet.

"You," they replied at the same time.

"Well I need a shower so you can continue talking about me then." I headed towards them but they didn't budge. They stared up at me. Waiting for what, I wasn't sure. Should I do a song and dance? Maybe a little performance would get them to move.

"We need to talk," Hope insisted, ringing her hands in her lap.

"Fine." I crossed my arms under my chest. "Talk."

"Xander, we should talk alone."

"I'm sure Caiden has shit to say as well." I glanced at him. "Don't you? So get it out. I'm listening."

They both looked at each other before turning back to me but they of course, said nothing. Why would they? It would only make sense when they said they wanted to talk.

"Geeze, would someone say something already?" I snapped.

"Why don't we go inside?" Caiden suggested, rising from his spot on the step.

"Okay." Hope chewed her bottom lip, looking at Caiden. Something passed between them.

Caiden nodded once and headed back into the house, leaving us alone.

I followed him when Hope stepped in front of me blocking the path. Like so many times before, she had blocked my path. In life. Where I could never move on. From her. From our time together. My limbs felt heavy, the palms of my hands going sweaty.

Hope stood a foot away from me but as the wind whipped around us, I could smell her. She never wore perfume when I knew her years ago. Her natural scent was enough to drive a sane man mad. Peaches and cream. The aroma wafted into my nose and I inhaled deep. Memories from when we were kids invaded my mind. Her laughing and telling me to stop smelling her like a dog. Me chuckling and barking, tickling her until she gave in. It was fun. And I never realized how much I had missed her until now.

"Xander." She took a step towards me.

"Ten years," I whispered, clenching my fists at my sides.

She looked away, a lonely tear rolling down her cheek.

I had to the fight the urge to wipe it away, to pull her into my arms and tell her how I felt. How much I loved her. But I couldn't. A part of me needed to hurt her as much as she had hurt me.

"I'm sorry. I'm so…" Her breath hitched. "Sorry."

"Sorry doesn't make it better. Sorry doesn't give me back

those ten years." I gripped my shirt, struggling to breathe in the air that flowed around us.

She stepped closer to me until she was mere inches from my body.

The air crackled and fizzled between us. We were attracted to each other before but now, this lust, this undying want bouncing from her to me, electrified into something I couldn't control.

"Right now, sorry is all I can give you." She peeked up

at me through tear soaked lashes.

My fingers twitched. "Until what?" "You're ready for more."

"You sound like Caiden," I said, frowning.

Her cheeks flushed. "I missed you. So much. But I…"

Running my hand over my buzzed head, I let out a heavy sigh. "If you missed me, you would have contacted me."

"I wanted to," she cried. "I did. I tried contacting you." "Did you? Did you try, Hope? I sent you letters, I tried looking for you on Facebook. I called the phone number I had for you but it was turned off. Did you try to contact me?" My voice rose after each question. I didn't want to yell at her. I didn't want to hurt her but the uncivilized part of me reared its ugly head. I took a step towards her, forcing her back. "How hard did you try to get a hold of me? I don't know, Hope. The last time I saw you, you were pretty damn happy that you were moving. No tears. No nothing."

"I cried for you. God, did I ever cry." Her eyes welled, her chin quivering.

"Right," I said, slowly. "Listen, I don't know why Caiden called…" Realization dawned on me. The unjust twinge of betrayal erupted through me, gripping my spine

like a monster. Or demons. My demons. So many questions pounded through my skull, beating on the doors of my mind. My mind. So loud. So. Damn. Noisy. "How did he get your number? Have you kept in contact with him after all of this time?"

Hope lifted her chin defiantly. "Yes."

TWELVE

Hope

FROM THE MOMENT I had walked back into Xander's life a couple of hours before, my world had tilted on its axis. I had loved him. I still loved him but now that I thought about it, our relationship had been toxic. But not in the beginning. It was perfect. I was the girl who tamed the beast. Popular. Good grades. On the varsity team. Him? He was the bad boy. But he graduated. Barely. "Xander?"

His head snapped up. "How often have you seen him?" he asked, his words eerily calm.

"I…I…" I stammered. "You don't understand."

"How often have you seen him?" Xander repeated, his voice raising.

"Xander, it's not like that," I cried, taking a step towards him. My fingers itched to hold him, my palms tingling with the need to run them over his body. To soothe his demons. His internal battle he had been fighting since his parents died and left him alone. It wasn't their fault. I knew that. Caiden knew that. But Xander? He blamed them. You could see it in his eyes.

And he blamed me for leaving him right after. I totally accepted that.

"Caiden, get the fuck out here!" Xander shouted.

I jumped at the abrupt demand, pleading with him to calm down.

"You rang?" Caiden asked, casually leaning against the door frame.

"Have you kept in contact with her after all of this time?" Xander was shaking, dark accusation swirling in his grey eyes.

I wanted so hard to tell him it wasn't true. With everything in me, I tried to ignore the hint of jealousy that had taken up permanent residence deep inside of me over the bond they shared. I didn't know why it never bothered me before. Since finding out how Caiden actually had felt about Xander, it made me realize I could lose him forever.

Caiden scratched the dark scruff on his jaw, his deep blue eyes piercing through Xander. Challenging him. "So what if I have?"

Xander gaped at him. "After all of this time..." He shook his head. "Why didn't you tell me?"

Caiden moved to the steps and sat down, stretching out his legs in front of him. "Would you have wanted to know? If I told you Hope and I have remained friends, would you care?"

"Of course I would." Xander looked between him and I. "Why wouldn't I?"

"Let's see." He looked at his watch. "How much time do you have?"

Xander frowned. "Caid, I—"

"You and this 'I am an island' bullshit is wearing on my nerves." He rose to his feet abruptly, going toe-to-toe with Xander. "You won't accept help when it's offered to you."

"I'm fine. I am. Why can't you believe me?"

"Because it's not fucking true!" Caiden yelled. His nostrils flared, his olive skin turning a light shade of pink. "When you can admit that you are not in fact fine, come talk to me. Until then? I'm remaining friends with Hope and I will not apologize for keeping in contact with her."

"You are an asshole," Xander bit out. Caiden smirked. "So I've been told."

Xander opened his mouth to reply when Caiden cupped his nape.

Caiden grabbed my hand, pulling me between them.

The heat from our bodies being huddled close together enveloped around us. He let out a deep sigh. "You need us. The help we have to offer you, you have to accept or else the demons will threaten to destroy you." Caiden leaned his forehead against Xander's. "Please."

"Xander." I wrapped my arms around Xander's waist, snuggling into him. The scent of sweat, leather, and man wafted into my nostrils waking a part of me that had stayed quiet for years. But it stirred something deeper. Something I never thought I would feel. Lust and desire for the man in my arms. A possessive fire burned in my soul and if I wasn't careful, it would take control. Clearing my throat, I rubbed my cheek against his chest. "Caiden may not apologize, but I will. I'm sorry for not trying harder to keep in touch with you. Things were...it wasn't a good time for me after we moved."

"I could have helped you," Xander whispered.

I inhaled a shaky breath. "I know. And I'm sorry."

Xander wrapped his hand around the back of my neck, squeezing it gently.

"Give in," Caiden coaxed.

Xander pulled away from us both. He glanced down at me, his eyes darkening with the same lust I felt. The attraction between us had always been there but this time? It was intense. Powerful.

Ignoring the urge in my body to wrap myself around Xander, I hugged my arms around my waist. It had been so long since I felt his warmth, smelled the lingering scent of his skin and tasted the delicious essence of his body. Desire unfurled deep in my core, begging me to go to him. But I couldn't. He was pissed. Or he tried to be. And he wanted me to know it. Ten years. And his best friend had kept in contact with me after all of this time. Xander had always been selfish. Was he that selfish that he never paid attention? Maybe Caiden tried to tell him.

"Zee," Caiden pressed.

Xander spun on him. "What, Caid? What the hell do you want me to give in to? My feelings? Are we going to hold hands and sing Kumbaya around a fire and shit?" His voice rose as each question left his mouth. His body shook, vibrating with the need to, no doubt, hit something.

"Let's go inside and talk," I suggested tentatively. I reached for his hand, hesitating first before sliding my fingers between his.

Xander glanced at Caiden.

His gaze was on our joined hands. When he looked at me, my breath caught. His eyes were dark, sad even.

A part of me jumped for joy that he was the one that was jealous but then the bigger part, the part that loved them both, felt guilty. My chest tightened. What the hell was wrong with me that I wanted to make both of my friends jealous?

Caiden cleared his throat and headed up the steps.

"Come to the gym when you're done talking," he said softly and disappeared into the house.

"Xander," I said softly. "I think you need to talk to him."

"About what?" he mumbled and sat on the steps, pulling me down beside him. Dropping his head in his hands, he let out an aggravated sigh.

"I think you need to talk," I said, wrapping my hands around his bicep.

"We do talk," he insisted. "I don't know what else to say. I have no idea what he wants."

"He wants you," I said so softly, I wasn't sure if he heard me.

His head whipped around. "Me?"

I chewed my bottom lip and brushed my fingers over the tattoo of my name on his forearm. Caiden had offered years ago to pay for him to get it removed but Xander refused. Caiden had told me Xander insisted on needing the daily reminder of a time when he was happy.

"Talk to him. If nothing comes of it, at least you talked." I looked away before continuing. "He needs you more than you need him."

"What does that mean? What's going on? Is he sick?" "No. God no. He's not sick." Not that I knew of anyway.

"Then what? What's going on, Hope?" Xander demanded.

I didn't answer. I leaned my head against his shoulder, holding his arm tight in my hands.

"I know he's been hiding something from me," Xander blurted, his deep voice rough.

I wished Xander was yelling at me. Demanding why I didn't try harder to come see him, especially when Caiden and I had kept in contact. But he didn't. He talked to me like I never left. Like I didn't leave him alone and broken, taking his heart with me. Like my absence never turned him into a drug addict. But little did he know how much leaving him destroyed me. If the words would leave my lips, would he still want me? Would he even want this empty broken shell of the woman he once loved?

"He hides from people in general." I rose to my feet and stretched my arms above my head before smiling down at him, ignoring the little voice nagging me to talk to him.

"Let's go work out like old times."

Xander scoffed, his gaze dark and heating with lust as they bored into mine.

"Xander," I breathed, my voice husky.

His gaze landed on my full chest, my nipples hardening under the thin fabric. A slow grin spread on his face.

"I'm not talking about sex," I said quickly, taking a step back.

"No?" He rose to his full height before sauntering towards me. "Why did you suggest it then?" He took another step towards me, backing me up until I hit the brick wall.

"I didn't suggest it. I would never allow you to have sex with me when I just came back."

Placing his hands against the wall on either side of my head, he caged me in. He leaned down, brushing his nose up the length of my neck. "But you didn't come back. You've been here all along. I just didn't know it."

I shivered, arching my back. God, I missed him. Never once would he act like this when we were kids. He was a boy. Although he could be an asshole, he was gentle and loving. The Xander standing in front of me, was a man in need of breaking his woman. Forcing her to submit to the ultimate desire of seduction and pleasure. "Xander, I...I told you."

"You didn't tell me anything," he said roughly, inching his body closer to mine.

Being this close to him sent a flutter through my belly. A heat spread over me, intense to a point I never felt before. Not even when I was with him years ago. I became hyper aware of how my body reacted to him. My heart raced. The tiny hairs on my skin stood on end, tingling from the scent of him.

"Tell me," he ground out, peaking his tongue out to lick along the line of my jaw.

"T-tell you what?" I asked, grazing my hands down his chest.

"Tell me you want me." He nipped the soft spot under my ear, igniting a moan to leave my lips.

I whimpered, gripping his shirt in my hands. "I..."

"Tell me," he demanded, pushing his knee between my legs. The heat from his body washed over me, blanketing me in crazed lust. Moving against me, he dug his fingers into my hips.

I groaned, undulating against his thigh. "Xander," I panted.

"Say it," he growled, pushing into me hard.

"I want you," I cried out, shaking against him.

A wicked grin spread on his face. "You were saying?" he asked when he released me.

My mouth fell open before they flattened into a thin line when I realized Xander was only leading me on to the point I would beg for his mercy. "Xander."

In a quick move, he wrapped a hand around my throat.

I gasped at the abrupt movement, my head jerking back against the wall.

He leaned down to my ear. "If you ever lie to me again, I'll bend you over my knee and spank your gorgeous ass." He released me and headed into the house.

I stood there panting and shaking. What the hell just happened? I made a promise with myself that I wouldn't jump into his arms at the first moment I saw him but something had switched between us. The lust had grown so strong in the few short hours I had been around him that my body reacted first before my brain could catch up. If our meetings would be like this, I would lose my control and fast.

***
(Xander)

I had to fight the urge not to run back to her and dive into her sweet as hell body. I knew right away she was lying when she told me she wouldn't have sex with me. Even from the little power play between us, she gave in right away and that no doubt pissed her off even more.

I headed down to the basement, the sound of fists hitting a punching bag banging in my ears.

Caiden hopped from foot to foot, his knuckles landing hard against the swinging item before him. He was graceful on his feet as he danced with the bag. "You do something to piss her off?" he asked, not bothering to look at me.

My back stiffened. "How did you know?"

"Because I know you. You haven't seen her in ten years. You want her to hurt as much as you hurt."

I opened my mouth to respond when he raised a hand, stopping me.

"Don't bother asking how I know. I'm not stupid. I've

seen it in your eyes since she left you."

"Alright, Yoda. Care to enlighten me on any more shit you think you may know?" I snapped.

Caiden chuckled and grabbed a hand towel, wiping the sweat from his face.

My body tensed, his laughter pissing me off. "What the

hell is your problem? You laughing at me now?"

"I'm not laughing at you."

"Then what the fuck gives?" I asked, raising my voice. "Nothing." He glared. "It's fine."

"Like hell it is. I know something's going on."

He snarled and pushed me up against the wall. "You don't know shit." He stared me down, his cold dark eyes daring me to challenge him.

I pushed out of his grip and shoved him back. "I know you've been acting weird."

Caiden's nostrils flared, his fists clenching and unclenching at his sides. Suddenly, his hand was wrapped around my throat, tilting my head back. "You think you know," he growled in my ear. "You think you know how I feel. What I want. Who I want."

"I...I..."

His grip on my throat tightened, his mouth mere inches from mine. "You're a selfish bastard."

My eyes widened. Never in our whole friendship had Caiden treated me this way. He was so close, I could see the purple hue of his dark eyes. His skin was smooth, aside from the bumpy ridges of his scars.

"You can't even see what's right in front of you." His voice was low, deep and eerily calm as he continued to hold me up against the wall.

I couldn't help but stare. I probably would have been able to fight him off of me but something warned me not to.

He gave off an air of uncontrollable rage, his lean but strong body shaking. Other than that, he was calm, cool and collected. The scent of mint mixing with salty sweat wafted into my nose, my blood heating and roaring through my body.

"Caiden." Hope came up beside us. "Let him go."

Caiden leaned down to my ear, the scruff of his jaw scratching against my cheek. "If only you knew." He released me and walked away but not before whispering something to Hope.

She nodded, patted his arm and kept her gaze locked with mine.

At that point, something inside of me snapped. I was like an elastic band being pulled so tight, eventually doing the only thing I could. I broke.

THIRTEEN

Hope

WHORE. SLUT. TRAMP.

All the words I feared Xander would call me when he found out the real reason why I left him. As the name calling flowed from his lips, I could tell he no longer had control. His lips were flapping, going ape shit as he laid into Caiden and me.

Xander gripped his head, beating his fists against his temples. He was losing it. Shattering before us and I had no idea how to fix it.

We stared at him wide eyed, his words no longer making sense.

"Stop!" Xander suddenly shouted, startling all of us. He fell to his knees, gripping his head. "Make them stop," he pleaded, rocking back and forth, when I knelt in front of him.

Wrapping my arms around him, I allowed the warmth to travel into me, heating my skin. It eased the racing of my own heart but Xander's mumbled words about demons and voices scared the hell out of me. They became louder and louder and I had no idea how to silence them. I couldn't make them out but I felt them poking at me. Jabbing me with the sharp edges of their words.

"Xander," I whispered.

"I…I can't," he choked on a sob.

Caressing his nape, I rubbed his back in smooth circles.

"Let it out, Xander," Caiden said gently, wrapping his arm around Xander's shoulders.

"We're here, baby," I said, soothingly.

Xander stiffened beneath me but didn't move.

"When was the last time?" I asked Caiden softly. I knew Xander had fallen into the pits of the drugs that he allowed to control him but I wasn't sure if now, he was going through withdrawal.

"Yesterday. Fell asleep with a joint in his hand," Caiden said, rubbing Xander's back. "Almost burnt down our apartment."

"Oh, Xander." My heart broke in two, aching for the trembling man in my arms.

"Give up, big guy," Caiden coaxed. "Once you submit, you can regain control."

Xander shook his head. "No," he croaked out. "I can't." Tears welled in his eyes. "Please. Don't make me." "Xander," my voice cracked. "I'm so sorry."

Shaking his head back and forth, he tugged and pulled at his shirt. "No!" He met my wide eyed stare. "If you were sorry, you never would have left me."

My mouth opened and closed before snapping shut.

"Xander, let us help you." Caiden cupped his jaw. "Let us in."

"How?" His voice was hoarse.

"By forgiving." Caiden released him and rose to his feet. "He needs a bath. It'll help make him feel better. I'll be in the basement if you need me." And with that, he left us alone, the sound of the basement door closing a moment later.

I nodded and took a deep breath. It wouldn't heal but it would help us become closer. "Come with me," I told Xander, my voice firm.

"Why would—"

"Come, with me," I repeated. "Now." I rose to my feet and held out my hand.

"And if I don't?" he ground out, his body still vibrating from his panic attack. If that's what you even wanted to call it. He was losing it. And I had no idea how to help him control it.

I winked. "As much as I like seeing a man on his knees, you need a bath."

He blinked slowly, his jaw dropping. "Since when do you talk like that?" he asked, slipping his hand in mine.

"Since always, but you never noticed." I helped him to his feet and slid my fingers between his.

"You never once talked to me like that. You were closed off. Shy," he said, allowing me to lead him to the spare room he was staying in.

"Xander, you had no patience." I stopped at the door. "I knew what I wanted and I told you constantly but you never listened." I hated to remind him of how he was back when we were teenagers, especially after his panic attack, but he needed to know sooner than later.

"What are you talking about?" he asked, rubbing the back of his neck.

I pushed open the door and headed in the direction of the bathroom. "Follow me."

He frowned. "You act like you've been here before," he said, half-joking.

My back stiffened. "That's because I have."

Well that stopped him in his tracks. "Hope."

"Whatever you are thinking," I turned to him. "Don't even say it."

"I wasn't thinking anything," he mumbled, following me into the room.

"Seriously?" I turned on the light and shut the door. "I don't know if you recall what you said to us not even ten minutes ago during your little panic attack but you accused me of fucking your best friend."

He squeezed his eyes shut, letting out a heavy breath. "I didn't."

"Yes. You did." Walking over to the large white claw bathtub, I turned on the water. "Strip."

"Excuse me?"

I pointed at him. "You can't bathe in clothes. Strip."

"If you want me to fuck you, all you have to do is ask," he said, taking a step towards me.

I held up a hand, stopping him and rolled my eyes. "You may have had the upper hand during our little moment outside but this," I waved my hand between us. "Is not about sex. Now take off your clothes."

He pulled off his shirt, keeping his gaze locked with mine. He was ripped in the most delicious way possible. He had grown since I saw him last. Thick around the edges and smooth in the curves of his muscles. My tongue tingled, aching to lick every inch of the man standing before me.

I could feel the burn in my cheeks but kept my face passive, not needing to inflate his ego any more than it already was.

Xander pulled down his pants, giving into the moment of defeat.

I was surprised he didn't argue. Giving up so quickly was not a norm for him but the dark bags under his eyes suggested he was exhausted. I prayed this little experiment would work. I couldn't wait to get my hands on his skin and my fingers digging into the knots of his tight muscles.

"Get in the tub," I said, my voice strong and firm when I was a racing pile of nerves on the inside.

"I can wash myself." He stepped into the scalding hot water, a hiss escaping his lips as he sank down into the tub.

"I know you can wash yourself but I am washing you." I knelt behind him and grabbed a cloth before dipping it into the water. "Lean back."

"Hope, I—"

"Damn it, Xander. Let me do this for you. Please. For once in your life, loosen that control." My chest rose and fell, my face red hot.

He huffed and turned around, crossing his arms under his chest.

"Don't pout. It's not sexy."

The corners of his lips tugged.

"Oh my gosh. What is that? Is Xander Brant smiling?" I teased. "Careful, your face might crack."

He laughed and rubbed the scruff of his jaw.

"And a laugh too! I don't know if the world can handle this," I cried, feigning shock.

"Shut up," he mumbled, fighting back a grin.

I giggled, running the cloth over his shoulder.

"What made you come back?" he asked, letting his body relax against the side of the tub.

Thankful for the distraction, I fought back the raging thoughts of jumping into the tub with him. "I've always been back," I said softly. "You just haven't seen me."

He grunted.

"What's going on with you, Xander? You are not the boy I once knew." I glided the cloth across his collar bone to his other shoulder, trying to wash away the pain. So much pain.

His skin became pink from the heat, other parts of him aware of my touch. My gaze landed on the area between his legs. His length jutted forth, pulsing in the water. I cleared my throat.

Xander placed his hands between his legs, shielding himself. "You aren't the girl I once knew either."

"What happened to us?" I asked, running the cloth over his deliriously hard abs. Up. Down. Left. Right. His skin, although shielded by the small square, was enough to make my panties melt.

"You left," he said, leaning his head against the lip of the tub.

I inhaled sharply. "I told you—"

"No. You see, that's the problem, Hope. You didn't tell me anything. You came over to my apartment, fucked me and then said you were moving. That's it. How did you expect me to react?" He sat up. "Would you have preferred I didn't react at all? Would you have

106

preferred I shrugged it off? Not caring that my girlfriend of over a year was leaving me and not giving a damn?"

My stomach twisted, tightening into a ball of agony inside of my gut. "I did care, Xander, but I couldn't do anything about it. I didn't want you to hate me but I also didn't want you stewing over me. I was trying to make it so you could move on and not hurt." I reached for him, pulling him back against the edge of the tub and wrapped my arms around his shoulders. "I'm sorry," I whispered against his neck. "It was stupid of me to think if I showed no emotion, it would hurt you less." I leaned over him, my eyes filling with unshed tears. "I am sorry," I said, brushing the back of my hand down his cheek before cupping his jaw. "I am. I didn't want you to hate me but I'd rather that than for you to lose yourself because of me."

"I did lose a part of myself," he whispered, tilting his head. Licking his bottom lip, he watched me.

My nostrils flared, my breath catching at the small movement. Screw it.

He opened his mouth to say something when my lips covered his in a hard demanding kiss. Not even hesitating, I pushed my way into his mouth. It was hot, desperate, as our tongues meshed and danced as one. I inhaled the sweet scent of his breath, taking it down into my lungs.

My grip on his jaw tightened, the kiss deepening.

Under any other circumstances, I would have jumped into the tub and allow him to have his way with me. But the kiss, this kiss was perfect. It was enough. For now. His lips were soft, moving against my own.

My chest rose and fell with ragged breath, my body tightening and quivering like never before. Desire and pent up passion erupted around us, enveloping us in a blanket of pleasure.

I released him, his eyes sparkling with lust. "I'm sorry. I—"

In a quick move, he turned around completely and cupped my cheeks.

My eyes widened.

A slow grin spread on his face before he captured my mouth in a kiss of undying want. He swallowed my moan, wrapping his hand around my nape and poured everything into that kiss.

My arms circled around his neck, leaning into him as our kiss became frantic. "Xander," I breathed against his lips.

"Shh." He deepened the kiss, silencing me.

Thankful for the interruption, I didn't want any words passing between us. I didn't want to talk about how wrong this was. How much I needed him at that moment.

His hands grazed down my back before cupping my ass. God, I missed him. I had forgotten how perfect his hands felt on my body.

Messaging and kneading, he dug his fingers into my flesh. Suddenly, he pulled me into the tub.

I gasped into his mouth.

He chuckled, which came out husky and filled with desire. Water sloshed over the side of the tub, my moans and purrs erupting around us.

I leaned back. His eyes were dark and stormy, billowing with a lust so strong, it took my breath. I glanced down, warmth spreading over my skin.

He followed my gaze. His cock stood at attention, throbbing and full, ready for my touch.

Licking my lips, I lowered my hand into the water when he stopped me. "Let me please you," I said, frowning.

"No. Not until I can have you completely." He brought my hand up to his mouth and kissed my knuckles.

"Xander." I rose to my knees, straddling his lap and pulled my shirt up and over my head.

His dick twitched at the sight before him, begging, pleading for him to bend me over and do what he did best. What he had wanted after all of these years.

My full breasts rose and fell, hidden by a white lace bra. My pink nipples hardened to sharp peaks, hinting for him to suck and bite them.

Xander ran a finger down the middle of my chest before cupping my breast. Pulling the cup down, he latched onto my nipple.

I jumped at the hard rough tug, throwing my head back and arched into his touch.

Hesitation shone in his eyes although his actions kept bringing me over the edge. His hands gripped the cup of the bra now covering my one breast and ripped it clean off my body. With a growl, he covered the other nub, biting into it like he couldn't get enough.

I whimpered. Reaching between us, I tried touching him but he only pulled back. Frustrated, I pushed him. "Let me touch you. Please," I pleaded.

Xander growled and crashed his lips to mine. His tongue invaded my mouth, dancing and sliding over mine. The kiss was hard, bordering on possessive while his hands roamed down the length of my body. Gripping my soaked jeans and panties, he pulled them down to my knees.

"Xander," I said against his mouth.

"Shut up," he snarled. Leaning back, he cupped my naked ass. His hand slid into my hair, gripping it tight and held me restrained against the side of the tub.

I stared up at him wide eyed.

His finger trailed down the length of my torso, reaching my mound. A wicked glint flashed in his eyes when he pushed a finger into my trembling body. "Is this what you wanted?"

A hard moan escaped me while he thrust into me slow and deep.

His palm rubbed against my throbbing clit while his finger pumped into me.

Reaching out for him, I pulled him down to my mouth. But he didn't kiss me. He rubbed his face into the crook of my neck, giving my body the pleasure I craved.

No words passed between us as the onslaught of a release exploded through my being. I cried out, shaking against him, wishing I could have given him the same.

Xander released me and wouldn't meet my gaze. His jaw clenched. Bringing his fingers up to his mouth, he licked the juices from my body off of them.

My core quivered at the sight but I ignored it, needing him back with me. "Hey." I cupped his cheek. "Talk to me."

Leaning into my palm, he placed his hand over mine. "If we don't stop, I won't be held accountable for what I do to your delicious body."

"Seriously?" I raised an eyebrow, attempting again to reach between us. "You want to stop?"

"No." He grabbed my hand, pulling me away from him. "I never said that. I said we should stop. Not that I want to."

"Why? What's the problem?" My free hand wrapped around the base of his dick. "Clearly you want me."

He hissed out a breath at the unexpected contact, his hips bucking.

"I know you've thought about me all of these years." I licked up the length of his jaw, my hand gripping him tight. "Did you jerk off to thoughts of me?"

He growled, wrapping his hand around mine that had a firm hold on his dick. "Yes. Every single fucking time. Is that what you wanted to hear? You want to know how just now, I had to control myself from turning you around and fucking you stupid?"

My brows narrowed. "Tell me how you've abused yourself. The alcohol. Drugs. Women. Is any of that as good as me?"

"No!" he snapped. "None of it is as good as you." Rising to his knees, he kept his hand wrapped around mine, squeezing his cock to the point it brought tears to his eyes.

"Xander." I gasped, trying to struggle out of his grip. I didn't want to hurt him. Challenge him, yes. But hurt him? God, the abuse he was making me inflict on his body, it brought bile to my throat. But I couldn't stop. He was too strong.

His hold tightened as he forced me to give him pain. Goosebumps rose on his skin, his breath leaving him in short bursts of air.

I could only stare at him as I helped push him over the edge of self-destruction.

He crushed his mouth to mine. A snarl escaped him, rumbling from his chest. Our hands picked up speed when he came hard on a roar, my name leaving his lips. Our pace didn't let up as he jumped over that edge a second time, coming hard into our joined hands. When he finally came down from the intensity of the release, he let me go.

My eyes were filled with unshed tears, my cheeks hot. Suddenly, before I could even begin to comprehend what was happening, I slapped him.

FOURTEEN

Xander

"DON'T EVER MAKE ME do that again!" Hope cried, beating her tiny fists against my chest. "How could you? How could you make me hurt you like that?" A sob escaped her lips.

Pulling her into my arms, I wrapped myself around her, holding her as she cried. What the hell was I thinking?

Going into this, I never expected the outcome. I never expected to even hold her again let alone coming in her hand. I was an asshole. I didn't know what had come over me but as soon as she had touched me, something inside of me snapped. "I'm so sorry," I whispered into her hair. My flaccid cock throbbed with a slight twinge of pain, resting against her inner thigh.

"Why would you make me do that?" she asked, pulling back.

I wiped the tears from under her eyes. "I needed to feel something," I said softly. I leaned my forehead against hers, running my hands down her arms. "I needed to be reminded that this hole in my chest can be filled."

"So you wanted me to hurt you? Are you wanting to fill it with pain?"

I shrugged. "It was better than the emptiness inside of me." Like I had felt for so long. Giving her the release I knew her body craved was one of the happiest moments I had in years. But it wasn't enough. The next time, I would take her and I wouldn't be able to stop myself. If only she knew how little control I had over my actions. If she could handle me, great. If not, it would ruin what we ever had and it would leave no chance for a future.

Fresh tears welled in her eyes before she rose to her feet. Stepping out of the bathtub, she grabbed a white terrycloth robe off the wall hook and wrapped it around herself. She turned away from me and with a little maneuvering, her wet pants finally fell to her feet with a wet thud. "Caiden told me you were different. He warned me," her voice cracked. "But I had no idea you were so…"

"What?" I asked, pulling myself from the tub and wrapped a towel around my waist.

"Broken," she said so quietly, I almost didn't hear her.

I walked by her and opened the door, being met with the scent of musk and leather.

Caiden stood at the doorway, his hand in the air. "I was checking to make sure everything was okay." He looked between us, frowning. "What happened?"

I grunted and pushed past him, letting go of the towel. A breath caught behind me but I ignored it, not sure who it was in the first place. Not that I cared. At that moment, I needed a fucking drink.

Soft voices scratched at my mind. Wishing they would shut the hell up, my pulse raced. "If you're going to talk about me like I'm not even here, the least you can do is leave."

"Hope was telling me you forced her to hurt you."

I roughly pulled on sweatpants and spun on them.

"Why don't you tell him you made me come as well? Does it make you feel better, telling him every single detail?" I demanded of Hope. "Did you tell him I fingered you? Why don't we announce it to the whole fucking world!"

"Shut the hell up," she glared at me, her cheeks reddening. "Stop accusing me of shit. I don't tell anyone anything. I told him I hurt you and I felt bad. That's it."

"Don't feel bad. I made you do it, remember?" I ground out but all I could think about was her tight body wrapped around my finger. God, she had felt so good.

Trembling in my arms. Moaning through the release I allowed her. If only I could make love to her. Show her how much I had truly missed her. Would it be like before? Like when we were teenagers? No. Because I knew more now. I knew what would make her tick. What buttons to press.

Which spots to kiss and lick and suck.

"Hope, can you give us a moment?" Caiden asked. His voice was calm and although it was said as a question, we knew not to argue when he spoke in that tone.

I sat on the edge of the bed, dropping my head in my hands.

The sound of the door closing made my heart jump when the bed lowered beside me. "She still loves you," Caiden muttered.

"Yeah. And I keep fucking it up," I bit out but she sure as hell wasn't making it easy. She apologized for leaving me but did I ever apologize to her? No. Because I was an asshole. And I owned that title. Unwillingly.

Caiden cupped my nape, brushing his thumb up and down the side of my neck. "She came back to you. You can't expect everything to be back to normal right away."

"Was it ever normal?"

His thumb stopped. "What do you mean?"

"I…she said I never listened to her. I assumed she wasn't upset when her parents forced her to move. She said she would rather I hate her than for me to lose myself because of her. But I already had." I swallowed past the hard lump in my throat.

"She was trying to remain strong for you."

I never thought of it that way. "God, I'm such a dick."

Several minutes passed without us saying anything. My heart had gone back to a normal rate. My muscles no longer tense and tight.

"Why did you make her hurt you?" he asked, releasing me and moved up the bed. He leaned against the headboard and patted the empty spot beside him.

"I don't know. I…I couldn't control the urge to have her hurt me," I said, sitting beside him.

"Why?"

"How the hell am I supposed to know?" I stretched out my legs in front of me, rubbing my hands on my thighs. My palms tingled, my fingers itching with the need to touch Hope again. *I don't know what's going on.*

"I wish I did." Caiden scrubbed a hand down his face, his eyes taking on a faraway look.

My head snapped around, not realizing I had spoken out loud.

"You aren't alone," he said soothingly.

My vision blurred and I swallowed repeatedly past the lump burning my throat.

"Xander," Caiden's voice became firm. "You are not alone."

I winced and looked away.

A strong hand cupped the back of my neck. "You're not alone."

"What are you doing?" I demanded, trying to pull from his grip.

"You're not alone."

"Caiden, stop this shit." Whatever he was doing, it wouldn't work. Him and his guru Yoda shit could go to hell.

"You're not alone." He pulled me into a hug, his arms wrapping around my shoulders.

"Stop. Let me go," my voice cracked. I pushed against him but he wouldn't budge, his hold tightening.

"You're not alone," he repeated.

His words vibrated into my body, annoying the ever living shit out of me. What did he think he was going to accomplish by repeating himself over and over again? I wouldn't give in. I couldn't. He could kiss my white ass if he thought I would break.

"Xander, you are not alone," he said slowly.

"Stop. Please, God, stop. I can't take it." A sob escaped me unexpectedly but I still continued to fight him off. I couldn't deal. His words. Those three little words. Fuck me, they hurt. They hurt because they were true and I was too dumb to see it in the beginning. I shut everyone out. When my parents died, I wished I would have died with them.

God, I missed them so much. So damn much.

"You're not alone," he breathed against my neck.

"Caiden, please. Help me. God." Tears rolled down my cheeks, my body slumping against his, admitting the ultimate defeat. I submitted to his words. Gave in completely, letting the sorrow of being trapped inside of myself take over.

"You are my best friend." He pulled me against him, keeping his arms locked around my shoulders. "I love you, Xander. In ways you will never understand."

My body racked with sobs and I would have asked him what he meant but at that point, I no longer cared.

Whichever way he loved me, however he loved me, it was still love. No one had told me that in so long, I let it soak in.

When the cries diminished, my eyelids became heavy. Resting my head against his chest, I curled an arm around his waist, falling asleep to the soothing beat of his heart.

***

I woke to a warm body resting against me. It was soft and firm in all the right places. Rolling over, I found

Hope staring back at me. Her lips parted, her pink tongue licking along the curve of her mouth.

"Hi," she whispered.

I swallowed hard. "Hi."

She cupped my cheek and kissed my forehead. "How are you doing?"

Inhaling a shaky breath, I let it out in one long exhale before I replied. "I'm alright. Where's Caiden?"

"He had some errands to run. I came in about an hour ago to check up on you and he asked me to look after you."

My chest ached at the loss. After I broke down, I fell asleep in his arms but I remembered his soothing words. I dreamt of them, fading in and out as he continued talking to me. He loved me. Was he in love with me? Did it matter? Not to me. Love was love. He told me I wouldn't understand his love for me. Whatever that meant.

"What are you thinking about?" Hope asked, pulling her robe tighter around her.

I glanced down at her. The robe opened at the top, revealing the swell of her breasts. Her tanned skin peeked out at me. My lips tingled, my tongue vibrating with the need to lick every inch of her.

"Xander."

My gaze shot to hers at the husky use of my name. Clearing my throat, I rolled over onto my stomach.

"Don't shut me out," she pleaded, placing a hand on my shoulder.

"I'm not!" I pulled myself from the bed. Sitting on the edge, I dropped my head in my hands. The onset of another panic attack was rearing its ugly head. My heart raced. My chest constricted to the point my breath barely reached my lungs.

"Breathe, Xander." Hope wrapped her arms around my shoulders, whispering softly in my ear. "Breathe."

I can't take this. I don't know what's wrong with me. I want...I need a fucking drink. I need something. Anything.

"Xander, please." Hope's voice cracked. She slid into my arms, straddling my waist and cupped my cheeks. Forcing me to look at her, she placed a soft kiss on my mouth.

My racing heart eased, beating to a slow rhythm. I inhaled deep, breathing in the scent of her. Running my hands up her back, I deepened the kiss. I pushed my tongue between her lips, sliding it into her mouth.

She jumped, a slight moan leaving her when our tongues came into contact. Her hands gripped my shoulders, digging into the flesh of my muscles as her hips began to undulate against me.

A growl escaped me and the next thing I knew, I had her on the bed beneath me. I swallowed her gasp, pushing against her. The kiss turned rough, needy, while I circled my hips into the heat of her core.

Hope released me, tilting her head back, panting. "Oh God. Xander."

I ripped open her robe, staring down at her naked flesh. Licking my lips, I took a nipple into my mouth, tugging and pulling until she was writhing beneath me. My teeth grazed over the hardened nub, biting down hard enough to make her yelp. I pulled the robe a part completely and grazed a hand down her middle. "You are so fucking beautiful and I'm going to have fun destroying every inch of you." My voice. It didn't sound like my voice as the rough vibrato rumbled from my chest. My mouth trailed along her skin, biting and sucking, nipping and licking a path in its wake.

Her breathing quickened, her eyes dilating to the point of black. So dark. Her rosy cheeks reddened, the purrs and moans leaving her full mouth erupting around us.

"What do you want?" I asked, making my way back up to her mouth.

"You. God, I've never wanted you this bad."

A moment of hesitation fluttered through me but I held it back. Those words stung. She had me before. But wanted me more now? Either way, if she wanted me to fuck her, I would. And there would be no way in hell it would be making love. "You want me?" I purred, nipping the soft spot under her ear.

She nodded. "Yes," she breathed.

I grabbed both of her wrists and held them in one hand above her head. Grabbing a condom out of the end table drawer, I ripped it open with my teeth.

Hope watched me the whole time, her mouth parting, her breathing picking up with baited anticipation. The Xander Brant she once knew no longer existed. I would fuck those thoughts out of her if she was thinking she would get him again.

I pulled my pants lower, sheathed myself and lined up to her hot entrance. "This is not making love." With everything in me, I had to force myself not to thrust forward and wrap myself in her warmth. I wanted to tease her. I wanted her to beg more than she already had. I wanted her to submit, giving me her undoing.

"I want you to fuck me," she said huskily. "Not love me."

In one smooth thrust, I filled her. "Fuck." Her snug core tightened around me, gripping me like a fist and if I didn't take control, I would come within seconds.

She cried out, squeezing her eyes shut.

"I do love you, Hope," I growled, pulling out of her. A hot shiver travelled down my spine.

"Don't," she panted. "Don't love me. Just fuck me. Please, Xander."

Grabbing her waist, I pulled her further under me and thrust into her hard. Keeping her wrists in mine, I sped up my hips. "You think demanding me to fuck you means I don't love you? Because you ripped my heart out," I pushed into her as deep as her body would allow. "It means my feelings disappeared?"

She whimpered, wrapping her legs tight around my waist.

"I've loved you since the day you walked into my life and I've loved you since the day you walked out of it." I pumped in and out of her, her pussy squeezing me, gripping me tight as her body got ready for its release.

"Stop!" she cried. "Stop talking. God." Her body shook, trembling beneath me.

And that was when I released her. I sat back on my haunches and wrapped my hand around the base of my dick.

Her eyes darkened, watching me. "What are you doing?"

"I'm reminding you who's in control," I said, squeezing myself. "I have shit going on in my fucking head but it doesn't mean anything. You and Caiden both need to remember that."

"None of us are in control." She rose to her knees, letting the robe fall off of her slender body. "But we are in control of right now."

"What do you want from me?" I heard myself ask. I had tried so hard to fuck her and get it over with but as soon as I was inside of her, that nagging part of myself reared its annoying head.

Hope grabbed my hand and kissed my knuckles before lowering her body onto me.

I groaned, gripping her hips and met her thrust for thrust.

She threw her head back, circled against me and road me hard. "Oh God."

Wrapping my arms around her, I took her pebbled nipple into my mouth, sucking and pulling until it was swollen and red under my touch.

She cried out, my name leaving her lips on a soft scream.

Holding her tighter, I quickened my pace, needing some control.

"Please. Stop," she panted. "I can't take anymore."

She could and she was going to until I was good and ready to let her go. She may have fallen in love with me as a boy but I would make her fall in love with me as a man and if the first way to do that would be by fucking her into exhaustion, then so be it.

Cupping her shoulders, I pushed into her hard, thrusting in and out of her. I sunk my teeth into her nipple, igniting a scream to leave her lips. "That's it, Hope."

"Oh God, you feel so good."

"Better than before?" I asked, pulling out of her.

She watched me, her eyes dark with lust and desire.

Pulling her to the edge of the bed, I pushed her onto her back. "You don't have to tell me. I know you're thinking it. What would you say if I told you I fucked my way through woman after woman trying to get over you?" I nipped her inner thigh and wrapped my arms around her waist.

"I would say you're an asshole." She held the sheets tight in her hands, lifting her hips towards my face.

I chuckled and blew across her mound. "I know right now, I could do and say anything and as long as you got the release you crave, you wouldn't care."

"I already came. I'm satisfied," she said, glaring down at me.

"Are you now?" Spreading her folds with my thumbs, I pinched her clit.

She gasped, arching under me.

"How satisfied are you?" I covered her core before she had a chance to respond and thrust my tongue deep inside of her.

Her hands wrapped around my head, forcing me into her harder.

I growled, the acidic taste of her sweet body washing down my throat. Peaches and cream. It was all I could think about while I ate her. She was right where I wanted her. She thought she was in control. She thought she had me backed into a corner. I wouldn't beg. Not yet. Right now, she was mine.

"Xander, please."

"Tell me," I demanded, releasing her with a smack.

"More. God, I've never…" Her chest rose and fell with ragged breath.

"You've never what?" I ground out. "Seen you like this."

A wicked grin spread on my face. "I'm not the boy you once knew, remember?" I shoved my face into her hot pussy and sucked her clit between my lips.

She was coming within seconds, my name leaving her lips and bouncing off the walls of the room.

Before she could come down from her release, I flipped her onto stomach and thrust back into her body.

"You may think you have control, but know that neither of us do," I whispered against her neck. "If you're smart, you'll leave me alone. You'll stop trying to take care of me and let me be."

"Never," she cried out.

"I didn't think so." I rose to my full height and smacked her hard on the ass. "That's for lying to me earlier."

Hope frowned and glared daggers up at me. "I didn't lie to you."

"No? You said you wouldn't fuck me when you got back." I smirked. "Well it looks like I'm seated nice and deep inside of your beautiful body."

She pushed back against me. "You are an asshole."

I covered her body with mine and sped up my hips.

She was right. I was being an asshole but I couldn't control the words leaving my lips. I couldn't control the urge to make her hate me. Make her see I wasn't worth it. But I knew deep down she wouldn't listen. She would try and fix me like Caiden had tried. If only they would both leave me alone. Then I could go on and wallow in my self-pity and smoke my way into oblivion.

FIFTEEN

Hope

IT HAD BEEN A couple of hours since I felt him inside of me. Full and throbbing. Thick and rigged. I could still feel every vein, every pulse. My body shivered.

Xander wrapped his arm around me, pulling me tighter against him and sighed into my hair.

Caiden had told me he was having nightmares. About me. About his parents. About life in general. I wanted to be the happy in his dreams. The sunshine in the darkness that threatened to swallow him whole.

"Sleep, baby," he whispered in my ear. He groaned, rolling over, his back stiffening.

I followed his movement and kissed his cheek. "Dream of me, Xander. Hear my voice."

His eyes remained closed, his brows narrowing.

"Hope," he said in his sleep filled state.

I pulled the covers up higher around us and snuggled into him. "Dream of me."

He let out a contented sigh and rolled over again, with half of his big body on top of mine.

Brushing my fingers over his upper back, my eyes became heavy. "I love you," I whispered, before I allowed sleep to take over.

***

(Xander)

Letting Hope sleep, I left the house a couple of hours later and started jogging down the driveway. I looked up from my perch on a picnic bench, not remembering how I got there. Dropping my head in my hands, I let out a heavy sigh.

"You alright?"

My head snapped up at and I found Shana walking towards me. Her look of concern would usually annoy me but right now, I needed it. "I have no idea."

She nodded and hopped up on the table, sitting beside me. "I have days like that. My grandma always asks me if I'm okay and when I tell her I don't know, she gets mad at me."

"Why?"

She shrugged. "Not sure. I guess in most cases people do know how they are but when you say you don't know, it throws them off. Like you're supposed to say, I'm fine, no matter what."

"Life's biggest lie," I muttered.

"Exactly." She tilted her head, closing her eyes. "I miss the sun."

I grunted. The gloomy weather fit perfectly with my mood so it didn't bother me at all.

"You still coming to my recital? It's next Wednesday." "Sure." I nodded. "Tell me where and I'll be there."

"Sweet." She clapped her hands together and grinned. "So tell me, Mr. Bitter, what do you like to do?"

"What do you mean?"

"Well clearly you like to go for runs but what else? What interests you?" She looked up at me, waiting.

My mouth opened and closed, a flutter swimming in the pits of my gut. "I...I'm not sure."

She frowned. "Do you like to read? Watch movies? What's your favorite movie?"

I shook my head. No one had ever asked me what I liked to do or what I was interested in. Everyone assumed I would go with the flow or I wanted to be constantly high. My chest ached and I gripped my shirt. "I...I should go," I said, rising from the table.

"No. Please don't go. I'm sorry." She grabbed my arm, stopping me. "My grandma tells me I'm too forward sometimes. Just tell me to shut up."

"I would never tell you to shut up," I whispered, rubbing a hand over my buzzed head.

"Where do you work?" she asked, genuinely interested in what I had to say.

I rose from the table and paced back and forth in front of her, embracing the bite of the cool crisp air flowing around me. "I don't have a job. That's why I live with

Caiden. I'm not a mooch but I can't keep a job with all the shit going on inside of my head. But I refuse to live off the system. I guess..." I needed help like Caiden and Hope said but I didn't know how to ask for it. I wanted to fight my demons on my own. I needed to.

"Maybe try working from home? Or do you have any hobbies that you could make any money off of?"

I scoffed. In another life, I would sell myself for sex but that wasn't doable. Unless…I shook myself. God, I was such an asshole. "I like to draw and paint but I…I have several problems I'm dealing with and no one understands. I'm alone. I'm trapped inside my head and I can't get out." Once those words left me, a lead weight was lifted off of my shoulders.

Shana stared at me, her face passive. "I…I think I know how you feel."

"You're fourteen years old. You shouldn't know how I feel." I found myself wanting to destroy anything threatening to hurt her.

"I know but I do." She looked away and rose from her spot on the table. "Please come to my recital," she said softly.

I nodded. "I wouldn't miss it."

***

Hanging out with Shana for a couple of hours each day allowed me to be myself. No judgment. No contempt. I felt normal. Or as normal as I could feel given my current situation. Why that was the case, I wasn't sure. Why couldn't it be like before? Caiden, Hope, and I hanging out. Shooting the shit. Being best friends. All throughout school, we were inseparable. My parents called us The Three Musketeers. Although it wasn't original, it stuck and I loved it. It was like no matter what happened in life, Caiden and Hope would always have my back. They flew through school with honors, awards and high grades. While I barely made it. I graduated but probably because my teachers felt sorry for me.

My parents were never home. I was alone most of the time. I loved them. I did. But they weren't the best role models. If only I could tell them how I felt. But that day...that horrible afternoon, left me alone for good. And ever since their accident, I closed myself off from the rest of the world. Even from my best friends.

My thoughts travelled around me, pounding inside of my head like a hammer. So many questions of what if and if only. I couldn't live life this way but it was the only way I knew how.

Turning up the volume on my phone until all I heard was the screaming of the guitars and heavy thump of the drums, I landed my fists against the punching bag. Circling the large swinging item before me, I envisioned that it was my demons. Black and billowy, laughing in my face, egging me on to the point I broke. But I refused. I wouldn't let them control me.

Beads of sweat rolled down my back, covering my skin like a second layer. My muscles burned with my rough movements, twitching and jumping inside of me.

It had been a couple of days since Hope and I had sex. Since I felt the delicious warmth of her body. I was rough but she gave it back as hard. She was with me like she needed to be and I was with her because I couldn't breathe without her. But did I ever tell her? No. I was stubborn. I could think the words I had wanted to say for so long but every time I got the balls to tell her how

I felt, they froze on my tongue. It was such a sad cliché but it was true.

Hope had kept her distance from me, no doubt still pissed at the way I treated her. Although she never stopped me, I knew we needed to talk. But once I was seated deep inside of her, all thought process fizzled out. She felt safe. She was my home. If only I could tell her.

Caiden had also kept to himself, probably giving up on me. We never talked about my breakdown or him telling me that he loved me. He spent most of his time in the basement, doing who knows what. I still didn't know what was down there and even though I was curious, I didn't care enough to research further.

As if he could read my mind, Caiden arrived in front of me and grabbed hold of the punching bag. His gaze locked with mine but he didn't do anything. He held the bag while I punched the shit out of it.

After a half an hour of self-torture, I stopped and hunched over. Taking deep breaths to ease my racing heart, I pulled the ear buds from my ears.

"How do you feel?" Caiden asked me, handing me a bottle of water.

"I forgot how much pain a punching bag could inflict." I shook out my limbs and stretched.

He chuckled. "No doubt."

"Where's Hope?" I asked, drying my face off with a towel.

"She's…around." Caiden made his way to the door and turned back to me. "I want to show you something." My heart jumped. "Okay…"

"Follow me." Caiden headed down the hall to the set of double doors leading to the basement. He pushed them open, took a deep breath and walked over the threshold, not looking back to see if I was behind him.

I followed, because curiosity got the better of me and I wanted to know what he did while he holed himself up in the basement.

The thick silence wore on, the only sounds being the shuffling our feet made against the deep red plush carpet. The walls were painted black with gold light fixtures hanging from the ceiling. The cool damp air circled around us, sending a shiver down my spine. It reminded me of a dungeon although it didn't look like one.

Once Caiden reached another set of double doors at the end of the long hallway, he turned to me. "I'm showing you this part of myself because you need to know." He grabbed the gold door knob. "Open your mind, Xander, and trust me." Not giving me a chance to respond, he pushed open the doors and stepped into a large room.

I followed in behind him, my gaze instantly landing on Hope. My jaw dropped. She looked absolutely stunning.

She was wearing a white floor length dress, her auburn curls piled high on her head. Her full lips tugged at the corners but she didn't do or say anything as I made my way further into the room.

My gaze danced around the vast expanse, not understanding what I was seeing. "What's going on?" I asked, my heart racing hard against my rib cage.

"For the past couple of years, I've been practicing Kinbaku." Caiden moved to the wall holding a coiled up rope. "Do you know what that is, Xander?"

I shook my head.

"It's a form of rope play. I found out a while ago that my grandfather practiced it. When I was a child, I walked in on him binding a woman and I was intrigued. But what amazed me even more was the look of pure and utter love and submission written all over her face. She trusted him completely."

I had no idea. I had met Caiden's grandfather once but never in my life would I have thought he was into kink.

"Now I know what you're thinking but this is not a form of kink," Caiden said as if taking the thought right from my mind. "It's more than that and I have had the pleasure of sharing it with Hope."

My head whipped around, my brows furrowing.

"Before you get all jealous and cave man on me, we have never had sex, so don't you fucking say shit," Caiden's voice hardened, his dark eyes taking on a glacial look. "This is your problem, Xander," he pointed at me. "You assume and jump to conclusions before you ask questions. I know you're still pissed I've kept in contact with her but there are reasons for it that you don't understand."

"Then enlighten me," I bit out, crossing my arms under my chest.

"I will, but not right now. Right now, we need to share this with you." Caiden stood beside Hope and handed her the coiled up rope.

"Why? What is this going to do for me? You going to bind me, restrain me so I can't do anything? So I submit like a pussy?" I said, my voice rough.

"Listen to me when I tell you," Caiden glared.

"Submitting is not a form of weakness. It does not mean you are a pussy if you give your control over to someone else. Domination and submission is all about trust and communication."

"So you tie your partners up, Caid? Is that it? Is that the only way you can get them to fuck you?" My mouth snapped shut as soon as the words left my lips. What the hell was I thinking? He was trying to help me. Trying to make me see I could be more than an empty shell that needed drugs and alcohol to get any sustenance.

In a quick move, Caiden was in front of me. He cupped my neck in a rough hold. "I know you're going through shit." His fingers grazed my temple. "I know there are demons inside of you that you can't control but don't you ever accuse me of forcing myself on the people I fuck."

"I didn't mean...I never—"

His brows narrowed to hard points. "You know what I've been through but what you don't know is the nightmares I've had. The moments where I wake up screaming because all I can feel is the fire burning my skin. The agony of losing my family over a stupid accident. You lost your parents in a car crash. That was not your fault and yet you blame yourself. Why, Xander?"

I swallowed hard.

"You need to stop. I lost my parents and little brother because of the fire I lit in the fireplace that got out of control when I fell asleep. But do you see me feeling sorry for myself?" His voice rose. "Do you see me drowning myself in a bottle or ingesting shit that would eventually kill me? No. You want to fucking know why? Because I know it was not my fault. I know it was an accident and that my family would not want me to destroy myself because of it."

Something flashed in his gaze and he quickly looked away.

My eyes burned and I tried to pull my head from his grip but his hold tightened.

Caiden leaned his forehead against mine, cupping the back of my neck with both hands. "I know you remember what I told you a couple of days ago."

My chest ached. I couldn't say anything because I didn't feel the same way. And he knew it. I loved him like a brother, a friend. I wasn't gay but he was the only man I've ever been comfortable enough with to show a part of myself that had been closed off for so long. That I've ever displayed my vulnerability in front of and I've ever allowed to hold me the way he had.

"I know you don't return the feelings I have for you," his voice lowered so only I could hear him. "And I don't want you to lose any sleep because of it."

"I'm...I'm sorry," I whispered, looking down.

"Don't. Don't you dare apologize. You can't force feelings. Not with me. Not with Hope. Not with anyone. Look at me, Xander."

I met his gaze and swallowed back my words. What would I say? What could I say?

"Don't worry about what I told you. Right now, I don't want anything. I want...this." He kissed my forehead, letting his lips linger.

My eyes fluttered closed and I knew right then that I could never give him what he needed. But I could be that friend. That one that would be there for him no matter what. That would support him in any decision he made.

"Besides," he pulled back, smiling softly at me. "I have someone to curb my cravings."

My eyes widened.

He chuckled. "Yes. You'll meet her soon I'm sure."

"Her?" I asked, frowning.

His smile faded. "I'm not gay, Xander. Yes, I've been with men but because I was attracted to them, not their gender."

"Oh…"

He laughed. "I know it's confusing but I like to refer to myself as pansexual." He grimaced. "Some think that means we are attracted to anything and I do mean anything, no matter the species or age but that's not true. Well not in my case, anyways."

I nodded, understanding. I glanced at Hope before looking back at him. "So basically you fall for the heart whether they're male or female?"

"Exactly and when you meet her, you'll understand more," he said, motioning for Hope to join us. He stepped out of the way, keeping a distance. "Now, enough about me. Hope, you remember everything I taught you?"

"Yes," she said, her voice firm. She stepped in front of me and placed her hand on my chest. "I know we've had our issues and I know you have so many questions about why I left and how I could leave without fighting my parents. I will tell you. I promise you this but right now? I want you to trust me. I need you to trust that I will never hurt you again. Can you do that?"

I swallowed hard, my heart racing. "I…" I cleared my throat. "I want to."

"Good. That's all I can expect right now." She walked around me, allowing her hand to graze ever so slightly over my arm, my back, my stomach.

"Zee, I know you enjoy your music. It's a form of therapy for you," Caiden said, holding an MP3 player in his hand. "If you listen to this music, will you allow yourself to feel?"

All I could do was nod.

He handed me the small player and pulled a black scarf from his pocket. "I'm going to blind fold you. I want you to turn the music up as loud as you can. We need you to drown out those demons."

My palms became sweaty at what he was asking of me. Blind to the outside world and what they would be doing to me and deaf to the sounds of them talking and moving about. Would they be discussing me? My issues?

Caiden squeezed my shoulder. "Anytime you need us to stop, I want you to shout out, Charming."

"Charming?" I repeated, the word tasting funny on my tongue.

He nodded.

"It's your safeword, baby," Hope said softly, linking her fingers in mine.

For the first time since she had been back, the term of endearment we had for each other didn't bother me. I craved it and welcomed it with open arms, needing it now more than ever before. "Okay."

"Put the ear buds in your ears and turn on the music.

It's on shuffle. You will know when it's time to turn it off." Caiden held the scarf in his hands and brought it up to my eyes. "Remember your safeword."

I placed the buds in my ears and pressed play as my world darkened.

He tied the scarf tightly around my head, cutting off my vision completely.

The two senses of me not being able to see or hear anything except for the music, made everything else hyper aware. My skin tingled, coming alive with anticipation. My lungs constricted with each baited breath.

The music flowed into my ears, washing over me like a lover's touch. I jumped when warm fingers pushed underneath my shirt, grazing lightly over my abs. It was hard not to speak as I gave myself to Hope in ways I never could imagine.

She linked her fingers in mine and I knew it was her by the way her hand fit perfectly in my palm. With a gentle tug, she pulled me to my knees and lifted both of my arms above my head. Next thing I knew, she pulled my t-shirt off of my torso, the cool wind sending a shiver down my spine.

A soft peck was placed on my back between my shoulder blades and I sighed, leaning into the touch. The ear buds were suddenly pulled from my ears. "I was supposed to let you listen to the music, allowing you to dive into the melody but I need you to hear my words," Hope said softly and kissed my cheek.

I nodded and reached up to pull the blind fold off of my face.

She came into my view, smiling. Her beautiful eyes twinkled, dancing under the flicker of the dim glow in the room. "Caiden trained me to make you fly." She pointed to the ceiling.

I looked up and frowned. A gold hook hung from it with a rope and lever attached. I didn't know exactly what I was looking at.

"It's to help me lift you when I'm by myself. He had it installed a couple of days ago."

"I never thought you would be into kink, Hope," I blurted, cupping her cheek. My thumb grazed back and forth along her jawline and my lips tingled. I wanted to kiss her again. I wanted to make love to her body, her soul, her mind and never let her go. She was the light in my sea of darkness. Even before she came back. Thinking of her kept me going.

"I want to do this for you. I want to help you battle your demons," she said, her voice firm.

I glanced around us, noticing for the first time that we were alone. "Caiden told me he loves me."

She placed a hand over mine and leaned into my palm. "I know. That's why I told you to talk to him."

I sighed. "I love him but not the way he needs me to."

Hope nodded. "He has someone who will take care of him until…"

I met her gaze when her words trailed off. "Until what?"

She swallowed a couple of times before looking away. "Never mind." She rose to her feet, her crotch lining up perfectly with my face.

My dick stirred and I cleared my throat. Memories of her taste flowing down my throat while I swallowed her orgasms slid into my mind. "Hope." My voice came out guttural and husky. This was not the time to be thinking about throwing her down on the floor and fucking her until she forgot her name.

Hope giggled, grazing a hand over my buzzed head.

My eyes shot up to hers. "Did you giggle? Are you laughing at my misfortune?"

"I'm laughing at the fact that right now, you are probably thinking about throwing me to the ground and having your way with me but you can't because Caiden could walk in at any time."

I nodded. "Yup, exactly, but he probably won't walk in. I swear that guy has Jedi mind tricks up his sleeve."

Her laugh hardened. "I love your Star Wars references." She sighed, pinching my chin and tilted my head. "I've missed them."

I shrugged. What could I say? I was a sucker for those movies. Light sabers. Aliens. Yoda. Oh my. "I've missed you," I whispered, not sure if she heard me.

Her eyes saddened but she took a step back, holding the coiled up rope in her hand still. "Will you allow me to make you fly? No blind folds. No music. Just you and me."

"Yes."

A deep sigh escaped her, a lonely tear running down her cheek. "Stand and take off your pants."

My heart gave a thump at the firm tone of her voice and I did what I was told. I stood in my boxers, waiting for her next instructions.

"Take them off," she demanded, pointing at my waist.

Her cheeks were flush, her voice dripping with arousal.

Under normal circumstances, I would have played into it but right now, I found myself wanting to feel. I wanted to embrace whatever she had to give me.

"I want you to keep your eyes down. Do not talk unless I say. If you need to speak, you must ask for permission first." She walked around me, keeping her hand on my body no matter which way she moved. "Take off your boxers," she repeated.

I slid them down my legs, kicking them to the side.

Never being ashamed of my nudity, I would usually brush it off but right now, I felt opened. Bare. Stripped of all things that could stop her from seeing me. The real me.

"Anything you want to say before we get started?" she asked, stopping in front of me.

"What made you decide to..." I motioned around us. "Get into all of this?"

She chewed her bottom lip, her cheeks reddening. "I accidentally walked in on Caiden tying up a woman. My story is pretty much the same as his. I was intrigued. And I instantly thought of you."

"Me?" My brows furrowed. "Why?"

"Because...I want to help you regain control of your life. The guilt is going to destroy you and that...that scares me." Her breath hitched. She closed the distance between us. "Kneel."

That word. That one small word. One syllable. One meaning. Submit.

My legs gave out beneath me of their own accord and I found myself on my knees before I could even begin to protest.

"Eyes down," she demanded.

I looked at my hands folded in my lap. Unfolding them, I placed them on my thighs and then folded them again. I was antsy and I had no idea what to do with them or what would be the outcome of this night.

"Don't worry, baby." She petted a hand over my head. "I'll guide you."

Her words were soothing, caressing me as if they were actually touching me themselves. "I'm ready," I whispered.

A thud sounded behind me, my heart jumped along with it.

"I'm sorry," I blurted a moment later.

Hope grabbed my hands, pulling my arms behind my back. "Why are you sorry?"

"For being rough. Earlier," I added, linking my fingers. "If I wanted you gentle, I would have told you." She kissed my shoulder, sliding the rope around my wrists until they were bound and pulled taught. "I liked knowing you couldn't control yourself. That you needed me as much as I needed you." The ends of the rope slipped over my shoulders when Hope crisscrossed them over my chest. "I hadn't planned on having sex with you but you were right. Seeing you again brought all of these feelings back. I tried to move on. I tried to get over you but I couldn't. It was impossible."

Her confession threw me off. I figured after all of this time, she would have married and had a house full of kids by now but knowing that was not the case made my inner alpha stand at large. I was happy to know she had been as miserable as I was, even though she deserved better.

Suddenly, my head was pulled back, the rope slipping around my throat.

Her eyes darkened, taking on a hint of lust and possession. "If you want to breathe, I suggest keeping your head back."

Holy. Hell. My dick lengthened at the threat in her voice and fuck me if it wasn't hot as hell. Swallowing was difficult as the rope tightened around me but it was exhilarating. Submitting all control to Hope was new. She had never been the authoritative figure type but so much had changed in the past ten years, who knew what she was like now. My thoughts conjured up images of her dressed in black leather, holding a bullwhip and cracking it hard against me as I crawled around her.

"I think you like my rope," she whispered in my ear, sliding it under my semi-hard erection. "Caiden had this rope specially ordered. Its type is called, Jute and it won't scratch or harm your skin." She tucked it between my legs, the smooth fibers of it brushing over the heavy sack beneath my length.

A moan escaped me, my heart racing hard. The blood pounded in my ears but all I could focus on was Hope's voice and the rope kissing my body with each touch.

"That's it, love. Feel me touch you through the fibers of the rope."

Her words swirled around me. My vision became hazy, my throat dry. The air left my lungs on quick bursts as the rope wrapped around and around me. My torso.

My chest. The heavy length between my thighs. My arms were bound behind my back. Snug and in place, not being able to move an inch.

"Are you ready to fly, Xander?" Hope asked, caressing her hand down my cheek.

"Yes," I breathed, swaying towards her touch. My eyes fluttered closed but not before I saw her head towards a lever on the wall. Suddenly, I was lifted, my body swaying gently a few feet from the ground.

My body tilted, my feet dangling behind me.

"Bend your knees," she demanded softly and wrapped the rope around my ankles.

My muscles became tight, jumping under my skin with delicious anticipation.

"He's ready," I heard Hope say.

I jumped when a liquid heat grazed down the length of my back.

"Look at me, Xander," she said, placing a soft kiss on my lips.

My eyes slowly opened, landing on the beautiful woman before me. The dim lighting gave her an unearthly glow much like the Hope from my dreams. Only this time, she was more beautiful than I ever could have imagined.

"Hope," I breathed out, purring as the hot liquid ran down my spine.

She smiled against my mouth. "Let yourself go for me." Her hand slid down my torso before gently grazing over my cock.

I bucked against her, groaning as her fingers scratched me lightly while it mixed with the powerful heat running over my body.

"Embrace the hot bite of the wax, Xander." Caiden's voice.

"I'm not trained in wax play," Hope said gently, noting my confusion. Her mouth covered mine in a hard bruising kiss, her tongue sliding between my lips. "Let go. Not for me. But for you." Her grip on me remained soft and gentle, while the kiss screamed for her to go harder. But she didn't. And I found that I didn't want her to.

The heat bit into my skin, tingling over my body as Caiden continued to pour the melted wax onto me.

The sensations mixed, swirling around me, tugging at the recesses of my mind. "Hope." Her name left me on a breathless moan.

Her tongue pushed into my mouth, silencing me. "Let go."

My body shook and tugged against the restraints, my muscles straining and tightening. "Please."

"Shhh…" Her kiss softened, her thumb grazing over the head of my length. "Come, baby."

I groaned. A tingle shot down my spine, as I came hard and fast into the palm of her hand. The euphoria was so strong, my vision blacked out.

"That's it. Fly for me. Embrace the heat of the wax." Her words. So soothing and caring, but firm and demanding, washed over me.

I couldn't help but listen and submit to her ways. It was the ultimate freedom as I gave her all of me.

The hot sting of the wax on my skin simmered, erupting into a delicious roar.

Hope released me. She looked up when the door behind us closed softly before meeting my gaze.

My eyes became heavy, fluttering open and closed repeatedly.

She winked and brought her hand up to her mouth, licking the essence from my earlier release off of her hand.

"I love you," I whispered, finally giving in and allowing sleep to take over.

*****

(Hope)

As much as I didn't want to leave Xander after the pure and utter submission he had given me, I needed to head to the hospital to see my dad. Although a part of me felt my mom only told me to come and see him because she wanted control. Maybe that was where I had gotten it from. The need to control and overpower someone. But for my parents? It was all about keeping me under a tight leash.

With me? I wanted to control Xander but I wanted to help him more. I wanted to help him heal and trust me again. I wanted to make him see he could control his demons. He could ignore those voices in his head. He could move past them. But little did I know, I should probably listen to my own advice. I needed to tell Xander about my alcohol issue. About the control I never had in the first place once I left him.

I never would have thought we both would have addiction issues. After him losing his parents and then me, I guess I figured he would have moved on rather quickly instead of diving into the fiery hell of a bottle.

A chime sounded, indicating an incoming call and I pressed the Bluetooth on my phone. "Hello?" "Morning."

My heart fluttered at the deep voice coming through the speakers. "Hi," I breathed, gripping the steering wheel tight.

"I was surprised to not find you beside me when I woke up," Xander said, his voice rough and gravelly.

Clearing my throat, I let out a heavy sigh. "Yeah. My dad had a heart attack. My mom called me yesterday." "Shit, Hope. I'm so sorry."

"Me too," was all I said.

"Listen," Xander coughed. "About last night…" "It was wonderful," I blurted, my cheeks heating.

"Yes," he said, his voice smug. "It sure as hell was."

I laughed, shaking my head. "How are you doing? Are you mad at me or anything?"

"No. Why would you think that?"

I quickly pulled into a parking spot once I reached the hospital and turned off the car. "Xander, you gave a piece of yourself to me that…that…"

"Hope, it makes me hard giving you my control," he said, his voice low and husky.

Oh sweet mother of all things holy. "I…" I whispered.

"I can't stop thinking about your warm body wrapped around mine or me bound for your control. You've given me pleasure I've never felt before. You've given me something I didn't think I would ever get again."

"What's that?" I asked, my heart racing hard against the confines of my rib cage.

"Hope. That's what you've given me," he cleared his throat. "Hope."

"Xander…"

"You should have woken me. I would have come with you."

"I wanted you to sleep. You've been through shit. What you gave me is exhausting, Xander." My body heated, picturing him lying naked in bed. "I also was hoping to wake you when I got back."

"So you are coming back?"

"Of course." I frowned. "Why wouldn't I be?"

"I don't know." His accusation went unsaid but me leaving years ago caused him to believe I would leave him again. I understood why he felt that way but it hurt. It stung worse than him yelling and screaming at me.

"I'll be back soon," I said softly, swallowing past the hard lump in my throat.

"Hope?"

"Yeah?"

He took a deep breath. "Thank you."

We said our goodbyes and I disconnected the call before I left the safety net of my car. Knowing I had to get this done and over with, I headed into the hospital. Under any other circumstances, I would visit my dad voluntarily. Although he was controlling at times, he was nothing like my mother.

"Can I help you?" a nurse asked me once I reached reception.

"Yeah, I'm looking for John—"

"Hope. It's about time you got here."

I grimaced. My mother's voice grated on my last nerve. "Hello, mother," I mumbled, turning towards her.

Her blonde hair was perfectly wrapped in a tight bun on top of her head, her light peach business outfit smooth and chic like she had just gotten back from the office. Even though she was retired, she didn't dress like it. All business and no pleasure when it came to that woman.

"Don't mumble," she said, pulling me in for a tight hug. "It's not lady like."

I bit back a scoff. If she only knew. "Where's dad?"

"Your dad is resting. You can see him in an hour or so." She pulled back, holding me at arm's length. "You need to do something about your unruly hair," she said, frowning and tried finger combing my blonde curls.

I slapped her hands away. "They're curls, mom. They're supposed to be unruly." And that was why I hardly saw her anymore. So judgmental and critical.

"You should get your hair straightened."

"Mom," I snapped, shoving out of her grip. "You did not call me here to talk about my hair. Where is dad?"

"He's resting." Her eyes narrowed. "What's with you? Are you seeing someone?"

I huffed and turned to the nurse. "Which room is John Charming in?"

"508-D."

"Thank you." I pushed past my mom and headed down the hall.

"He's resting," she repeated, calling after me. "I know that!" I quietly stepped into the room, stopping in my tracks when I saw my father pulling on his jacket.

He paused, glancing at me. "Hi, Hope." His eyes shone, twinkling in the fluorescent lighting of the hospital room.

My jaw clenched, my hands curling into fists at my sides. "Hi, daddy." I spun on my mother as she walked into the room. "I thought he was resting."

"He was." Her eyes darted quickly back and forth.

"If he was resting, than why is he getting dressed? You made it sound like he was going to be here for a while."

"What?" my dad scoffed. "Please. It was a case of indigestion. No big deal."

My mouth fell open, shock settling in at the lie my mother had said. "So you told me he had a heart attack to get me here didn't you?" I accused my mother, pointing at her.

"Angela, you did what?" he asked, his eyes wide.

"It was the only way I could see you. She never comes over anymore," she told her husband. "You never come over anymore." Her eyes filled with unshed tears, her bottom lip quivering.

"This is why I don't come over," I cried.

"Are you spending time with that Xander boy again? Is this why you never come over?" she asked, ignoring me.

"No! God, do you ever listen to what I say? Xander has nothing to do with this."

"Have you told him why you left him yet?"

Looking away, I mentally counted to ten. She knew how to get me right where it hurt. I wished at the time that I would have joined a convent instead of moving away. I thought being the good child and telling my parents what had happened would make them respect me and look at me as an adult but I only got contempt and judgment. "No, I haven't told him. I'm not ready to yet."

"You probably should. You don't want to go to your grave with that secret."

I stared at my mother, my mouth opening and closing but no words would come out.

"I wanted to see you," she said finally.

I shook my head. I tried so hard to be nice. But after years of having someone breathe down your neck over every move you made, she was making it difficult to love her. Being religious is one thing but forcing it down someone's throat was uncalled for. It made people rebel and hate you. I on the other hand, chose to ignore her instead.

Growing up, it was always my father who tried to instill the religion on me but as I got older, my mom took over the role. She tried so hard to mold me into the perfect child. As long as it made her look good, she didn't care about hurting me or anyone else for that matter. I loved her. I did but I didn't like her and I found myself especially not liking her at that moment. To tell me my father was not doing well crossed the line. "You criticize every move I make and you lie. You make it hard for me to like you." I let out an aggravated sigh.

"Please don't say that." A lonely tear rolled down her cheek.

A twinge of guilt swam through my belly but I stayed strong. I wouldn't console her when I was the one needing consoling for a change. "Daddy, I'm glad you are doing well. I'll call you later." I glared at my mom. "Mother." And with that, I stormed out of the room.

"Hope," she pleaded. "I'm sorry."

"Oh and one more thing." I turned back to her. "I'm an alcoholic. I have been for years. And I go to AA meetings too." The look of pure and utter shock on her face satisfied me as I quickly left her to stew in her own self-righteous misery.

***

(Xander)

Wednesday afternoon, I was lying on the couch with my head in Hope's lap. Her fingers brushed over my forehead, my cheek, jaw and back again. Caressing, gentle and loving. We had been talking for hours about nothing. It was nice. Not like the old days. Being in high school and a guy, I was all about sex. I wanted it as much as possible, not knowing how to control the urges of a teenager who discovered his girlfriend was tight and hot as hell.

Since the moment the three of us shared in the basement, I never felt closer to Hope and Caiden, than I did while being bound and restrained. My trust for them enhanced, growing into something I needed more of.

Holding Hope's hand against my chest, I let out a deep sigh. The small talk passed between us easily, even better than before.

When she got back from visiting her dad at the hospital a couple of days ago, she was upset, frustrated and angry.

Ranting and raving about how her mother was an inconsiderate bitch and looked out only for herself. I had never liked Angela Charming. Knowing she didn't like me either and she thought I wasn't good enough for her daughter when really, no one was.

A smile spread on my face remembering how I helped Hope calm down. Her moans and purrs of pleasure were music to my ears and I could never get enough. Breathing in the scent of her skin, I distracted her pain with the feel of me inside of her, holding her, making love to her sweet body until we were both spent and exhausted.

It had been a couple of days since we last had sex and I was fine with that. We talked, hung out and spent time together like any normal relationship. But there was still that huge ass elephant in the room. Why did she leave me? What made her not come to me?

The sound of the basement door closing interrupted our conversation as Caiden made his way up the stairs. "Mind if I join you?" he asked, nodding towards us.

"Not at all." I sat up, keeping my fingers locked with Hope's and snuggled against her. Although she was tiny, much smaller than I, I felt safe. Protected. At ease with myself. For the moment at least.

"I made something for you," Caiden said, his voice soft. He handed me a small frame.

Taking it from him, I frowned. My eyes widened when realization dawned on me as to what I was holding. "Is this...?"

His cheeks flushed and he nodded. I glanced at Hope.

She grinned. "He did a good job, didn't he?"

"Did you know about this?" I asked, looking back down at the black wax in the frame. It was in the shape of a rose. I had no idea how he did it, but it was beautiful.

"I did. I saw him take it off of your back." Hope brushed a finger down the glass and let out a soft sigh.

A moment of trepidation fluttered through me. Was she jealous?

She met my gaze. Chewing her bottom lip, her body tensed when she looked away.

Shit, no. She couldn't be. I couldn't deal with her jealousy. There was nothing going on between me and Caiden. He knew that. So did she. We were doing so well. "We're doing so good," I whispered.

Her gaze shot to mine. "What?"

"Nothing." I shook my head and rose to my feet, placing the frame on the fireplace mantel.

"Everything okay, Xander?" Caiden asked softly. "I have plans tonight," I told them.

"You do? What plans?" Caiden sat back, crossing his arms under his chest which was his way of saying, yeah right.

"I'm going out for a little bit so I need to borrow your car." I lifted my chin defiantly. "Please," I added when his eyes turned cold.

"Are you sure that's a good idea?" Hope rung her hands in her lap, staring at me hard.

"Why wouldn't it be? I won't be out late." I didn't understand what the big deal was and why they were giving me the third degree.

"I mean…it's…" Hope chewed her bottom lip which would normally turn me on but right now, it was pissing me the fuck off.

"Spit it out, Hope. Tell me exactly what you want to say. What do you think will happen tonight if I go out? Huh?" I asked, my voice raising.

Her eyes widened. "I don't know. I—"

"What? Do you think I'm going to drink myself into a stupor or find some drugs to inject? God, since you've been back, I've hardly thought about that shit. Do you not trust me at all?"

"Xander, we know your history," Caiden said, rising to his feet.

"What the hell is that supposed to mean? I haven't had one hit or even one drink since you forced me to stay here!" I shouted, taking a step towards him.

His brows furrowed. "No. But you've been thinking about it."

"Of course I have!" I threw my hands up in exasperation. What the fuck did he want from me? "You think it's easy going from drinking and smoking to nothing at all? You're lucky I'm not a fucking junkie."

"Maybe not but if I let it go any further, you would have turned into one. Junkie or not, you're still addicted." His voice was calm, cool, while he stared me down.

"I'm fucking addicted to her and I don't see you doing anything about it!" I yelled, thrusting my arm out in Hope's direction.

"That's because that addiction won't kill you!" Caiden shouted back.

"Give me the keys," I bit out through clenched teeth. "Tell us where you're going," Hope pleaded softly.

"We want to keep you safe."

"Is that it, Hope?" I turned to her. "Are you sure you don't want to keep me on a tight rope, controlling every single thing I do and say?"

Her jaw dropped. "That's not...how could you say that?" her voice cracked.

"Xander, that was a dick thing to say," Caiden growled, stepping towards me.

"Whatever." I held my hand out. "Keys. Please." When neither of them budged, I yelled out in frustration and headed to the door. "Fine. I'll fucking walk." "Tell us where—"

"I'm going to be at a high school hanging out with parents and kids," I snapped at Hope. "What trouble could I get into there?"

"Do you remember our days in high school?" Caiden asked, pulling his keys out of his pocket. "And why are you going to a high school?"

I let out a heavy sigh. "I didn't want to share this with either of you because I wanted something to myself. For a little bit." My jaw clenched.

"You were keeping something..." Hope's voice trailed off and she let out a shaky breath.

"Seriously?" I rolled my eyes. "Don't act so surprised."

"Xander, chill the fuck out." Caiden placed a hand on my arm.

"No!" I shoved him off. "I'm sick of this. I can't...I can't deal. Not with this...shit...and her jealousy."

Hope's gaze snapped to mine, her cheeks turning a bright shade of pink. "I'm not jealous."

"No? I know you wish you were strong enough to tie me up yourself. I know you wish you would have been the one to put the wax on me. I saw your eyes when Caiden handed me the frame." The words left my lips and I couldn't control them. I didn't even know if half the shit I was accusing her of was actually true or not. I said it. Not caring in the least what the repercussions would be. "I know you wish you could love me like Caiden can."

Her eyes welled, a lonely tear strolling down her cheek. "I'm not having this conversation with you when you're pissed."

"Well I'm sorry because we're having this conversation now whether you like it or not, baby." My chest rose and fell with ragged breath and I couldn't help but lay into her. Into both of them. "Tell me you're not jealous again. Lie to me. Again."

"Fine. Yes, I'm jealous," she snapped and shoved to her feet, closing the distance between us. "I'm jealous because Caiden knows you better than I do. I'm jealous because he got to spend all of these years with you and I didn't because I was scared. I was scared you hated me. I was fucking terrified you didn't love me anymore and I couldn't stand to see that in your eyes."

"I've always loved you," was all I said.

Her eyes softened. "I know that now. And I'm sorry for not coming back sooner—"

"You can't tell me you're sorry and expect everything to be back to the way things were!" I yelled.

"I know that, asshole." Hope pushed me, beating her small hands against my chest. "I didn't want to leave you but I had no choice."

"Then tell me why you left. Why didn't you fight your parents? You've never told me the reason, Hope. Did you think that when you came back, everything would be fine and dandy and our relationship would be back to normal?" "I don't want that relationship with you!" Her nostrils flared, her cheeks going red.

My mouth opened and closed and I shook my head. "What the hell does that mean?"

"I loved you. I did but you were an asshole. You only thought of yourself but I still wanted to be with you." Her voice was shaky as she stared up at me.

I glanced at Caiden.

He nodded once with encouragement, remaining silent.

"I...I don't know what you mean," I stuttered, confused as hell.

Hope sighed, gripping my t-shirt in her hands. "After your parents died, you changed. I understand why that happened but you wouldn't let me in. You shut me out. You shut Caiden out."

"Tell me why you left," I bit out, ignoring her. "Xander, I—"

"Tell me," I demanded, gripping her wrists.

She shook her head. "I don't think—"

"Tell. Me," I growled.

"You want to know the real reason I left? Fine. I'll tell you. I'll tell you that my parents never forced me to leave. I'll tell you they never once asked me to leave you. I decided to leave you. On my own terms."

Her words stung, wrapping around me in a tight grip, poking me hard like sharp tiny needles. "What..." I croaked.

Tears flowed freely down her cheeks but her voice remained calm. "I was pregnant."

SIXTEEN

Xander

MY CHEST CONSTRICTED. THE air flowed into my mouth, threatening to choke me when it didn't make its way to my lungs. It left me on a whoosh like I was punched in the gut. Her words…they struck home, I reacted to them but they didn't register. Pregnant. "Why…" I couldn't form a proper sentence. I couldn't ask her why she never told me. Was I that much of a dick that she was too scared to tell me she was pregnant?

"I'll leave you two alone," Caiden said, clapping me on the shoulder and placed his car keys in my hand. "Please be careful tonight," he whispered in my ear.

I wrapped my fingers tight around the keys. They dug into my skin, biting through the flesh of my palm.

"Come sit," Hope offered gently, taking my hand.

Allowing her to lead me to the couch, I slumped hard on it and dropped my head in my hands. Thoughts swirled around in my mind. So many questions. So many accusations. How could she keep something like this from me?

"Talk to me, Xander," she whispered.

"Where's the baby now?" I asked, slowly turning to Her eyes saddened and she looked down at her hands in her lap. "I lost it. I was so scared to tell you I think the stress of it all caused me to lose it." When she met my gaze, my heart dropped. "The baby wasn't yours."

Fuck. Something had told me it wasn't mine. That nagging little annoying piece of shit voice that talks to you when you do something bad. When you know you shouldn't be doing what you are doing, but you do it anyways out of spite.

"I'm so sorry." Her breath caught.

"You cheated on me?" I asked, even though I knew the answer already.

"We had a fight and I was upset—"

"Who was the guy?" With shaky hands, I scrubbed them down my face.

"I don't know," she confessed.

My head whipped around. "So you fucked some random guy because we had a fight and you were upset? You never thought to use a fucking condom?"

"We did use a condom," she cried. "God, Xander, that was so long ago. It was some guy at a bar—"

"That's supposed to make it better? You fucking random men like a whore?"

Her body shook, soft cries leaving her lips. "You told me to go to hell."

"I was mad!" It was so long ago, I didn't even remember why we had the fight in the first place. A thought crossed my mind, jarring my memory. "We fought because you wanted to go back to school and I didn't want you to. We both blew up. It got heated. I told you to go to hell and you fucked some guy at a bar. Tell me, Hope, did you at least take him home or go back to his place?" I looked at her when she didn't answer.

She stared out the window but wouldn't meet my gaze.

I laughed, shaking my head. "You actually fucked him at the bar didn't you? In the bathroom?"

"Yes," she answered.

"Of course you did." I rose to my feet. "You know, if you wanted to be fucked like a slut, all you had to do was tell me. At least then you would have known you'd be safe." I didn't wait for her to respond and left the house, slamming the door shut behind me.

***

(Hope)

I had been terrified to tell Xander the truth. Scared that he would leave me and hate me for what I had done. All because we had a fight.

A sharp pain erupted through my abdomen, forcing me to my knees. I cried out, gripping my lower stomach, tears stinging my eyes. "No," I pleaded, begging God to let the baby be okay. I knew I had done wrong. I knew I had sinned and cheated on Xander but it was not the baby's fault.

Please, God, don't take my baby away from me. Hurt me. Make me suffer. But keep my baby safe.

Another sharp pain exploded inside of me. I cried out, curling over. Something warm seeped into my panties and I knew. Right then, I knew. Because of my mistake, my baby was dying. Because I was too scared to tell Xander. So I left him.

Bone crushing sobs wracked through my body as I could feel the life pouring out of me. It was so unfair that a baby could be taken away just like that. I never had a chance to love it. I never even had a chance to feel it move. And now I was losing it.

Because of this, I swore I would stay away from Xander for good. A part of me blamed him. I was angry at the fact that we fought. Furious that he pushed me, forcing me into another man's arms. I didn't even remember the guy but I was carrying his child that was now being ripped from me.

I could feel my soul breaking, shattering into a million pieces. My baby. My unborn child. It was dying.

I was helpless, knowing there wasn't a damn thing that I could do about it.

"He hates me," I sobbed, trying to forget that horrible day of losing my baby. I curled my arms around myself and fell to my knees. "God, I'm such a horrible person."

"You are not a horrible person," Caiden said gently, rubbing my back in smooth circles. "Give him time."

"Time!" I yelled. "All we've had is time but I screwed it up. If we never would have had that fight. If I wouldn't have slept with some random guy." I hiccupped. "If I wouldn't have gotten pregnant." Cries wracked through my body. The guilt I felt for betraying Xander tore through me. I would have done anything to go back in time and change everything. Even if I would have still gotten pregnant, I would have confessed to Xander instead of leaving. Then I would have still given birth to the baby. My baby. My stomach twisted, a sharp pain tearing through my soul. "I wanted the baby to be Xander's. I prayed it would be." The tears flowed freely down my cheeks. "But the weeks didn't add up." I glanced up at Caiden. "I never meant to hurt him."

Caiden's gaze darkened with sympathy, his eyes saddening. "I know, Hope. He will forgive you. That's one thing you have to remember about him. His heart is big. He loves you. Although you've hurt him, he'll want your love more. Remember that."

I nodded, sniffing and wiped the tears from under my eyes. "When I lost the baby, my mother told me it was probably a good thing so then I wouldn't have raised a bastard child." I grimaced. "And she wonders why I can't stand to be around her."

Caiden winced. "Your mother means well but she needs to think before she speaks sometimes."

I scoffed and rose to my feet. "That's an understatement."

"Yeah." Caiden coughed, hacking until his cheeks reddened.

"You alright?" I asked, frowning. He nodded. "Yes," he wheezed.

My heart gave a start. "You need to tell him," I said softly.

"No." His gaze shot to mine. "And don't you dare tell him either."

"Caiden."

"Promise me!" he snapped. "He's not ready. We need to help him first. He needs…" He slumped down onto the couch. "He needs me."

I sat beside him and wrapped my arm around his. "I know."

Caiden pulled from my grip and wrapped his arm around my shoulders instead.

Leaning against him, I curled my feet under me.

"There's so many things he has to learn and that I have to teach you. God, this shit sucks," Caiden's voice cracked. He scrubbed a hand down his face, finally letting the tears flow down his cheeks.

I held him while he cried. If only Xander knew.

Knowing would make it easier, but I was afraid Caiden wouldn't talk to Xander until it was too late.

They say life is too short. Live every day like it's your last. One morning you could wake up and your world could be ripped out right from under you. In Caiden's case, his world had been tipped on its axis for years. But he never told anyone. Only me and that was going to piss Xander off even more.

***

(Xander)

Where I was headed, I had no idea. The only thing I knew was that I needed to get away. I needed some control in my life. I needed sustenance. I needed things to be normal. I had Shana's recital to attend later that evening but I wasn't in the mood. I wanted to dive into myself, curl into a little ball and hide.

Tears burned my eyes and my throat became thick. My skin tingled, my muscles jumping and twitching under my skin. But I walked. And walked. Heading in the direction of an open grassy field surrounded by trees. The cold wind whipped around me, biting into the flesh that wasn't covered by my clothing.

I started running, pounding my feet hard into the ground. My chest constricted with the air I tried so desperately to breathe in. Shit. "Fuck," I yelled out, stopping abruptly and fell to my knees. "Why, Hope?" A sob escaped me. If only she would have told me. If only she would have come to me for help. I would have loved the baby like it was my own. Yes, I would have been pissed, hurt, angry, but eventually I would get over it. I would forgive her. But she never gave me the chance. And her stress and worry over my reaction caused her to lose a life. A precious little gem growing inside of her. All because of me. Was I hard to deal with? Was I hard to approach? I thought I was always a reasonable person. Did I have a temper? I didn't even know. Why the hell didn't I know?

Leaning on my knuckles with all of my weight, they pushed into the ground. The gravel bit into my skin, the sharp sting sending a warmth over my body. Pain. So much pain. Good pain. Bad pain. All of it surrounded me.

Memories of the wax being poured onto my body by the hands of Caiden seared its way into my mind. More.

I always wanted more. All through high school I was never satisfied. "Why?" Hope being with another man made bile rise to my throat. I had been with women. Many women. But it never occurred to me that Hope would be with anyone else but me. It was unrealistic but a part of me liked to think I had ruined her for all men. The Dominant Alpha inside of me reared its ugly head over the fact some other dick put a baby in her. Something I couldn't give her because the fear of my reactions caused her to leave me.

Knowing I was the sole reason for her departure made my stomach twist and turn with gripping agony.

Why the fuck couldn't I have a normal life? Why couldn't Hope and I be happy and together? Why did Caiden have to love me? "Why!" I screamed, hitting my fists against the ground.

"Why?" It came out as a whisper.

Something soft touched my arm and I jumped.

Spinning around, I found Hope kneeling behind me, tears streaming down her face. I wanted to yell, scream and beg. Demand answers I knew I had no right demanding in the first place. So I did the only thing I could think of. I pulled her into my arms, wrapping mine around her and held her. Hugging her like my life depended on it, I poured all of my feelings into that touch.

Her body stiffened at the abrupt movement but I only held her tighter. She finally relaxed, curling herself around me and cried softly into the crook of my neck. "I am so sorry," she said softly, her voice hoarse like she had been crying for a while.

Something poked at me, jabbing at my soul. Something was wrong but I didn't know what. Pulling back, I cupped her cheeks, brushing my thumbs under her eyes.

The wind whipped around us, curling under our clothes and brushing through her hair. The mid-day sun shone down on her, casting a halo around her beautiful body. "I've been in love with you since the moment you stepped into my life," I whispered. "I'm sorry you felt you couldn't talk to me and that it caused you to lose the baby." My breath hitched but I continued. "If you would have come to me, I would have helped you raise it. I would have loved it like my own."

"I know," fresh tears flowed down her cheeks. "I know that now. And I am so sorry. I'm sorry for that fight we had. I'm sorry for leaving you and not trusting you. I'm sorry for the pain I caused you." She looked away, a dark shadow passing over her face.

"Hey," I pinched her chin, forcing her to look at me. "What was that?"

She chewed her bottom lip. "There's something else you don't know. After...after I lost the baby," she swallowed hard. "I started drinking. I couldn't control myself. One night I ended up in an alleyway and this girl found me. She brought me to an AA meeting and I've been going ever since." She looked away again. "That was five years ago."

A heavy feeling fell into the pit of my gut over her confession. "You should have called me."

Hope frowned. "What do you mean, I should have called you?"

"I mean, I would have gone with you," I offered gently.

"You are the first one to say you don't need help. That you're not addicted to alcohol and drugs. At least I knew I had a problem. I still have a problem. I think about drinking every damn day and I can't do anything about it," the words flowed effortlessly from her mouth, an underlining bite of contempt filling her voice.

"What's your problem? I'm saying I would have joined you. We could have gotten help together."

She shoved roughly out of my grip and rose to her feet. "Don't patronize me, Xander," she said, storming back to Caiden's house.

"What the hell are you talking about?" I grabbed her arm, spinning her towards me. "What is this? Why are you acting this way?" I should have been the one upset and yelling and accusing her of shit. Why the hell was it the other way around?

She laughed, a cold maniacal sound leaving her lips. "I never should have come back."

My eyes widened. "What the fuck, Hope?" I cupped her nape, crashing my lips to hers before she could protest.

Her body melted into mine, her arms wrapping around my neck. She pushed her chest against mine, her nipples pebbling under the touch.

I swallowed her moan and deepened the kiss, needing to show her coming back was meant to be. Fisting my hand in her hair, I pulled her head back, giving me better access to her delicious mouth. Inhaling her sweet scent, I breathed it down into my lungs. If I could live off of her, I would.

She was my drug. The fix I needed. I was a junkie and I craved her. Cupping her ass, I pulled her tight against me, molding myself against her soft form.

Hope's body fit perfectly against mine. Where she was soft, I was hard.

"Xander," she breathed, scratching her nails into my shoulders.

Picking her up, I wrapped her legs around my waist and carried her to a shady spot in the field. Trees surrounded us and when I laid her gently on the ground, I released her.

She stared up at me, her eyes dark with lust, her lips pink and swollen from my rough kiss. "I love you. I love you so much it hurts. I love you to the point I can't control what I say or do."

"It's fucking toxic," I finished for her.

She nodded, fresh tears welling in her eyes. "So what do we do?" she asked, her voice cracking.

"I loved you as a kid, but now? I need you more than I need my next breath," I said, brushing my thumb over her swollen mouth.

"What I feel for you scares me." She cupped my cheek. "Being with you after all of these years..." My breath caught. "I..." I trailed my fingers down her jaw and kissed her softly on the mouth.

"I know," she said, softly.

I didn't know what was going on or what had changed.

We fought. We argued. We were both so indecisive.

"Xander?"

I glanced down at her.

"Kiss me. Please...let me feel."

Brushing my mouth along hers, I licked between her lips, swallowing her breath. I poured everything I felt for her into that kiss. It was nothing like before. This time, it was pure. Raw. Real.

We made out under the clouds, in the thick of the woods. Nature surrounded us. No walls. No bedroom. No nothing. Stripped bare until all we felt was the love we had for each other. It was so deep and powerful, we were terrified it would ruin us before bringing us close together.

A love so strong, turning dark and possessive, bordering on obsession.

***

"Xander?"

I sat up abruptly at the female voice and found Shana standing a few feet away from us. Rubbing the grit out of my eyes, I glanced down at Hope who had curled onto her side, sleeping soundly in the grass.

"Hi," I said, my voice rough from sleep. "Everything okay?"

"I don't know," I shrugged. "How long have you been standing there?"

"I just got here. I was walking to your friend's house to remind you about my recital tonight but then I found you here. Is that Hope?" she asked, nodding towards us.

"Yes." I looked down at Hope, brushing her curls off of her forehead.

She sighed, pushing back against me and remained sleeping.

"You guys make up?" Shana asked, sitting on the grass in front of me.

"We still have some shit to work through," I grumbled, leaning back on my elbows.

"You should bring her tonight too," Shana suggested, her eyes brightening.

"What about Caiden?" I lifted Hope's head, resting it in my lap and rubbed circles on her back.

She stirred, meeting my gaze and yawned. "Who are you talking to?"

"Hope, meet Shana Chase," I nodded towards Shana.

Hope looked behind her and sat up. "Hi." She yawned again and held out her hand. "It's nice to meet you."

"Nice to meet you too. I've heard so much about you," Shana said, returning the handshake.

"Oh?" Hope glanced at me. "What have you been told?"

"How much Xander loves you but that things have been difficult." Shana shrugged. "I hope everything works out for you."

"How old are you?" Hope asked, leaning against my chest.

"Fourteen."

"How did you two meet?" Hope grabbed my arm, curling it around her waist and stifled another yawn.

Shana told her about our several run-ins and about me being miserable. Hope laughed every so often at Shana's description of me being moody and face planting several times during my runs.

Hearing her laugh, even though it was at my expense, made me happy.

"So where are we going tonight?" Hope asked, leaning forward.

"It's Shana's recital. That's what I was trying to tell you and Caiden earlier." Before it blew up into a fight.

"It's a date."

SEVENTEEN

Hope

FINALLY TELLING XANDER THE real reason why I had left him all of those years ago took a huge weight off of my chest. It felt so good to not hold any secrets between us. But the kiss in the field...even though it was just a kiss, it spoke more words than we could ever say. It left us open, vulnerable, stripped bare of all emotion as we laid our feelings on the line through that small touch.

We walked hand-in-hand back to Caiden's place, silence falling between us. When we reached his house, I frowned. Embree's tiny blue car sat in the driveway.

Xander stiffened beside me, pausing in his steps when she slid out of the vehicle.

She raised her hand to wave when she glanced at me but her face fell.

My heart started racing, confusion settling deep inside of me. "Xander, do you know her?" "Yeah. Do you?"

I looked between them as Embree came towards us. "She's the woman who found me in the alley I was telling you about."

Xander's eyes widened. "She brought you to the AA meetings?"

I nodded, stepping in front of him when Embree closed the distance between us. "What are you doing here?" I asked her, gripping Xander's hand tight in mine. At that point, Caiden stepped out onto the porch, frowning when he saw Embree. They knew her but I didn't know how. "You called me, asking me to bring you a bag of clothes, remember?" she said, handing me my gym bag.

"Right," I took it from her. "Thank you." But that still didn't explain how they knew each other.

"Is this the ex you told me about?" she asked, nodding towards Xander.

"Yes." I looked between them. "How do you know each other?" I asked even though I didn't want to know the answer.

Embree chewed her bottom lip, glancing away.

"You slept with him didn't you?" I released Xander's hand and took a step towards her.

She nodded.

"She slept with both of us," Caiden said, joining our little huddle.

Shaking my head, I crossed my arms under my chest. "Why am I not surprised?"

"I am so sorry, Hope. I had no idea Xander was your ex. I swear if I would have known, I never would have slept with him. Please believe me," she pleaded.

"I...you should go. I need some time to process this." I walked past her. "I'll call you later," I muttered and headed into the house.

"Hope," Xander called after me. "Please stop."

Ignoring him, I headed to his room and started packing my clothes. This was a bad idea. I never should have come back.

"What are you doing?" He grabbed my hands, stopping me and pushed me onto the edge of the bed. "Please, you can't run because another wrench was thrown into this...this thing we have."

"Another wrench!" I pushed him so hard, he fell back on his ass. "You fucked Embree. Did you know she goes to my AA meetings to pick up men? And women? She has a sex addiction. She'd be the first one to tell you that but did you ask her? No. Probably not because you were too focused on getting your dick wet."

"I didn't know you were friends," he yelled. "I didn't even fuck her the last time she offered. I couldn't. And I didn't know why until now."

"Why? Why couldn't you fuck her?"

"Because I couldn't stop thinking about you," he shouted. "And I felt like it would be cheating on you if I did. But that's never stopped you, now has it?"

Before I could control myself, my hand landed against his cheek. My palm tingled, his skin going red from the impact.

"Hit me again," he growled, his eyes going cold.

I geared up my hand but pushed him instead.

He grabbed my hand, pulling me into his arms and held me while I fought him.

Beating my fists against his chest, I broke. "I don't know why it bothers me so much but knowing you were with her disgusts me." I finally stopped struggling against him and let him hold me.

"She never touched me," he said softly. "What do you mean?" I asked, frowning.

"No one has touched me since you. I wouldn't let them." He pinched my chin. "I know that doesn't make it better or easier but it's the truth. You are the only one I allowed to put their hands on my body." His mouth brushed along mine. "You are the only one I allowed to have any control."

I sighed, leaning my head against his chest. "What is wrong with us?"

"We're in love." The way he said it, made it sound like a bad thing. But this lack of trust, this constant fighting was either going to tear us apart or bring us together. I just wished I could figure out which and soon.

"Guys?" Caiden said from the doorway. "Embree has left and won't be back. Hope, your bag is in the hallway."

"Thank you," I said.

"Will you come to a friend's recital tonight?" Xander asked Caiden, helping me to my feet.

"Of course." Caiden's gaze met mine. I swallowed hard.

His skin was pale, dark circles forming under his eyes. He coughed, the sound crackling in his chest.

I opened my mouth to say something when he shook his head, warning me to leave it alone. But I couldn't. At the moment I would but eventually, I would tell Xander everything if Caiden wouldn't. No more secrets. And even though it wasn't my secret to tell, Xander had every right to know what was going on with his best friend, even if it would end up destroying him in the end.

***

(Xander)

Once the three of us arrived at the school, it brought back memories of a time where I was at my best. I hated school but I was happy. Before my parents passed away, taking a piece of me with them, I would come home, leave them notes every so often about a passing grade. They were always proud of me. And I would give anything to hear them tell me how much they loved me one more time.

Seeing Shana with an older couple who I assumed were her grandparents, my chest tightened. She laughed, hugging them both and squealed when another couple approached her. "Mom! Dad!" she shouted, running into their open arms. They whispered something softly to her, her nodding every so often.

Shana pulled back, wiping under her eyes and caught my gaze. She waved us over. "I never thought my parents would be here," she said as we approached her. "I thought they would be too busy."

"I'm glad they could be here," I said, my voice thick.

Hope kept her hand in mine, squeezing it encouragingly.

"So am I." Shana surprised me by wrapping her arms around my middle. "I wish your parents could be here for you." She motioned for me to bend down. "But you have Caiden and Hope. Don't screw it up." She released me and headed to the stage. "I'll introduce you after," she called out, making her way to a group of kids who were lining up.

I shook my head at her honest but refreshing words. Don't screw it up. I had already done that a million times over.

"Let's sit," Caiden offered, clapping a hand on my shoulder.

We followed him to a row of empty chairs and waited.

The lights dimmed in the auditorium while the first teen made their way up onto the stage. They ended up doing some slam poetry about love, crime and hate. It was powerful in the emotion he brought forth and received a standing ovation at the end. A couple more kids performed, some sang, some rapped, some even played instruments.

I tried to focus on the words and the acts they were doing, but all I could focus on were Hope's fingers linked in mine and Caiden's arm on the back of my chair. My friends. My two best friends and the only family I had. My parents may have passed away sooner than I would have liked but God gave me Caiden and Hope. He gave me a blessing in disguise and I tried so hard to throw it all away.

When Shana finally walked up to the center of the stage, she took a breath. "This is for my new friend. You know who you are. If you know this song, I hope you enjoy my version of the words I know you want to say to her but can't. And if you don't know it, sit back and just feel."

I sat forward, a tingle shooting up my spine when the slow music flowed through the speakers above us.

Once the words left her lips, I squeezed my eyes shut, letting them caress me.

I am addicted to you.

Your love. Your touch. Your being. Everything about you draws me in. I am captivated by you.

The heat in your gaze. The beat of your heart. I am addicted to you.

It was a coincidence. It had to be for her to sing the one song I had dedicated to Hope so long ago. "Hope."

"This song," Hope said softly from beside me. Her breath caught, tears welling in her beautiful eyes. "Is this about us?"

I nodded, swallowing past the hard lump in my throat.

From the moment we touch, I crave you.

Your kiss. Your breath on my skin. The warmth of your embrace.

I am bound by the ropes of your love. Restrained by your powerful passion.

Your caress. Your hold on my body. The possession that seeps from your soul.

I am addicted to you.

When the words ended, Shana hummed out the rest of the melody. Her voice, much like the singer from the band that created the song, flowed effortlessly over the beautiful words.

I didn't know what to say. I didn't even know how to react.

Hope shifted in her seat beside me, grabbed my hand and held it tight in hers.

Caiden clapped when the song ended, squeezing my shoulder after. "Perfect," was all he said.

I glanced at him, frowning when I saw the glassy look in his eyes. "Are you alright?"

He stifled a yawn. "Tired." He rose to his feet and wavered.

I caught him as he landed hard in the chair. "Shit, man. Are you sure you're okay?"

"Yeah." He pulled from my grip. "I'm fine."

"I'll say goodbye and then we can head back." I squeezed his shoulder. "Okay?"

Caiden nodded, rubbing his hands down his thighs.

My throat constricted, a slight twinge tightening in my chest but I ignored it and searched out Shana. Leaving Hope with Caiden, I couldn't help but wonder what the hell was going on with him.

"Xander."

I spun around and found Shana coming up to me. "Hi." "Did you—"

I pulled her into my arms and lifted her in the air, spinning her around in circles. "Thank you."

She laughed, returning my hug. "You are welcome. Now put me down, big guy."

I chuckled and did as she said. "Listen, I have to go but thank you so much. You have no idea what that song means to me."

A huge grin spread on her face. "I have an idea but you Can tell me about it sometime okay?"

I nodded. "I will."

***

(Hope)

My body was vibrating, the need and want for Xander heating my skin on fire. We had said our goodbyes to Shana and left the high school. Something was up with Caiden but he shrugged it off, saying he needed some rest.

I didn't know any more than Xander did but I couldn't focus on anything else if I tried.

When we arrived back at the house, I quickly headed into Xander's room, pacing back and forth. Those words. From that song. So beautiful and meaningful. I knew Xander had difficulty with words but to hear them in a song…it made me want to show him exactly how I felt in return.

"Hope, what did you want to do for the rest of the night?" Xander asked me as he stepped into the bedroom.

He closed the door behind him and pulled off his black leather jacket. "Caiden's gone to bed. I don't think he's feeling well. Want to watch a movie or something?"

"Or something," I whispered, pulling off my sweater. "What?" he asked, glancing my way. His nostrils flared as I continued stripping for him. "Tell me," he said, his voice husky.

"I want you." I removed the last bit of clothing, leaving myself standing naked in front of him. "I want you deep inside of me, bare and rigid." I reached out for him when he closed the distance between us. "I want to feel you."

He lifted me in his arms, crashing his lips to mine. His fingers dug into the flesh of my rear, squeezing to the point of painful. It brought tears to my eyes but the pain felt so good. Oh so delicious like he couldn't get enough of my body.

"Lay on the bed, baby," I said against his lips. "I want to ride you."

"Fuck. Me," he growled, placing me on my feet.

I pushed him back on the bed and cupped him over his jeans.

In a quick move, he had his pants undone and his cock free. "Hope." The veins in his neck strained as he forced everything in him not to throw me down onto the bed.

Licking up his neck, I inched a hand under his shirt. "I'm on the pill."

"Shit, Hope. Fuck. Please." He trembled beneath me, lining up his thick length with my opening.

Moving down his body, I brushed my soaked entrance over the thickness between his legs.

He groaned, bucking his hips and squeezed his fingers into my waist. "Please. Fuck me."

Wrapping my fingers around his cock, I leaned back against his bent knees. "Tell me." "Hope, damn it!"

I impaled him hard, igniting a yell to leave his lips. My body stretched to meet his size but I didn't stop. My hips slammed against his pelvis as I rode him with everything in me.

"Shit. Harder. Hope, fuck. Please. Faster." His back bowed off the bed, sweat coating his brow.

Undulating my hips against him, I took him deep, past the barrier of comfort. A slight pain erupted inside of me. He was hard and swollen. Deep and powerful as his thrusts quickened, bringing me over the edge of ecstasy.

He called out my name, pouring his hot cream inside of me, filling me with his essence.

I moaned, throwing my head back and whimpered, not letting up my movements.

"God, you feel so fucking good." He groaned, sitting up. His hands massaged and kneaded over my body, pulling me tight against him.

My hips slowed.

"You didn't come."

"That's because I was focused on you." I placed a soft peck on his lips and rose from his lap.

He rose with me and inched a hand between my thighs, brushing a finger through the folds of my core. "I want you to always come for me." He purred against my neck, inserting a finger into me. Thrusting once and then twice before bringing it up to his lips. The tip was red, showcasing a drop of blood. "Did I hurt you?"

I shook my head, watching his every move.

"No?" He licked his finger, swallowing our mixed pleasure from the tip before backing me up to the dresser. He pulled off his jeans and the rest of his clothes, turning back to me a moment later. "I want to spend the rest of the night making love to you. I want you so sore that all you feel is my thick cock throbbing inside of your hot body." He brushed his nose up the length of my neck. "Your pussy is going to swell for me. Your tight heat is the only liquid I want from now on. No more alcohol. No more drugs." He wrapped his hand around my throat, tilting my head back.

"You are my addiction."

We stood there for what felt like hours, staring at each other. No clothes. Skin against skin and our scent mixing as one. I could still feel him inside of me as his warmth seeped down my inner thigh. "I want to pass out in your arms," I whispered.

A wicked grin spread on his face. He lifted me, placing me on the dresser and pushed his way between my thighs.

His fingers dug into my skin, spreading my legs wider as he made his way back into my body. For the rest of the night, like he had promised, he showed me over and over again through his touch, how much he loved me. How much he had missed me. And how much he needed me. No words were said as we massaged, kneaded, caressed. He claimed me as his, marking me from the inside out. He ripped open my soul, forcing new feelings from deep within me.

I loved him and his rough touch. I couldn't get enough of him. He was my addiction. He was pure, unlaced, dripping with lust and ultimate seduction.

He filled me with life, hope and dreams. He used me until I was sore and broken, submitting to the delicious pleasure.

EIGHTEEN

Xander

I WATCHED HER SLEEP. I watched her tanned back rise and fall with each soothing breath. Her leg hooked over mine, her core brushing against my thigh. Her dark curly hair, fanned out on the pillow, tickling my shoulder.

My dick twitched, hardening from listening to her breathe. I couldn't get enough. Although I had spent the night buried deep inside of her warm body, my length swelled to the point of painful. I groaned, reaching a hand underneath the covers and wrapped my fingers around myself, trying to calm the raging hard on. But my touch made it worse. The soft skin was pulled tight, tender from the many times I had taken Hope throughout the night.

"Shit," I breathed, my hand moving up and down the rigged length. The throbbing muscle sprung free from my body and I couldn't control the actions I inflicted on myself.

"Are you thinking of me?" Hope whispered in my ear.

Squeezing my eyes shut, I nodded, gripping my cock tight in my hand. "Fuck. You're going to be the death of me."

She purred, sinking her teeth into my shoulder. "Make yourself come for me."

"Baby, I need you." My hips thrust forward.

"You have me." Hope slid her hand up my inner thigh, cupping my balls. She gave them a light squeeze, massaging and kneading. "Come."

Her soft command set me off as I spurted my release onto my lower stomach. A satisfied sigh left my lips. I rolled over, snarling into her neck and placed a soft peck on her mouth. "You make me come so fast like a prepubescent boy."

She giggled, brushing her fingers over my forehead.

I deepened the kiss when a bang from outside the door made us both jump. I quickly rose from the bed, cleaned myself off and pulled on sweatpants.

Hope got dressed and followed me out of the room. My heart raced, my gaze landing on a crumpled Caiden. "Caiden!" I yelled, running to him. He was shaking, his skin cold and clammy. His eyes rolled into the back of his head, his body convulsing hard against me. "Hope!" I screamed.

She had a phone to her ear, her mouth moving over words I couldn't hear.

My life flashed before my eyes. A life without Caiden. A world without the man who had saved me. "Caiden," I pleaded. Please, God. I sent up a silent prayer, asking for what, I wasn't sure. I didn't know what was going on. I didn't know why Caiden was having an attack but I knew something was wrong as he stared up at me with a glazed look in his eyes.

***

"Hope, if something happens to him…" I couldn't even get the rest of that sentence out without wanting to throw up.

"I know," she whispered, holding me tight.

It had been an hour since the ambulance picked up Caiden. We were now sitting in the waiting room…waiting. And it was driving me fucking insane. We had no answers. No matter how many times I had asked the EMT what the hell was going on, they wouldn't tell me.

Caiden was now undergoing some tests but no one would give us any damn information.

The control slipped through my fingers, making me want to dive into the bottom of a bottle that much more.

"Are you here for Caiden Yeo?"

I looked up at an older man dressed in white, a stethoscope wrapped around his neck.

"Yes, we are," Hope answered for us, gripping my hand tight in hers.

"Caiden is resting. We have to run some more tests before we can find out what exactly is going on," the doctor said gently.

"Can we see him?" I asked, my voice hoarse. "Why don't we come back tomorrow," Hope suggested, rising to her feet.

"No," I insisted. "Please. I don't care if he's sleeping. Let me see him."

The doctor nodded. "Come with me."

"Xander, do you want me to wait for you here?" Hope asked, chewing her bottom lip.

"No. Please come with me. I..." I kissed her forehead. "I need your strength."

She nodded, holding my hand tight.

We followed the doctor to a private room. He motioned for us to enter and closed the door quietly behind us.

Caiden was lying in bed, his large body wrapped under a white blanket. His olive skin was pale, his jet black hair mussed. He turned to us, his dark eyes sad.

"Caiden," I whispered, heading towards him.

"Hey." He sat up, coughing several times before letting out a deep sigh. "Sorry for scaring you."

"You have no idea." I sat in the metal chair beside his bed. "Do you know what's going on?"

Caiden glanced at Hope before looking back at me. "Yes."

My heart raced when he didn't continue and I looked back and forth between them. "Don't..." I rose to my feet, pushing the chair back abruptly. "She knows."

Caiden nodded.

"Xander," Hope said, reaching out for me.

"No!" I snapped. "Fuck this. You...I can't deal with this shit again. Why haven't you told me that something's wrong? Why do you feel the need to keep this from me?" I demanded from the both of them. Secrets. Lies. I couldn't wrap my head around it. I couldn't control the urge to rip into them, begging for their mercy and the truth.

"I'm sorry," Caiden said, sitting up higher in bed. "I asked her to keep this to herself. If you need to blame anyone, blame me. I will tell you more when I know but right now, you need to go home and take care of yourself. Go home, Zee."

I shook my head. "No. Not until you tell me what the hell is going on."

"I had cancer," Caiden blurted.

I blinked a couple of times, my brain not processing what I heard. Cancer. That horrible C-word destroyed millions of families. "Cancer."

Caiden nodded, letting out a heavy sigh. His shoulders slumped. "I fought it once. It's that time of year. It's probably the flu."

"You...why didn't you tell me?" I slumped back down in the chair, grabbing his hand.

"Because you have enough shit going on in that head of yours. I didn't need to add my problems to the mix."

"But your problems are my problems," I said, reaching out for Hope in the process.

She slid onto my lap, covering our joined hands with hers.

"I love you both," Caiden said softly.

"Don't," I pleaded. "Please don't." My chest constricted and I leaned my head against Hope's back. I couldn't...not like this. Please, God. Not like this.

"Go home. I'm fine. I'll be home before you know it." Caiden swallowed hard. "Please. It'll give me something to look forward to, knowing you both are there waiting for me. Besides, I have to introduce you to my girl."

***

(Hope)

The drive home was long and silent. The air crackled and fizzled around us with built up tension. I was waiting for Xander to explode over me not telling him about Caiden's illness but when he hadn't, it set my nerves on edge. It would only be a matter of time before Xander laid into me.

"Why didn't you tell me?"

And there it was. I slipped out of the vehicle, slowly trudging up the steps to the house. "Because I made a promise to a friend and it wasn't my secret to tell." I turned back around when another vehicle came up the driveway.

Xander walked up to the car when the driver handed him a package. He slipped something into his hand and turned to me as the vehicle backed out of the driveway.

"What is that?" I asked, pointing to the item in his hand.

"It's not drugs, if that's what you're wondering," Xander said, pulling a bottle from the bag. The golden liquid swirled inside the glass bottle.

My mouth watered, itching for a taste of the amber bliss. "Xander," I breathed.

"You want some of this, baby?" he asked, holding it between us.

"You...you know I can't," I said, not taking my eyes off the item in his hand.

"Well I can and I'm going to." Xander pushed open the door, walking past me. "Caiden having cancer is funny to me."

"Excuse me? How the hell is it funny?" I slammed the door shut, placing my hands on my hips.

"Because he's such a good guy. It proves no matter how good of a person you are, life fucking sucks." Xander ripped open the lid and threw it on the kitchen counter.

Tilting the bottle towards his lips, he took a long drawn out swig. "Fuck me, that tastes good." He coughed, wiping his lips.

At that point, I lost it. I ground my teeth, my muscles quivering. "Does it taste as good as me?" I yelled, pointing at him. "You said I was the only thing you wanted from now on. No alcohol. No drugs."

"That was before I found out my best friend had cancer and my girlfriend never told me!" he shouted, taking another swig from the bottle.

I charged at him, pulling the bottle from his grip and ran to the sink. I refused to let him drown himself in the evil of that bottle.

"Give it back to me." He grabbed me around the waist, reaching for the bottle.

I stomped on his foot, shoving out of his grip. "I won't let you drown in tequila. Use me. Take out your anger on me," I screamed. "But don't you dare give in. Please. God, Xander, don't give in."

Xander hooked an arm around my middle, lifting me over his shoulder and grabbed the bottle out of my hand. "I already gave in the moment you stepped back into my life."

"Put me down." I beat my fists against his back, struggling out of his tight hold.

He threw me on the couch, took another gulp of the gold liquid and crashed his lips to mine.

The sweet scent of the alcohol wafted into my nose when liquid poured into my mouth. It burned my throat, heating my belly as I swallowed. "You fucking asshole." I shoved him off of me, coughing. "I haven't had a drink in five years and you forced it down my throat."

He smirked, sitting back on the couch. His eyes were glassy, no doubt already drunk as he continued downing the contents of the bottle. "Cancer. Alcohol. Drugs. Sex. It's all the same." He shrugged. "Eventually, one of them will kill us." His words were slurred. He didn't make any sense.

None at all.

"I can't believe you did that." I wanted more. Thanks to the man I loved, I wanted to give into the powerful seduction of the bottle in his hands and ride that high with him.

Fuck it.

Throwing myself into his arms, I took the bottle from him and brought it up to my mouth. Ignoring the voice in my head screaming, five years, I gulped down the burning liquid.

"That's right, baby. If I'm going to lose this battle, so are you." Xander tilted the bottle, forcing more of the liquid down my throat.

My head spun, my stomach reeling. The room swayed, my vision fading in and out. A warm tongue licked up my jaw, cleaning up the drops that had spilled out of the corner of my lips.

"So fucking good." Xander lifted me in his arms, carrying me to his bathroom. Laying me in the tub, he crawled in with me and knelt between my legs. With both hands, he cupped the vee in my shirt and ripped it in half.

I arched under him, pushing my chest into his hands.

He grabbed the bottle and poured the liquid onto my torso before lapping it up with his tongue. "Open, baby," he said, bringing the bottle up to my lips.

I swallowed some of the liquid before he replaced it with his mouth. Kissing him like never before, it bordered on rough.

His hands pulled at my body, digging into the flesh of my muscles. Ripping into my hair, he tugged my head back, swallowing my cry of surprise.

We were high with the need for each other and drunk off of the tequila we consumed. Everything mixed as one. My thoughts. My feelings. My actions. I couldn't control anything as my drunken body took over.

My vision faded in and out. Every so often, I would get snippets of what was happening. I couldn't focus. Grunts.

Screams. Whimpers and purrs of pleasure erupted through the room, bouncing off the walls.

Eventually, Xander had me bent over the tub, covered in his scent and the tequila. In a crazed lust of alcohol and passion, his thrusts turned violent, ripping into me with a powerful force I craved.

I didn't know how long it lasted. I could only imagine we continued into the night, taking out our pain and frustration on each other, allowing the tequila to be the one to fully take control.

NINETEEN

Xander

THE NEXT MORNING I woke sore and stiff in places I never even knew existed. Muscles hurt that I've never used before. Even my hair hurt. Fuck. What the hell happened?

Opening my eyes, I squinted, breathing through the onset of a headache and swallowed past the impending nausea.

A soft body was wrapped around mine. Hope. Alright. Well that was a good start. Looking around the room, I realized we were in the tub. "Hope," I said, my voice hoarse.

She stirred, groaning and sat up. "Holy shit. Who drove a stake through my head?"

I chuckled and pinched her chin. "Hey, beautiful girl."

"Hi," she breathed, her voice coming out husky.

Our eyes locked and that was when I saw them.

Bruises. Red marks. Bile rose to my throat. Her clothes were ripped, hanging off of her in shreds. "Hope," I gasped.

She followed my gaze, her jaw dropping. "Oh my."

"I'm...I'm so sorry," I said.

"Don't..." Her gaze snapped to mine. "Oh God. You made me drink."

My eyes widened. "What? I did?" Memories of me drinking the tequila, kissing her and then pouring the liquid into her mouth invaded my mind. "I...I'm..." I stuttered. I couldn't form the words. She was a recovering alcoholic and because of me, I set her back. What kind of man was I?

She rose from my lap and stepped out of the tub. Her back was rigged as she stripped completely of the tattered clothes. Stepping into the shower, she turned on the water but not before I heard the soft crying.

Pulling myself from the tub, I took off my clothes, sticky from sweat, alcohol and us. Heavy guilt settled on my back as I joined Hope in the shower.

Her shoulders shook, the scalding hot water turning her skin pink.

"I'm so sorry," I said finally, wanting to touch her but kept my distance.

"Five years, Xander. Five years since I had a drink." She looked at me over her shoulder, her eyes cold. "I'm not like you. I don't have control over the alcohol I drink. That's why..." Her breath hitched. "When I lost the baby, I became depressed. So many times I had picked up the phone to call you. I needed you. And last night, I needed you more and yet you threw my need in my face."

"I'm sorry," I said, my voice low. It was all I could say. I didn't know how to make it up to her. What more could I do? I had done enough already.

"You may say you're sorry but..." She shook her head. "I understand you're mad I never told you about Caiden. But if he told you to keep something to yourself, would you?"

"Yes," I said without hesitation.

"Exactly. I was helping out a friend. I know how much you mean to him and him to you...I didn't want to do anything to rupture that bond." Her chin quivered. "I'm going to leave, give you guys some time."

"No!" I fell to my knees, wrapping my arms around her legs. "Please. I'm sorry. I'm so fucking sorry."

"I can't...I can't keep doing this." She pulled out of my grip and knelt in front of me. "If you loved me—"

"I do love you!" I shouted, pounding my fist against the tiled wall. Sharp pain shot up my arm but I ignored it. "I love you more than life itself. I worship the fucking ground you walk on."

"Xander, we need some time a part or something. Look at us."

I crushed my mouth to hers, pulling her into my arms.

She moaned but pushed against me. "Stop. We can't keep doing this. If you loved me, you never would have forced the alcohol down my throat."

"I was drunk!" I insisted. "I never would have done that sober."

"Exactly!" she screamed. "Now you know why you can't drink."

Realization dawned on me, punching me hard in the gut. "I..."

"That's what Caiden has been trying to tell you. This is why I don't drink anymore. I lost a part of myself when

I lost the baby but I know if that baby would have been yours, it would have killed me."

"I wish I could have been there," I said, rubbing my face in the crook of her neck. "What can I do to make you stay? Please, I'm begging you. Tell me."

She cupped my cheeks and placed a hard peck on my lips. "Let me go."

"No. I refuse. I won't ever let you go." I gripped her tight, holding her against me.

"Then love me. Help me. Be with me. But before you can, you need to help yourself, Xander."

"Tell me how. Please," I begged, running my hands up her back.

"I—"

A hard knock sounded on the bathroom door, interrupting us.

"One minute," I called out, frowning.

"Is that Caiden?" she asked, turning off the water.

"I assume it is." I wrapped a towel around my waist, made sure she was decent and opened the door.

Caiden stood there in front of me, a smile on his face. "Hi."

My eyes widened. Shaking my head, I pulled him in for an embrace. "Hi? That's all you have to say? Why the hell are you out of the hospital?"

He chuckled, returning my hug. "They let me go but I have to be back next week for more tests and if something like last night happens again, I have to be back sooner. Do you have any idea what time it is?" His head peaked around me. "What the hell were you guys doing last night?"

"Nothing we can't work through," Hope said, wrapping her arms around his middle.

I prayed she was right.

"Well get dressed and meet me in the living room. I want you to meet someone." Caiden left the room.

"Hope," I said, slipping on blue jeans and a white t-shirt.

She didn't answer and pulled on a white bra and panty set. She reached around behind her to clasp the ends together on the bra when I stopped her. Her back stiffened but she let out a sigh. "Don't pressure me."

I clasped the bra closed, letting my fingers brush over her smooth skin. "I won't." I turned her in my arms and kissed her hair. "I love you. I'm an asshole and a dick. I can never expect you to forgive me for what I did last night," I pinched her chin, kissing the salty tears falling freely down her cheeks. "But please know I will do everything in my fucking power to earn your love back. I will make you trust me again. If I have to spend my every breath, telling you over and over how sorry I am, I will."

"Xander," her voice wavered.

"I mean it, Hope. There is no excuse for what I did last night. No excuse. No matter what happens, I shouldn't have done that to you. I shouldn't have forced you to drink. I am sorry."

She nodded and stepped out of my embrace. Pulling on black tights and my grey zip up hoodie, she sighed.

My blood stirred at seeing her in my clothes. Gripping

her shoulders, I kissed the side of her neck. "Do you hurt?"

"It's a nice pain," she said, her cheeks reddening. "I can feel you every time I move."

My dick twitched. Clearing my throat, I kissed her forehead. "Good."

The corners of her lips tugged into a smile but she didn't say anything. She grabbed my hand and kissed my fingers. "These fingers," she grabbed my other hand. "These hands have done so much hurting." Her voice wavered, her eyes filling with unshed tears when she looked at me.

"I…" I swallowed hard. "I can't control it." I realized then it was the truth. I had a good childhood. I wasn't abused. I wasn't shit on by my parents. But when they died and Hope left me, my world was ripped apart. The bellows of Hell opened up and sucked me in, forcing me to my knees and giving into the submission I didn't have control of.

Hope placed light pecks on my knuckles, her thumb brushing back and forth over the rough and calloused skin. "I've never stopped loving you. I would go to bed each and every night, praying I would wake up next you. That it would all be some horrible nightmare."

Not knowing what else to say, I pulled her into my arms and whispered over and over how much I loved her.

Her back stiffened and she pulled out of my grip.

Grabbing my hand, she led us to the living room.

Not knowing what happened, I allowed her to guide me, to be my strength, to be that light in the tunnel I needed. After everything I had put her through, she still hung on.

She latched onto me like I was her…everything.

Once we reached the living room, I stopped in my tracks when I saw a small woman sitting on the couch beside Caiden. She was talking quietly to him, looking up at him with a gentle love in her deep blue gaze. She was pale in comparison to his olive skin tone. Her long straight honey blonde hair shone in the dim lighting of the late afternoon sun. Her gaze landed on us. She looked to Caiden. He nodded once and she rose to her feet.

"It's so nice to meet you both," the tiny woman said softly, holding out a hand. "I'm Erica but you can call me Erica."

Hope and I greeted her, shaking her hand in turns.

"It's nice to meet you, too," Hope said, remaining standing beside me.

Caiden rose to his feet and cupped Erica's nape. He whispered something to her and she nodded.

"How long have you been seeing each other?" I asked, sitting on the coffee table across from them.

Caiden and Erica looked at each other before glancing back at us. "Her brother is a friend of Lee's," Caiden explained. "We met one night at a club and have been talking ever since." Caiden shrugged like it was no big deal.

I guessed it wasn't but seeing Caiden with a woman was a little weird for me, especially when he told me how he had felt for me a couple of days ago. Did he still feel the same? Could he turn on and off his feelings like that? God, I was starting to sound like a woman.

"Caiden hasn't told us much about you but I know you must be something special," Hope said, sitting beside me.

Erica's cheeks reddened. "I try. Caiden is something special himself."

Caiden grinned and cupped her cheek, brushing his thumb along her bottom lip. "You are special. And you know why, kitten."

She nodded. "What have you told them about us?"

"Not much." Caiden looked back at us. "Erica has been working with me on my Kinbaku. Although I have trained Hope to help you, Xander, Erica is my new apprentice, so to speak."

"What does that mean?" I asked, frowning when a slight twinge of unease swam in my gut. I had never seen Caiden so loving and caring with someone. It was always fuck 'em and leave 'em, for both of us. Especially with Embree.

"It means I will make Erica fly until my time has come," Caiden said, his voice gentle but strong.

"Your time has come? Caid, what is going on?" I demanded, rising to my feet.

Caiden looked down at his joined hands linked with Erica's. "There are some things that are going to be changing rather quickly. I don't know when. But I do know you have to be ready for them. Promise me."

"I don't know what you're talking about," I said, shaking my head. "Please tell me what's going on."

Hope gripped my inner thigh, squeezing with reassurance.

"Do you know what he's talking about?" I asked her, desperation in my voice.

She looked away. "I...I don't know enough."

I stood up abruptly, pacing back and forth. Gripping the collar of my shirt, I pulled and tugged at it. My chest constricted, my lungs aching with the need to breathe.

"Xander…" Caiden came up behind me and cupped my nape.

"Something's wrong." I spun on him. "But you won't tell me. Am I not strong enough? Do you think I'm going to lose it? Because, Caiden, I'm already fucking losing it."

His eyes softened. "You are strong but I don't want to do anything to set you back. Look at what you've been through already. Have you fought your demons yet? Have you forgiven Hope yet? No, you haven't."

"You don't know what I've done, Caiden. You don't know all and see all. Stop acting like you do."

"I don't know all." He chuckled. "God, Xander. If I did, I would have built this house years ago."

"What the hell are you talking about?" I asked, my brows narrowing.

He shook his head. "It doesn't matter."

"Yes, it does!" I shouted. "You've accused me of shutting you out. Well stop doing the same to me. Tell me what the hell is going on. We've been friends for years and I just find out you have fucking cancer. All this time, I thought you were gay and then I find out you don't have a preference. Why don't you talk to me?"

"I do talk to you! But you don't fucking listen." He took a step towards me, forcing me back. "If you would listen, you would know I've been sick. You would know I've been in love with you for years. You would also know I only fucked Embree because it was the closest thing I could get to fucking you!"

My eyes widened at his confession.

Several gasps sounded from the living room but he ignored them and continued. "I know you love me like a man should love his brother. I get that, but I realized it's not enough for me. Am I in love with Erica? I've given everything I can to her that I've wanted to give to you. She understands this but…" He stopped, his body mere inches from mine.

My mouth opened and closed, my heart jumping.

"Caid…I'm sorry," was all I said. I couldn't wrap my head around what he was telling me. I knew how he felt about me but I also knew it wasn't enough. I couldn't give him what he needed. I couldn't force myself to love someone the way they deserved.

"Sorry doesn't stop me from loving you," Caiden said, leaning against the wall opposite me.

"So what do we do?" I asked, my voice small.

Caiden brushed a hand through his hair, not meeting my gaze. "I'm leaving."

"What?" My eyes widened. "You can't leave."

"I'm going to stay with Erica for a couple of days," he said, ignoring me and pushed from his spot at the wall.

"Caiden." I grabbed his arm. "Please. We can work through this."

He looked down at my hand gripping his bicep and took a deep breath. "Let me go."

"No. Please. I will do anything," I pleaded.

"You can't do anything because you can't love me like you love Hope. I tried ignoring the way you are with her. I've tried. But it fucking hurts!" he snapped, shoving from my grip.

"That's not my fault!" I yelled, pushing him. "You can't make me feel guilty over giving my heart to someone.

If I could give it to you, I would. You can't force me." "I know it's not your fault." He pushed me back, shoving me up against the wall. "But it's not my fault you fucking stole my heart."

"I never asked for your heart," I growled, punching his shoulder.

"Doesn't fucking matter." In a quick move, he wrapped his hand around my throat and crashed his lips to mine.

I swallowed a gasp at the rough impact, my body stiffening and then relaxing into his touch. His warm mouth moved fluidly over mine, his velvet tongue slipping into my mouth. The scratchiness of the scruff on his jaw brushed against mine.

His fingers tightened around my neck, tilting my head back as he deepened the kiss.

Never in all of my life would I thought Caiden would ever kiss me. My heart jumped hard against my rib cage, my palms becoming sweaty. A tingle trembled down my spine. I loved the man who had his mouth on mine but I only loved him like a brother. I realized it now more than anything.

Caiden released me. His eyes dilated, desire swimming in the dark depths. "Xander," he breathed.

Licking my lips, I took a breath and shook my head. Before I could stop myself, before I could even think twice about what I was doing, I punched him.

TWENTY

I HAD DONE SOMETHING that I had wanted to do for years. Ever since I realized that I felt more for Xander Brant then just friendship. When I kissed him, I wasn't thinking of what his reaction would be. I wasn't thinking of how it affected him, Erica or Hope. I was thinking about myself. I was selfish and for that, I paid the price when he punched me.

The pain shot through the side of my face like I had been hit by a brick. Xander was bigger than me and he packed one hell of a hit.

I knew right then that everything would change. It would become weird between us no matter how hard we tried to stop it.

But I never expected him to hit me. Yell and scream at me maybe but punch me in the fucking face? God, I was naïve to think he would react any less.

As we continued our stare down, my heart beat hard against the confines of my ribs. I loved him. More than life itself. And without him, I would break. But without me?

The cancer would surely destroy us both.

Seeing him with her, ate at me until I had enough. I shouldn't have let it go on for as long as I did. I would never want Xander and Hope to break up but I couldn't handle seeing them together. I wasn't sure if it was because the cancer was back and it was messing with my head or my feelings were growing for Erica. Either way, I found myself wanting to be alone. But I couldn't kick Xander out of my house. Even though it was mine, I had built it with him in mind. He needed a place to stay after I was gone. I knew he could take care of himself. I got that. But he needed more. Hope had told me that he would always need me no matter what happened so I liked to think that when I was gone, a part of me would still remain with him. In this house. It would be hard, but he would make it work.

"Hit me back, fucker," Xander growled, his voice low so that only I could hear.

A slow grin spread on my face. "I love you, man, but you are being a dick," I said through clenched teeth.

These next couple of minutes would be a test. Of our friendship. Our brotherhood that he liked to remind me of constantly. But I didn't want to be his brother. I didn't want to be just his friend. But I would take it. Because if something happened where we couldn't be friends anymore? It would kill me faster than the cancer seeping through my body.

***

(Hope)

When I saw the impact of the kiss, I knew it was in a desperation of love and want. I had been there, so I knew how Caiden felt. He wanted to let Xander know his feelings for him weren't bullshit. I got that. But did Xander?

I was not expecting Xander's fist to fly at Caiden's face. The pain behind his eyes broke my heart but it soon flashed into something else. Pure hard rage and that scared me even more.

Everything next happened fast.

"Hit me again," Caiden bit out through clenched teeth, a dark bruise forming on his jaw already.

I rose to my feet as Xander geared up to hit him again but this time, Caiden charged at him, throwing him to the ground.

I screamed, begging them to stop. Erica and I rushed over, careful not to get mixed in their fight but tried our hardest to separate them.

The sound of fists hitting bone caused bile to rise to my throat but I pushed forth, pulling Xander off of Caiden.

"Stop. Please, both of you. Stop!" I fell back on my ass with Xander shaking in my arms. His cheeks were mottled pink, his nostrils flaring. He was seething mad but he didn't try and escape my grip.

"Leave, you fucking asshole." Xander laughed. It was cold and maniacal. "Run. Run like you've done your whole damn life."

"I never ran!" Caiden shouted. "I told you exactly how I felt. I helped you through your shit. I brought you and Hope back together and this is how you repay me? I should fucking kick you out but I can't because you have no place to go."

"I could find a place," Xander yelled.

Caiden threw his head back and laughed. "You almost burnt down our apartment. You have no job. You're a bum, living off of me because you're too damn scared to be out on your own. Well guess what, Xander? You're going to have to be on your own faster than you would like." He spun on his heel, storming to the door. He threw it open, paused and looked back at us. His eyes saddened. "You need to learn to take care of yourself."

"I can take care of myself," Xander growled.

"Can you? You don't like being alone," Caiden said, his voice coming out hoarse.

"That's because my head is too loud!" Xander snapped.

Caiden nodded once and left the house with Erica following after him. She stopped briefly to smile at us with sympathy and closed the door behind her.

"Caiden," Xander whispered. With shaky hands, he scrubbed them down his face.

"I'm so sorry." I kissed his cheek, wrapping my arms around his waist.

He turned in my arms abruptly, forcing me back. A look of pure unadulterated lust filled his gaze as his eyes traveled down the length of my body. "I want you to run," he said roughly.

"What?" I gasped, the small hairs on my skin tingling. "Let's have a bath, relax or watch a movie."

"No!" He shoved out of my grip. "I will fuck you right here if I have to. I don't fucking care but I will spend the night buried balls deep inside of your delicious body."

I rose to my knees and cupped his cheeks. "Xander…"

A wicked grin spread on his face when he pushed me face first onto the carpet.

My eyes widened, the nerve endings on my body exploding with delight.

"Tell me how much you want me." He ripped down my pants, landing a hard swat on my ass. "Tell me."

"I want you. God, I always want you," I cried, digging my fingers into the carpet.

Xander knelt between my spread thighs, fisted my hair and towered over me. "I love you. But right now, this is pure fucking. You got me?"

I nodded, understanding completely.

"I didn't ask for him to kiss me," he breathed hard against my neck. His voice was panged, like he was apologizing for the moment he and Caiden had shared.

"I know you didn't," I whispered. As much as it probably should have bothered me, it didn't. I was jealous of their friendship but seeing how that kiss played out and the aftereffects of it, I would never want that for me and Xander. It broke my heart that because Caiden had reacted first, it could in the end destroy their friendship.

"I'm yours, baby." A zipper lowered, a hard grunt filling my ears. "I need to show you who I belong to."

"I know… you…Oh, shit," I cried out when he thrust into me hard.

"Let me remind you," he growled, pumping slow and deep.

Whimpering, I spread my legs wider, opening myself to him. I gave him a part of me that no man ever had. He reached inside of me, pulled forth this undying want. It was so strong, I could feel it.

Xander was ferocious in the feral way he took me. He forced me over the edge of pure and utter bliss, taking me to new heights I never thought I would get from him.

Pulling my head back, he placed a hard kiss on my mouth. His tongue tasted of spicy smoke. He pushed deeper, claiming me and owning me with the demanding strokes of his cock. "Can you taste him?" he ground out, his voice rough.

I gasped into his mouth. My hips tilted, taking him deeper.

Xander growled, released my mouth with a hard smack and fisted his hand tighter in my hair. "I need you to coat my dick with your orgasm, beautiful girl." He tugged my sweater higher up my torso, inching his hand under my breast. His fingers pushed under the cup of my bra and twisted and teased my nipple into a sharp peak.

All I could do was moan and hold onto his free hand beside my head while he made use of my body. He took what he needed. Gave me what I wanted and left the rest for both of us to consume. I realized at that point I would never get enough of the man seated deep inside of my body. It was never like this before. Never like the love we once shared. This was carnal. Desperate with the need to mate and mark each other like property.

"Please," he whispered into the crook of my neck. That once broken man reared its ugly head as his hips slowed down. But I didn't want that. I needed him, the new him.

Even though he was still broken, I wanted to show him we could get through this battle inside of him together. I wanted to help him. I craved his touch like I needed it to live. I loved him so much it hurt. It was a physical ache inside of my chest and every time I wasn't near him, that ache grew. I realized this now as his desperate plea washed over me.

Pushing to all fours, I started hammering back against him, giving him all of me.

"Fuck," he groaned, digging his fingers into the flesh of my ass. "Faster."

I did as he demanded, throwing my head back.

Suddenly, he pushed me to the ground and thrust forth with so much strength, I screamed. An earth shattering release rocked through my core.

"Louder. Scream my name, baby," he snarled, slamming into me in hard moves.

"Oh God." I panted. "Xander."

"Your body is so fucking perfect." His thrusts slowed. "Perfect for my thick cock."

I moaned. "Please."

"Please what?" He cupped my knee, pulling it out to the side, spreading me open for him.

"Come for me," I whispered.

With his sweat coated cheek, he rubbed it along my neck, scenting me. "I want you to smell like me for the rest of your life."

"Our life," I corrected, linking our fingers.

"Damn straight. Tell me you want me. Tell me you want me like this." His words held a hint of a warning, daring me to say yes. So I did.

"I want you. Like this. Stripped bare for me. Giving me all of you." I purred out a moan as he pushed into me further, picking up his speed. "I love you more than my last breath. I need you. I need you so much it hurts." I told him how much I loved him over and over while he used my body for his pleasure.

He roared out a release, shaking violently on top of me, his body trembling. His orgasm spurted into me in quick hard bursts, filling me with a piece of him he had never given to anyone. "You are my life," he said softly, kissing my neck.

Xander released me and kissed my rear before helping me to my feet.

I kicked off the pants hanging from my ankle and pulled off the rest of my clothes.

His eyes grazed down my body, heating my skin from a look. His nostrils flared, his beautiful grey gaze taking me in like he couldn't control his need for me. "Bedroom," was all he said, wrapping a hand around his semi-hard length.

My eyes followed the movement. Licking my lips, I reached out for him when he stopped me.

"Bedroom," he growled.

This time I listened.

TWENTY ONE

Caiden

"FUCK!" I YELLED, SLAMMING a fist against the wall. A sharp pain shot up my arm, igniting my skin on fire. I paced back and forth, scrubbing a hand down my face. How could I kiss him? How could I cross that line? I was never one to let my feelings get the best of me. But with Xander, they took full control and now he probably hated me.

"Caiden." Erica came up behind me and wrapped her arms around my waist. She had driven us back to her place, the trip filled with unnerving silence. "Use me. Please. But don't you dare fall into yourself."

I spun on her and wrapped a hand around her throat.

Her eyes widened. "Please," she whispered.

Backing her up until she hit the wall, I caressed a hand down her face. "I need you."

She nodded.

For the rest of the night, I had made her mine. Marking her from within. Claiming her with the rough touch of my hands, my mouth. Every single inch of me.

She had given me all of her. Her mind. Body. And soul.

And that was when I fell in love with her.

***

(Hope)

The next morning I woke up on the floor. Wrapped in sheets and Xander, I kept my arms around him, holding him against me as I listened to the sound of his breathing.

Grazing my fingers up and down his back, I smiled as he shivered every so often. His cock bobbed against my hip, swelling from me not even touching him.

"I will fuck you hard and not be sorry in the least if I make you sore," he said, his voice raspy. He looked up at me and placed a soft kiss on my lips.

I smiled, brushing my hand down his cheek. "I will take you whatever way you want to have me." I kissed his chin. "But I'm already sore."

A smug grin formed on his lips when he pulled the covers off of me. His eyes inched down my body, taking me in.

I was self-conscious about my curves but the way he looked at me like he wanted to eat me alive, I got over

216

that little fear. "I love the way you look at me," I blurted, my cheeks heating at my little outburst.

His eyes shot to mine. "I love the way you see me."

The mood quickly changed, going from light to heavy in the matter of a couple seconds. He hadn't called Caiden since he left, spending the rest of the night doing exactly what he had promised to do. My body ached, my muscles sore and twitchy but if I made Xander feel somewhat better, I would give him every single inch of me a hundred times over.

"Xander," I said gently.

He cleared his throat and sat up, scrubbing a hand over his shaved head. "I don't know what to do about Caiden. I don't want to hurt him but I love you too much to…"

"To what?" I asked, sitting up behind him.

Xander placed his arm over my lap, leaning his head against the side of the bed.

"Did the kiss confuse you?" As much as I didn't want to hear the answer, Xander needed to talk about it.

"I…I'm not sure. If it was anyone else, I probably would have shrugged it off."

I raised an eyebrow. "If some random guy came up to you and kissed you, you would shrug it off?"

He huffed. "I don't know," he snapped. "What I'm saying is because it was Caiden who kissed me when I know how he feels about me, it fucked with my head. I don't feel that way towards him. I don't. I have no issues with anyone who wants to be with the same sex or whatever. I'm not homophobic in any way but I felt like he kissed me to piss me off, not because he wanted to."

"I'm sure he did want to kiss you. He did it because he thought it could change your heart," I offered, shrugging.

Xander searched my face. "Do you think that?"

"No, but…" I chewed my bottom lip, thinking over my words carefully before Xander and I got in a fight as well. "I would step aside—"

"No!" he shouted. He grabbed my arms, pulling me towards him. "Don't you dare say that. Ever. Promise me." "Okay. Okay." I cupped his cheeks. "I'm sorry. All I'm saying is, I want you to be happy. If it meant being with him, as much as it would destroy me, I would step aside for you. I love you both too much to be in the middle of…whatever this is."

"No," he whispered into my hair. "I would spend the rest of my life alone first."

"You can't say that." I sat back. "Caiden would be good for you."

His jaw hardened. He brushed the back of his knuckles down the center of my body before gripping my hip.

Although we were both naked, it wasn't sexual in the least. "It's dangerous."

I scoffed. "Please. Like our relationship isn't? It's toxic." I pushed a finger into his chest. "You have said that over and over again."

"That's different," he muttered, grazing his hands down my back.

"How? How is it different, Xander? We take one step forward, everything is fine and then something happens, setting us back. We're both addicted to something that will eventually kill us if we're not careful."

I inhaled a shaky breath. "I'm not strong enough to fight my addiction."

"Yes. You are." His hold on me tightened. "You fought it for five years—"

"Yes, but then one night with you and all that hard work blew up in my face," I cried, dropping my head in my hands.

"Are you blaming me?" When I didn't answer he tugged my head back. "Are you blaming me?" he repeated slowly.

"Yes," I blurted. "I can't help but blame you. I want you so much. I love you more than I should. This…this thing I feel for you isn't normal."

"Yes, it is. It's perfectly normal."

"Is it? I'm addicted to you. I can't get enough. Every time I'm not with you, it hurts. I get this tightness in my chest…it's a physical pain…I…I can't…" My breaths started coming out in quick bursts, tears filling my eyes.

Xander wrapped his arms around me, holding me tight against him. "I know," he whispered.

"It hurts. Being with you hurts but being without you hurts more." A sob escaped me. No more words were said as we held each other. I didn't know if you could love someone too much but what I felt for Xander, what I had always felt for him, was worse than the alcohol I was addicted to. He was right. I was strong enough to fight it. But when it came to Xander, I was weak. And I would give in every single time.

TWENTY TWO

Xander

BEING WITH HOPE WOULD eventually destroy me. Her taste. Her dewy skin. Her peaches and cream scent. I didn't know if it was possible to love someone too much but with her, it bordered on pure and utter obsession. I couldn't go on with my day without thinking about her. I couldn't eat. Sleep. Every time I had a shower, I touched myself. I woke up hard, full and throbbing for her warmth. She was the only thing that could satisfy me and even then, it wasn't enough. I lost control when it came to Hope Charming. She knew it. She never admitted it but I knew she enjoyed the control I gave her.

It had been a week since Caiden kissed me. And a week since he left us alone at his house. Hope called him every so often but I refused to talk to him. I was scared.

I was man enough to admit it. I didn't want to lose him as a friend but I also didn't want to confront the fact I enjoyed the kiss. It was nothing like what I shared with Hope and it never would be, but it was nice. Desperate but…nice. It was something that had to be done even though nothing would come of it. It was meant to be, a final goodbye and that thought ripped me apart.

"You have to talk to him," Hope said, interrupting my thoughts.

I slammed my fist against the heavy weight swinging from the ceiling in front of me. "He doesn't want to talk to me."

"Yes, he does but he's waiting for you. He's giving you control, Xander," she said softly.

Control. Were any of us ever truly in control? Of life. Our jobs. Our own damn personality. Everyone you come across has some impact on you. So this shit about being in control or giving it up, it didn't fit. It didn't work.

My fists continued ringing blows on the punching bag, sharp pain shooting up my arms each time. If he wanted to talk to me, he could come to me. But I wasn't making the first move.

"He loves you."

"I know!" I yelled, spinning on her.

Hope lifted her chin defiantly, crossing her arms under her chest.

"And I love him," I continued. "But I love you more. I can't love him the way he needs. He knows that."

"Does he? Have you actually talked without yelling at each other? No. Because both of you are too pigheaded and you let your alpha males come out." She grabbed my hand and slapped a cell phone in it. "Call him."

"No need."

My gaze snapped up at the deep voice coming from the doorway. Caiden leaned against the frame, his arms crossed under his chest. "Hope? Can you give us a little bit?"

She nodded. "I have to call Embree anyways." She gave my hand a light squeeze, her eyes filling with warmth.

A cold draft washed over my skin when she let me go. Her touch was always my safety net. It kept me grounded. Made me feel somewhat normal. My parents would be so ashamed of me. Letting the bottom of a bottle control me in ways I never would have imagined. But if they were still alive, I would never need to drown myself. God, I missed them. I missed them so much. More and more each day.

People told me it would get easier. But it hadn't. And it probably never would.

"We need to talk," Caiden said, closing the door behind him.

"I know." I brushed my hand over my shaved head. "Listen, I'm sorry for punching you. I—"

"I don't want to talk about that." Caiden closed the distance between us and cupped the back of my neck.

"There's something I need to tell you. Something I haven't told anyone."

My eyes searched his face. His scars were more pronounced, the purple hue in his gaze no longer filled with life but utter defeat. My heart skipped a beat. "What's wrong?"

"The cancer..." He swallowed hard. "It's back and there's nothing they can do."

"What...what does this mean?" I asked, staring intently into his eyes. I knew exactly what it had meant but I needed to hear him say it. I needed to know that my ears weren't playing tricks on me although I wished they were. He looked away. "It means it's only a matter of time."

The air left my lungs on a suffocating whoosh. I gripped my chest, gasping for breath as the words sunk in. "No...it's not possible. You're strong. You can fight this. You have to fight this. Please. For me."

Caiden gripped my neck, squeezing his fingers into my flesh. "I can't fight this. Once it's at the level where it's at now, there's nothing they can do."

"No! Get a second opinion. Get...no...please." My lungs burned as I struggled to breathe.

"Xander," he said, his voice firm.

"You can't leave me. I won't let you." Before I knew what I was doing, I crushed my lips to his.

He gasped into my mouth, momentarily surprised before he took full control. He pushed me back, deepening the kiss and scratched his fingers into my nape. "Xander," he said, breathing heavy and released me.

I reached for him again but he stopped me.

"Stop," he held me at arm's length and shook his head. "You don't want this."

"I...I do." I gripped his wrists, licking my kiss swollen lips. I was willing to do anything. I needed some sort of connection with him. It didn't make sense but a part of me felt that if I was with him, he would stay. I was losing my ever-loving mind. The thought of losing my best friend to the evilness of cancer tore at my soul and made me act out in a fit of desperation.

Caiden smiled sadly. "No. You don't. It would be cheating on Hope."

A lump burned in my throat. "I want...I want you here. Forever."

"Having sex with me will not save me," he said softly.

At that point I fell to my knees submitting to the wrath of the unexpected. Caiden was strong. He was the strongest person I knew. But even then, the strongest person could lose in the end. "I would give you my last breath if it meant saving you."

He let out a sigh and knelt in front of me. "I've been battling this disease for years. I should have told you sooner. I am sorry. I thought I could control it like I control everything else. But I was wrong. I'm so sorry, Xander. Please forgive me."

My head snapped up. "Forgive you? Of course I forgive you. How could you...God, Caiden. I wish you would have told me. I could have supported you. I could have been there with you during all of your appointments. I..." My eyes filled with unshed tears. He was still here, still in front of me but I felt like I was losing him already. A life without Caiden Yeo, my best friend, a part of me would forever be filled because of him. It was the ultimate destruction. Not alcohol. Not drugs. The loss of my best friend would be the true destroyer.

"Stop thinking. Whatever is going on inside of that head of yours, stop it." He cupped my cheek and kissed my forehead. "I'm not gone yet."

A sob escaped me and I threw my arms around him. Bone crushing cries wracked through my body as tears flowed down my cheeks.

Caiden held me tight, crying along with me.

"I don't want you to go," I whispered eventually, wiping the tears from under my eyes.

He leaned his forehead against mine and ran his hands up and down my arms. "When I go, you'll be ready. As hard as it will be for all of you, you will come out strongest in the end."

I wanted to argue and scream and shout that he was wrong. I was not strong at all. There was no way I would be able to handle him dying on me but a light knock on the door stopped me from lashing out. It was probably a good thing. Too many hurtful words had been said already.

"Guys?" Hope peeked her head into the room. "Erica is here, Caiden."

"Thank you." Caiden rose to his feet and held out a hand, helping me up. "Remember what I told you."

I nodded, fighting back unshed tears that threatened to escape. Again.

In a solemn like daze, I followed Caiden out into the living room where he greeted Erica with a hug and a soft peck on the lips.

She smiled up at him, wrapping her arms around his waist and snuggled into his touch.

My stomach burned with anxiety and I walked into the kitchen instead. Taking a deep breath, I started pacing back and forth. Never needing a drink more than at that moment, I slid to the ground, circling my arms around my bent knees.

Control it, Xander. You got this. I chanted to myself over and over but I didn't have this. I didn't have anything. No control. No urge to move forward. I felt stuck in time. Stuck in this depressed like state where the only thing that would cure me and bring me out of this funk was diving into the pits of a bottle or smoking the shit out of a joint. My mouth watered. Grabbing my phone out of my pants pocket, I quickly sent Lee a text. When he replied he would be over in less than five, my heart sped up. My palms became sweaty, a laugh escaping my lips.

"Xander?" Hope came into the kitchen, frowning when she saw me sitting on the floor. "Everything okay?"

I grinned. "It will be."

***

(Hope)

After I finally approached Embree, even though it was only over the phone, I felt like a weight had been lifted. She and I had been friends for years. We weren't as close as I would have liked but that was my doing. I was guarded, only ever wanting to let Xander in and even then, I found it difficult to truly open up. I was working on it. I had to. For him and for me. But he needed to give as much as I did.

But as I watched Xander pace back and forth in front of me, I realized there was more to life than this. One moment we were happy. The next, something set him off and we would be back to the beginning. It was constantly a game of Tug of War.

His big body shook, his hands clenching into fists at his sides. His eyes kept darting to the front door, like he was waiting for something or someone to show up.

"Xander?" I said, tentatively, taking a step towards him. "Are you okay?"

His phone buzzed. He quickly checked it, a sigh leaving his lips as his gaze slid over the words staring up at him from the small screen. In an abrupt move, he shoved the phone back into his pocket and grabbed my hand. He kissed my knuckles. "I'm sorry," he said so softly, I almost didn't hear him.

"Sorry? Sorry for what? Xander, what's going on?" I asked as he pulled from my grip.

He ran out of the house as Caiden and Erica came out of the kitchen. Hand-in-hand, Caiden held onto her tight. My heart skipped a beat at seeing him with her. Knowing how he felt about Xander, it was odd to see him with someone else. Much less someone who knew about his feelings.

"What's wrong, Hope?" Caiden wrapped his arm around Erica's tiny frame, leaning on her for support.

"I'm not sure." I didn't know what he and Xander had talked about. It wasn't my place to pry but when they came out of the gym, their eyes were red and bloodshot, their bodies stiff and broken. I would always remember the look Xander had given me and the feel of his lips on mine when he kissed me. He claimed me with a touch. He had also asked me again if I could taste Caiden. I never would have thought they kissed again if Xander never would have said anything. But the taste of the spicy smoke on his lips made my stomach twist and turn with unease.

"Hope, are you sure you're okay?" Caiden asked softly.

My gaze slowly slid to Caiden's. I put on a brave face.

He had been through enough and if my gut was right, he was still going through some crap. His cheeks were sunken in, his scars more pink and pronounced. I felt my feet move of their own accord and I didn't know what I was doing until I had my arms wrapped around his waist. "I'll help him. In any way I can."

Caiden kissed my hair and leaned his forehead against mine. "Please be patient with him. He needs you now more than ever."

"What's going on?" My stomach gave a nervous flutter.

"I'll tell you later." He yawned.

"You need some rest," Erica said, squeezing my arm gently.

Caiden nodded and hugged me again. "I promise we will talk later."

"Okay," I said and watched them disappear down the stairs, the basement door quietly shutting behind him. How Erica did it was beyond me. I didn't know her. I hardly knew anything about her at all but there she was, a woman who cared for a man who was in love with another man. Was she jealous? Did it hurt her? She clearly knew about Caiden's feelings for Xander but she acted like everything was fine. Like everything was normal. Life wasn't normal. Life was hard and it took a beating every single day to survive it and move on to the next.

Grabbing a book off the bookshelf, I sighed. It felt like a lifetime since I had picked up a good book and dove into a world that wasn't my own. Giving myself over to words allowed me to fantasize and dream up a life that wasn't reality. I was never into the romance books. I was more a classics girl but sometimes a person needed a good dirty smut-tastic book to bring her out of a funk. But right now, I didn't think anything would help. Licking my dry lips, I shook my head, my control slipping away from me.

It had been at least ten minutes since Xander had left the house. I frowned, wondering where he had gone.

Moving towards the door, I jumped when it banged open. A tall skinny guy stood in front of me, his hair shaggy and falling into his eyes. My heart thumped hard against my rib cage, my stomach twisting.

"Well aren't you a pretty thing?" he purred. His tongue slid along his bottom lip, his eyes raking over my body.

I rolled my eyes. "Where's Xander?"

"He's busy," the guy sneered, taking a step towards me. He wavered on his feet and pulled a small silver flask out of his jacket pocket. Tilting it to his lips, he took a few pulls of the liquid. "He asked me to come keep you company."

"Yeah. Right. Tell him I'll be in his room when he's done doing whatever he's doing." I walked by the larger guy when he grabbed my arm, spinning me towards him.

"Shit. You smell good," he slurred, brushing his nose along the side of my neck.

"Let go of me," I cried, attempting to pry his fingers off of me.

"Don't be rude. I want to talk." He pulled me against him, cupping my ass and squeezed. "Don't you remember me? I sure as hell remember this ass."

Lee. I whimpered at the twinge of pain and pushed him, struggling against his rough hold. "Please. Stop."

"Did you know Xander and I shared Embree? That hot friend of yours fucked her way through all of us. Even Caiden. I always thought he was gay but I guess a woman like her could make any gay man straight for an hour." He fisted my hair and crashed his mouth to mine. "Now I think you should be polite and give me some of what Xander has been getting all along."

"Stop!" I shouted, gearing up my knee. I moved to kick him in the balls but he was soon pulled away from me. Shock tore through me as a large figure came into view.

Xander was calm as he shoved him against the wall, his fist flying into the other guys face. Blood spattered his white shirt, the man submitting to his full wrath.

Caiden ran up the stairs at the commotion, yelling for Xander to stop. "You're going to kill him!"

Xander pushed the guy again before he was on me. I gasped, my eyes widening as Xander threw me over his shoulder. "Xander, put me down!"

He ignored me and carried me to his bedroom all the while I beat my fists against his back. He slammed the door shut, clicking the lock into place and tossed me onto the bed.

"Xander," I said, sitting up.

He wrapped a hand around my throat, tilting my head back. He was eerily calm as his eyes travelled down the length of my body.

"Xander," I whispered, struggling out of his grip. "Please."

He leaned down to my ear, the scent of liquor wafting into my nose. He didn't say anything as his lips brushed along the side of my neck.

Squeezing my eyes shut, I breathed past the unexpected nausea swimming in my stomach. Stale alcohol and smoke forced their way into my lungs.

Xander pulled me further under him and slid his fingers into my hair. Gripping my head, he pulled it back, forcing me to look up at him.

His eyes were cold, the gun metal gray going dark. But he still didn't say anything.

My heart thumped hard. I opened my mouth to speak when he suddenly rose off of me.

He pulled me off the bed, his fingers wound tight in my hair.

I cried out, grabbing his hand gripping my curls and fell to my knees in front of him.

"Did you enjoy kissing him?" he asked roughly.

"What? No!" A sob escaped me as a slight twinge of pain screamed through my head. "Please, Xander. Stop this. You're drunk."

He pulled my head back abruptly, staring intently into my eyes. "You're mine. I will remind you who you belong to," he said, unbuckling his belt.

My gaze caught the movement and I struggled against him. "No. I'm not having sex with you when you're like this."

A wicked grin spread on his face. "Who says anything about sex? That mouth needs to be reminded."

"Stop. Please," I cried, scratching my nails into his hand. "I don't want this. You don't want this."

Suddenly the door crashed open, revealing a red faced Caiden. His nostrils flared, his clothes disheveled but the look of pure hard rage in his dark eyes stole my breath.

"Xander!" he barked. "Let her go."

"Not until I remind her who she belongs to," Xander snapped, his fingers gripping my hair tighter.

"She knows that she's yours. You want to fucking keep her, let her go." Caiden wedged himself between us, forcing Xander to let go of my hair.

"Get out of my way, Caiden," Xander growled, pushing him back.

"Hope. Get out of here. Now," Caiden demanded, shoving Xander up against the wall. He leaned down to his ear, whispering something to him.

I couldn't make out what he was saying but by the way Xander's eyes widened, I knew it wasn't good.

Leaving the bedroom on shaky limbs, I was met by Erica in the hallway. She grabbed my hand, leading me down the stairs to the room where Caiden and I had tied up Xander. Where he had given a part of himself to me that he had never shared with anyone. Not willingly and definitely not because he felt the need to. But that night, that beautiful moment we had shared, it brought us closer together faster than I thought it would. It brought us three together in ways I never would have imagined before all of this.

"Shhh…" Erica said softly, patting my hand. She wrapped her slender arms around my shoulders, holding me against her.

And that was when I broke. I gave Xander everything. Every single piece of me and this was how he treated me. He thought I wanted to kiss that guy. He thought I welcomed it. I cheated once. Would he always accuse me of it from now on? Would it be a thing? Would he never be able to get over what I had done to him years ago?

"He loves you," Erica whispered gently.

And he hated me as well. Love and hate. It was a constant battle. If only I knew which one would win out in the end.

TWENTY THREE

Xander

"YOU WANT TO HURT her. You want her to suffer as much as you have suffered. You want to rip into her, erasing her memories of the previous men she has been with and replace them with thoughts of you. You want her to feel you."

I swallowed hard and nodded at Caiden's words, licking my dry lips. "I do." When I saw Lee kissing her, something deep inside my bitter soul snapped. Before I knew what I was doing, she was lifted over my shoulder and on the bed. I couldn't fight the urge to hurt her. To make her see I was enough for her. To pound into her with a fervor I couldn't break away from. I wanted to destroy her.

"You want her to beg for your mercy. You want to show the little slut what it's like to be in pain. Don't you?"

I nodded again but than my eyes snapped open. "What? No. That's not true."

"Come on, Xander. Tell me. You want her to hurt. Would you have stopped if I wouldn't have come in here and interrupted you two?"

"Yes. Of course I would have." I shook my head, ridding the sound of the hate in his words.

"Would you? She said no several times before I kicked the door open. Xander, you wanted her ripe and swollen, begging for you."

"Stop. Please, stop. That's not true. I wanted to remind her. She's mine." I pleaded with him, trying to make him see that I wasn't a horrible person. That I wouldn't have really hurt her. I only wanted to scare her.

His breath washed over my ear. "I don't believe you. She's a whore, Xander. She hurt you once. She will do it again."

"No! I hurt her. I forced her to drink. I never meant to. I…" A sob escaped me and I couldn't fight them anymore, the cries winning out. "I wanted to forget. I wanted to drown out the noise in my head. I want her. That's it."

"Do you? You keep going back to her and then pushing her away. One of these times, it will be too much and you'll push her away for good." His forearm pushed into my throat. "Do you want her? Or are you comfortable with the idea of her?"

"I want her. God, do I ever want her. I want to marry her. I want to spend the rest of my life with her. I want her to have my children. I...I want her." Caiden released me and I slid down the length of the wall, crashing my head in my hands. "I want her."

"I know."

I looked up at him through my eyelashes.

He smiled softly. "Now that you know that, man up and be there for her. Trust her. Love her. Give yourself to her. No more of this I-can-handle-everything-all-on-my- own shit. She loves you and needs you. Be there for her. Be there for both of us."

A heavy weight had lifted off of me. A weight that had rested on my shoulders since the day I found out my parents had died. If it weren't for Caiden, I would have slowly died right along with them even though I was never in the vehicle. To hear his hurtful words and the names he had called Hope, it woke me up. He never meant them. He said them to jar something in my head. To make me see reason. The guy was good and I loved him even more for it. I only wished I could tell him.

I nodded, taking deep breaths. Caiden had begged me time and time again to ask for help, to give myself over. To submit before I could take control. I didn't know how to start so I said the one word that came to me. The one word that had any bearing. "Help."

***

(Hope)

"How do you do it?" I asked Erica an hour later. After my cries had diminished. After I felt like I could finally form a coherent sentence.

"How do I do what?" Her small frame moved around the dim room, lighting candles on the surfaces of the dark wood.

"How do you be with a man who clearly loves another…man?" I curled my feet under me, picking at a hem on my pants.

"He's good for me. He gives me what I need and I give him the same in return." She looked at me over her shoulder. "It doesn't matter to me who he loves. I know he's coming back to me."

"How can you say that? Caiden loves Xander and he has been with Embree, too, from what I hear. I…I don't get it." I dropped my head in my hands, curling my feet under me. "I could never be with Xander if he loved someone else."

"But he does love someone else, Hope." Erica gently took my hands in hers, kneeling in front of me. "He loves Caiden. He may not love him the way Caiden loves him but Xander feels something for him. That's probably what is screwing with his mind."

I thought a moment. "Do you think Xander is in love with Caiden?"

She smiled softly, shaking her head. "No. I don't."

A breath left me on a whoosh. "As much as I say I would step aside if that were the case, I'm happy to hear you say that." I glanced up at her. "Is that bad of me?"

"Gosh no. Not at all." She patted my hand. "You are in love with him. You have every right to feel that way."

At that moment, the door slowly opened. Caiden peeked his head in, his gaze moving between us. "Can we come in?"

"Of course." Erica rose to her feet and greeted him. He and Xander entered the room.

Xander caught my eye but I looked away. I didn't want to see him but I didn't have the strength to fight him. To tell him to leave me alone. Because in all honesty, I never wanted to be alone.

My phone vibrated.

I love you.

I smiled at the text I received from Embree and sent her a reply, telling her I loved her as well. We may not have been as close as I would have liked but she saved me. In ways I could never thank her. I wanted to help her. In any way I could.

"Did you and Embree make up?" Xander asked, sitting on the floor beside me.

I nodded, turning my phone on silent.

"Hope," he said softly, inching his fingers between mine.

Tears welled in my eyes, a lump burning my throat. "I can't."

His breath hitched. "Please."

"What do you want from me?" I whispered, still refusing to meet his gaze.

"I want you to love me. I want you to forgive me. I...I want you."

"Until the next time a guy hits on me. Or you get me drunk again. Or you get high." My head whipped around. "I can't keep doing this."

"I don't know what more to say." He paused, his jaw clenching. "I'm sorry."

A laugh escaped my lips. "Please."

"Do not fucking laugh at me," he growled, his eyes hardening.

Erica and Caiden quietly left the room, mentioning something about Caiden needing his rest but all I could do was stare at the man sitting beside me. The man destroyed everything in his path. He was worse than a tornado ripping up a town. He tore up my heart and stomped on it whether he realized it or not.

Rising to my feet, I paced back and forth before finally
stopping at a wooden table. "I can't keep doing this back and forth thing with you, Xander."

"What the hell do you want from me?" he yelled, taking a step towards me.

"I want you to stop yelling at me and love me. I want you to tell me how you feel," I cried when he closed the distance between us. I pushed him but he didn't budge.

"How I feel?" he bit out. "I'll tell you how I feel." He spun me in his arms and pushed me face first up against the wall. "You are the air I can't breathe," he said roughly.

"The words I can't say."

"That's not my fault," I whimpered, pushing back against him.

His breathing was hard as he inched his knee between my legs. "From the moment I touched you, I was done. I can't control myself when I'm inside of you." He lifted my dress to my hip, wrapping his arm around my waist.

Letting my head fall back against his shoulder, I ground against him. "I want you to talk to me. I want you to tell me how much you love me. I want you. No alcohol. No drugs. You."

"And I want you to let me fuck you." His fingers dug into the flesh of my rear. "I want to rip you open."

"Why?" I swallowed a moan as his hands continued massaging my ass. The needy hold on my body made me crazed with lust for this man but the little voice in my head told me this would be it. It was the final band in our relationship and if we didn't loosen it, it would snap.

But I wanted to play. I wanted him to be as desperate for me as I was for him so I pushed out of his hold and shoved him back.

A wicked grin spread on his face. "Push me again."

I didn't know what game he was trying to play but I did it anyways.

He grabbed my wrists, slammed me up against the wall and held my arms above my head. With a rough tug, he ripped my panties clean off my body. "I am going to show you what I want. I'm done, Hope. No more games. This is me. The real me and if you can't take it, if you can't handle me, than I suggest you leave."

"Show me. Give me you. Please." I was desperate. Desperate for his love and for him. My heart raced hard against the walls of my rib cage. I couldn't fight him anymore. Even if I wanted to, this was it. This was raw and gritty. And I needed it more than I ever needed anything in my life. More than the alcohol I was addicted to. "Xander, do it," I demanded.

"Shut. Up." He snarled against my neck. Sinking his teeth into my flesh, he bit down hard enough to leave a mark.

I cried out, the sharp pain springing tears to my eyes. "Xander. Please."

He lowered his zipper and roughly pulled out his length. Stroking a hand up and down, he firmly grabbed onto the base. "Tell me."

"Please," I said, arching against him.

Xander spun me and covered my mouth with his hand. "I'm going to make you feel good," he growled and pulled me back against him. "I'm going to take what I want from you and give you what you need."

I jumped when his fingers inched between my legs, pushing deep into my body. Whimpering, my hips moved of their own accord.

"You're so wet for me," he whispered against my ear. "I need help, Hope, but I need you to be patient with me. Please."

I nodded, breathing hard against his hand. Anything. I would do anything for the man using my body for his pleasure. We both had our issues. Our relationship was fucked up. Dangerous, bordering on the point of destruction. But it was ours. And I was damn determined to keep it.

"Let me in, baby," he said roughly.

Spreading my legs, I gave myself completely to him.

Utterly and totally, he owned my body. My mind. My spirit.

Xander rubbed himself over my opening, teasing and hinting. Building the anticipation of what was to come. But I knew. I always knew. I had memorized him, inside and out, but every time I was with him, it was better than the last. It was perfect. Brutal but delicious. Painful and passionate. It was us.

Inching his way into my body, he wrapped his arm around my waist, holding me tight against him. His grunts of satisfaction filled my ears, his hips picking up speed like he could no longer control them.

Every so often, I was lifted into the air, my screams and cries muffled by his hand. He felt good. Oh so deliriously wonderful. I broke in seconds. My release shattered through me, encouraging him to pump harder and faster. The shackle of his buckle slapped against my thighs, the metal biting into my skin. But it only intensified the powerful force of the orgasm.

"Tell me. Tell me you love me," he demanded, loosening his hold on my mouth.

"I love you. God, I love you more than anything," I cried out, pushing my rear back against him. Meeting him thrust for thrust, I slammed back into him hard.

"Fuck, Hope." His hold on my waist tightened as he pushed into me as far as possible, my name leaving his lips on a roar. His release coated me, marking me. His hips slowed to a stop while he reined light pecks on the side of my neck. "I love you. I don't deserve you but I fucking love you. Shit, Hope." He released me completely and righted his pants before pulling me back into his arms.

Inhaling a shaky breath, I wrapped myself around him, allowing him to lower me to the floor. "No more. This is it."

He nodded against the crook of my shoulder. "Take me to your meetings. I need something." He leaned back and cupped my face. "I refuse to give up on us. I'm an asshole but I'm in love with you."

A lonely tear rolled down my cheek and I kissed him. "Promise me you won't give in to the bottle. If I can do it, you can too. Please, Xander. Or else I'm done. I can't be with someone who drinks and gets high all of the time. I'm tired."

Xander leaned his forehead against mine, holding my hands between us. "I had a dream you told me I was worthless. That I wouldn't amount to anything and that you were glad your parents took you away."

"Yeah, well none of that is true," I mumbled. "Promise me."

He hesitated. "I promise," he said finally.

"I know it's hard. I crave a drink every damn day of my life."

"Did I set you back?" he asked, rubbing a hand over the back of his neck.

"No. I set myself back." I met his gaze. Brushing my fingers over his face, I traced his features. I never noticed before but his nose was a little crooked.

"Caiden punched me years ago and broke my nose. That fucker may be smaller than me but he sure packs a hell of a punch."

I smiled and continued in my path of his beautiful features.

"What are you doing?"

"Engraining you into my mind so when we're not together, I always have the image of you to keep me safe. To remind me I am loved. And to remind me we will get through whatever life throws at us."

His breath caught. "I don't know how it's even possible but I think I fell in love with you a little more."

TWENTY FOUR

Caiden

FOR THE FIRST TIME since telling Xander that I was falling in love with him, I knew that this was it. The point of no return. Whatever I thought I had with him was over. We were just friends. And that was it.

As much as it hurt at first, I was fine with it. I got over it and moved on but a part of me felt that I didn't deserve to.

This moment was a test as I walked around Erica kneeling on the floor in front of me. Her eyes were down cast, her chin lowered. Her hands were palms up on her thighs. I knew I had to do something to get her to stay. I had to claim her. Make her mine.

After kissing Xander, she never said a word. Never judged. Never even questioned why I did it. She just let me use her. The kiss, although desperate, had turned me on and I took it out on her body.

Kneeling in front of Erica, I grabbed her hands, kissing each of her knuckles. "Look at me. Please."

She looked up at me through tear-soaked lashes.

I had been expecting this. I could never ask her to shut off her feelings for me. It was an unrealistic demand but I did it anyways. "I'm sorry for everything."

"No, it's fine."

"No." I pinched her chin. "It's not fine. I'm an asshole for thinking that you could go into this with an open mind. I told you that I was in love with another person and that I was dying of cancer. But yet, here you are. You're here...with me." My chest tightened. "Why?"

She chewed her bottom lip but she shook her head.

"Erica," I said gently. "Talk to me."

At that point she threw herself in my arms, wrapping her warm body around mine.

I returned the embrace, holding her tight against me. I was in love with her but I didn't know how to say it. I needed her but I didn't know what more I could do.

Picking her up in my arms, I laid her on the bed and brushed my fingers down her cheek.

"No toys. No controlling. I just want you tonight," she said, softly, placing a soft peck on my mouth. "I have something to tell you first though."

***

(Xander)

"You're drawing again?"

I glanced up at the sound of Hope's voice and smiled, placing my pencil down on the paper before me. It had been something that helped relax me when I was a kid. The stroke of the pen, paint brush, pencil…didn't matter to me as long as I could get an image from it. It had been years since I drew. After our moment in the basement, a weight had been lifted off of my shoulders and I found the urge to create.

"Come with me," I said, grabbing her hand.

She slipped her fingers in mine and allowed me to lead her outside. "Are you going to draw me finally?" She kneeled on the grass, picking a dandelion from the ground.

I smiled and placed a soft peck on her full lips. "Yes."

Her eyes welled and she let out a soft sigh.

A long time ago, she asked me over and over to draw her but I never could. I always used the excuse that I couldn't draw perfection. But I now knew it was because I was scared. If I drew her on paper, maybe she would leave me in real life. It was messed up and didn't make sense but until now, I could never draw her.

"Stay still, baby," I said, lifting my pencil.

"How do you want me to pose?" She folded her hands in her lap, crossing her legs in front of her.

I smiled, looking up from my sketch pad. "Relax and act natural. Be yourself."

Her teeth grazed over her plump bottom lip, her hands fidgeting. Her gaze darted back and forth and every so often, a heavy sigh would leave her lips.

I placed my pencil on the pad and reached for her hand.

Hope slid her fingers between mine, brushing her thumb back and forth over my calloused palm.

It had been two weeks since I had a drink. Two weeks since I promised Hope I wouldn't have another drop. And I felt...if I was being honest, it fucking sucked. But she said I had control over my addiction when really, I didn't. If I did,

I would never have forced her to have a drink in the first place. I wouldn't let my temper rear its ugly head and attack her when another man hit on her. "Lee has tried calling me," I told her.

"He always hit on me but never like that, Xander. It scared me." She traced her finger over a small scar on the back of my hand.

"I know," I mumbled. "I'm sorry for how I reacted. I know that's not enough but...I am sorry." So fucking sorry.

She nodded and lifted our joined hands. "These hands," she grabbed my other one. "They have brought me so much pleasure," she said, a smile spreading on her face. "They have also brought pain." Her gaze met mine. "A little spanking every now and again is hot but don't you dare ever hurt yourself again."

"I haven't. I promise. And I never will again." Self-inflicted abuse over the years was not by choice but by utter defeat. I knew now it was a way of me admitting I was finally giving up. Giving up control. But now? Now that Hope and I were making progress, I didn't need to hurt myself. I didn't need that twinge of pain that allowed me to feel something other than emptiness. I had her.

Her small hands fit perfectly in mine, her teeth chewing her bottom lip as if she were remembering. A happy memory? A dream? Even a fantasy. If it involved me, I would make it come true. All of her dreams. All of her inhibitions. I would give her the sun, moon, and stars.

"I don't know why," she said, releasing me and leaned back on her elbows. "But it makes me nervous that you're drawing me."

I leaned against the leg of the patio table and put pencil

to paper. "You've been wanting me to draw you for years." She shrugged. "I know. It's like…you're stripping me bare. Like once the sketch is done, all of my secrets will be revealed."

"I already know your secrets, Hope. I know what you like. I know what you feel before you tell me. I sometimes even know what you're thinking."

"How?" She raised an eyebrow. "How do you know?"

I rose from the spot on the grass and held my hand out for her.

She hesitated.

"Come with me," I pressed. "Please."

She let out a soft sigh before letting me help her up.

We walked to the patio door and I pulled her in front of me. "What do you see?" I placed my hands on her shoulders, wrapping my fingers around the base of her throat.

"Xander." She frowned. "Tell me what you see."

She huffed. "I see Caiden and Erica sitting on the chair, talking."

"What else?"

She thought a moment. "Happiness," she finally said.

A lump formed in my throat. She was right. Days had passed since Caiden told me the doctors couldn't do anything for him. We hadn't talked about it again but every day that came and left, I thanked God he was still with us.

I watched as Caiden laughed at something Erica had said. His hand cupped the back of her neck possessively while she snuggled against him. He kissed her hand, letting his lips linger. I turned away, not wanting to impose any longer on the private moment they shared.

"When I kissed him, I was expecting him to react differently," I blurted.

"What did he do?" Hope cupped my hands, leaning her head against my chest.

"He...he kissed me back and then pushed me away." As much as I thought I wanted it at the time, I was thankful he didn't allow it to go any further.

"Are you okay?"

Moving back to the couch, I picked up the pad of paper, motioning for her to join me.

"Xander?" She squeezed my arm gently.

"We're talking about me kissing someone else and you're wondering if I'm okay." I couldn't believe her sometimes. After all of the shit I had put her through, she still surprised me every single day. Her love, her patience, her seeing me. Even her touching me, made me wonder if this was in fact a dream.

"Of course." She let out a sigh and curled her feet under her before continuing. "Could you ever see yourself being with Caiden? Even if you and I weren't together.

Could you date him, sleep with him, do everything that a couple does?"

"No," I answered without hesitating. "I kissed him…as a goodbye."

"I know. If he wouldn't have pushed you away, would you have let it gone further?"

I glanced at the patio door. "No. A part of me knew he would push me away. So I wasn't worried."

Hope wrapped her arms around my shoulders.

"He…he told me the cancer is back."

"I know."

My head whipped around. "You know?"

"Well he never came out and told me but I had an idea." She placed a soft peck on my mouth. "Don't always assume the worst."

I looked away, guilt twisting at my gut.

"Draw me." She moved to the other end of the couch, stretching her legs out in front of her.

Putting pencil to paper once again, I finally let the image of her beauty flow through my fingers. Every detail. Every curve. Every inch of her skin, covered the paper.

She would ask me every so often to see the picture but I refused until it was done. "You can't rush art," I told her an hour into the sketch.

She scoffed. "Please. I'm boring and plain. I'm wearing your t-shirt and sweatpants. I think you can rush it a little bit."

I stared at her. "Are you fucking serious right now?"

"What? I'm stating the facts. My hair is too curly. My boobs are too small. My—"

"Stop." I held up my hand. "But—"

"No." I grabbed her feet, pulling her towards me.

"Look at this." I held the sketch out in front of her. Her eyes widened. "This is…it's…"

"You. This," I pointed at the image. "Is you. I drew your curls. The way they fall around your face. Each tight strand grazing your shoulder every time you move. It makes me jealous because I want to touch your shoulder. I want to be a permanent mark on your body. I'm jealous of your fucking hair, Hope." She opened her mouth to respond but I ignored her. This was it. I was laying it all out on the line.

How I felt. What I saw. How I saw her. I tapped the face on the paper. "Your freckles. The smattering of dots that I need to kiss every time I'm near you. But I won't for fear they would disappear."

Her cheeks reddened. "You rhymed."

A slow grin spread on my face. "I even captured the freckle right here," I said, brushing my thumb along the small brown spot between her breasts.

"I don't like it," she frowned, following my gaze. "I do." I pulled her to my side, wrapping my arm around her middle. Linking our fingers, I kissed her knuckles. "I like everything about you. I also know you have a freckle right here." I moved my hand between her legs, brushing a finger between the crease of her thigh and pussy. "And you sigh every time I kiss it."

Hope hugged my arm, leaning her head against the back of the couch. "You drew all of my imperfections." "No." I kissed her hair. "I drew all of your beauty."

Her breath caught. "What's changed?" She grazed a finger down the image staring back at her.

"You had patience. With me. Most women would have given up by now. But not you."

"I think I was born to love you."

My heart gave a start, my arm tightening around her waist. "The only thing I ever regret are the hurtful words I have said to you. If I could take them back, I would."

"I know." Bending her knees, she grabbed my hand and placed it on her thigh. "Tell me what else you know about me."

Her husky voice made my dick twitch. And now that I was an honorable man, I appeased her request. For the moment. I would give her a taste. A hint of what was to come later. It had been hours since I felt her warmth but it felt like a lifetime.

Cupping her jaw, I kissed the soft spot under her ear. "I love the way your body responds me. Your nipples pebble under my touch. Your pussy glistening, dripping with need for me." I licked the shell of her ear. "I bet you're wet right now."

Her full lips parted, her tongue peeking out to moisten her mouth. "Touch me. Please."

Inching a hand under the waist band of her pants, I brushed my fingers over her smooth mound. "I know you keep yourself bare for me."

"Always. Even before I came back."

"Did you think of me when you touched yourself?" I purred in her ear, slipping a finger lower between her legs.

"Y-yes." Her head tilted, her legs spreading wider. She cupped my hand and pushed it against herself, helping me thrust a finger inside of her. "Xander," she moaned.

"I love that you can't get enough of me. That you're so desperate for me, you have to take control." I replaced a finger with two, thrusting them slow and deep inside of her wet body.

She sighed, leaning against me and rocked her hips towards my hand. "I want you. God, I ache for you."

"How bad?" I sped up my hand, forcing her body to tremble and shake beside me.

"Bad. Oh God," she whimpered, moving to the rough thrusts of my fingers. "Xander. Shit." She shook against me, chewing her bottom lip.

"Harder, Hope. Show me how much you want me. How desperate you are to get me inside of you." I nipped her ear. "Fuck my fingers."

"Please. I want to come with you inside me. God, Xander. Please. I'll do anything."

Her rambling words set me off. Pushing her onto her back, I ripped her sweat pants off of one leg and ground my hips against hers.

She arched under me, cupping me over my jeans. "Please. I'm begging you."

I reached between us, ripped open my fly and growled when my dick came in contact with her heat. "Fuck, Hope. You're so hot."

Hooking her legs around my waist, she pulled me towards her. "I need you," she bit out through clenched teeth. "Now."

In one smooth thrust, I filled her.

She sobbed out a cry, digging her heels into my ass.

Brushing my nose along her neck, I inhaled, smelling her arousal and pleasure. This woman. This woman in my arms with me seated deep inside of her body, wanted me. Was desperate for me. Loved me.

"Please. Move," she begged, inching her hands under my t-shirt. Scratching her nails into my back, she tilted her hips, hinting.

"It makes me hard, knowing you would do anything to get my cock inside of your body." I pulled out and slammed back into her.

Hope cried out, her eyes rolling into the back of her head.

"It sets my blood on fire when you beg. My dick becomes so thick, all I can think about is taking you. In whatever way I want."

She panted, nodding at my words. "Yes. Please. Any way. I'll take you in any way."

"Promise?" I gently nipped her jaw, licking the spot soon after.

Her eyes heated, dilating to the point that all I saw were her pupils. "Oh. Yes."

"Fuck, I love you." I crashed my mouth to hers at the same time I sped up my hips. Slamming into her body, I gave her what she needed, what she had so desperately begged for and took what I wanted in return. Her mind. Her body. Her soul. It was all mine. Every single inch of her.

The air she breathed, was mine. The looks she gave, were mine.

Linking our fingers, I kissed her knuckles before covering her mouth once again. I kissed her slow and deep while my body took control.

Her pussy rippled, squeezing my dick in a vice-like grip, small moans of pleasure leaving her lips in the process.

"Come for me, baby," I coaxed, whispering in her ear. "Let me hear how good I make you feel. Coat my dick with your orgasm."

"Oh, God. You're so deep," she panted.

I grinned and pushed into her one last time before she broke. Swallowing her screams, I thrust my hips once, twice, before I followed her release. My come filled her, marking her, giving her what I had always wanted to. Me.

Once we both came down from our high, I kissed her face, remaining connected with her body.

"I can feel you harden inside of me," she said softly, brushing a hand down my cheek.

"You make me hard, baby," I said and sat back on my haunches.

Her gaze glanced between us and she licked her lips.

"If you keep looking at me like that, I'll never leave your pussy," I said, gripping her hips. Pulling out, I lowered my hand between our bodies and brushed a finger over her core.

She shivered, her eyes darkening.

"Taste us," I breathed and inserted the tip into her mouth.

Her eyes fluttered close, her lips wrapping around my finger.

Covering her mouth, I pushed my tongue between her lips, swallowing the sweet taste of our pleasure.

Hope moaned, a soft purr rumbling from the back of her throat.

"We taste good, baby," I whispered, releasing her.

She sighed. Righting her pants while I did the same, she looked up at me. "I love you."

"I love you," I said, grabbing her hand. Pulling her back in my arms, I kissed her neck. "Thank you."

She nodded, snuggling against me.

The air became thick around us in a matter of seconds. I knew we couldn't change the heavy subject by having sex. I had never even intended to fuck her on the patio but hearing her beg, her desperate words for me, I couldn't resist. She was worse than the alcohol and drugs I was addicted to. At least with them, I could stay away. But Hope Charming…I would never leave.

"I would give anything…" I swallowed hard. "To have my parents back."

"I love mine but they drive me insane. It makes me feel guilty when you and Caiden have no one."

"We have each other. I think that's why we became close. After the fire, he changed. It was so long ago but even I remember it. Hearing about it. Seeing it on the news. But I was a kid. I wanted to help him. I wish I could have been there for him. I wish…"

"Xander, there's nothing you could have done. You were a boy. Both of you were…boys."

"But I should have done more," I insisted. "When my parents died, he was there for me. At the funeral.

Everything. God, I'm so selfish. After all these years…" The words poured out of me, leaving me whole but empty at the same time. A relief flooded through me at the words I had wanted to say for years but couldn't. I never had the strength. I was weak. Powerless. Submitting to the thoughts threatening to destroy me every damn day of my life.

"You are not selfish." Hope rose to her feet and thrust the sketch towards me. "Look at how far you've come in only a couple of weeks. Look at what we've done. What you have said. Your feelings. You're talking. Finally. After all of this time, you're finally telling me how you feel. Look at what we did a moment ago. You made love to me in the best way possible."

"But I'm losing Caiden!" I snapped, throwing the sketch pad on the ground. "I have nothing if he leaves me." "You have me!" Hope yelled. She took a couple deep breaths, her chest rising and falling.

Letting my head drop in my hands, I broke. Again.

"Baby, you have me," she said gently, kneeling at my feet. "I love you. I will be there for you when…when…"

"Don't say it." I swallowed past the lump in my throat.

I couldn't deal. Caiden dying would set me back. Him leaving would destroy me.

"Xander," she said softly.

"I can't. I can't deal." My breath hitched, my chest constricting. "I'm not strong enough."

"Yes, you are."

"No—"

"Xander." Hope pulled my hands free from my face and cupped my cheeks. "You are strong. You are one of

258

the strongest people I know. Look at what we've been through. I know we still have shit to deal with but you are strong."

"I don't feel I am," I said as Caiden and Erica stepped outside.

"What's going on?" Caiden sat on the couch beside me, crossing his ankle over his opposite knee.

Hope sighed, holding my hand in hers. "Having a setback."

"I'm fine," I grumbled.

"Are you?" Hope frowned.

Her incessant badgering sent a tingle of need down my spine. Under normal circumstances, like if we were alone for one, I'd shut her up by kissing the hell out of her. Or other ways.

"Xander, stop looking at me like that," she whispered, sitting on the ground between my legs. She inched her hand under my pant leg and wrapped her fingers around my calf.

That touch, although soft and gentle, relaxed me.

"Talk to me," Caiden said. "I need you guys to talk...please just...talk."

Hope's grip on my leg tightened.

I sat still, staring out at the back yard before us. Erica started crying softly.

And Caiden? When we didn't talk, he walked out to the middle of the yard, his head tilting to the sky.

Was he praying? Was he demanding why God would allow him to die and so soon? Was he giving up? Please don't let him give up.

"Go to him," Hope whispered.

I stood up. Taking a deep breath, I held out both of my hands. "Come with me. Both of you." I made a point at looking at Hope and then Erica, my gaze finally locking with hers. "Please."

"Are you sure?" She slid her hand in mine, linking our fingers.

"Definitely." We needed to all be there for him. It wasn't me. As much as I liked to think in the beginning Caiden belonged to me, he wasn't just my friend. He belonged to all of us. "Caiden," I called out gently as we made our way to him.

Caiden was whispering, talking to himself as we all knelt around him. I wasn't able to hear everything but what I did hear, tore at my soul.

"Help him. Please, God, keep him safe."

At that point, I hugged him.

His back stiffened and then relaxed into my touch. "I can't do this. I don't want to leave you."

Fuck. I swallowed hard, clearing my throat several times before I was finally able to form a somewhat coherent sentence. "We are here for you. All of us. We will live every day to its fullest. But I refuse to live every day like it's your last."

"But it could be." He shook against me.

"And we will take them one day at a time." I cupped his nape, pouring the strength I didn't feel into our embrace. He was the strong one. He was the one who always told me things would be okay. That we would move on. Without him, I knew a piece of me would die. He was my rock. My best friend. My brother. Something more. I wasn't sure. I didn't care to ask or know the answer. I would treasure these moments with him. I would hold him until he pushed me away. I would touch him until he had enough. I would be there for him. I was determined to reach deep inside of myself, pulling from within every ounce of courage, every morsel of strength he had shared with me over the years.

We sat there, the four of us huddled together for what could have been minutes. Even hours. I didn't know. I didn't care.

"Caiden," Erica said softly awhile later. She looked at him through tear soaked lashes. "I know we said we wouldn't fall but I did. I fell hard. For you."

"Erica." Caiden cupped her cheek.

"I'm sorry. I tried so hard not to but…I'm falling in love with you. I need you to know that." She leaned into his hand and kissed his palm. "That's what I was trying to tell you earlier before we got distracted."

"I had a coughing fit, Erica. You can say it," he pushed. She shook her head. "I know."

Hope grabbed my hand, squeezing it gently. Telling me to be strong? To not over react? To let Caiden have this moment? I wasn't sure what she thought I would do but I squeezed her hand back in reassurance anyways.

"Erica, I don't…I…" Caiden fumbled over his words.

Shock fluttered through me. He never had issues saying what was on his mind. That was one reason why we got along so well. He never took my shit, always telling me straight up if I was being stupid or not. To hear him be unable to tell Erica exactly how he felt made me wonder if there was more going on besides them being fuck buddies.

"We'll give you two a moment," Hope suggested, making a move to rise to her feet.

"No," Caiden said, his voice firm. "I...I need to say this. To all of you." He took a breath.

My heart raced, my mind conjuring up what he could possibly say. But what I thought and what came out of his mouth were two different things.

"Marry me."

Erica's eyes widened, her mouth falling open.

"What...are...I..." Now it was her turn to stumble.

"I want to marry you. I'm in love with you." He took a breath. "God, it feels so good to say that."

Her eyes filled with unshed tears, the corners of her lips twitching.

"I've been in love with you since you stepped into my play room. The shy timid girl then has now turned into a beautiful strong woman kneeling before me. I don't want to die and have my...everything...all of this...go to the bank and shit." He glanced at Hope and I. "I set it up so I left something to each of you but it's not the same." Caiden placed a soft peck on Erica's lips. "I want to be yours," he whispered.

"I don't want you to marry me because you feel you have to."

I felt like we were intruding on their private conversation. When Hope and I tried to give them time alone, Caiden demanded we stay, telling us he needed us there. To test my strength. To see how far he could take it before I broke. Maybe he wanted to see if I could handle him being with someone else. Not like he was ever with me in the first place. Not on my end at least.

Was that why he was single for the longest time? Was he waiting? No. I wasn't worth the wait.

"I never do anything on a whim. You all should know that." Caiden scrubbed his hands down his scarred face. "When I lost my family, I had problems in school. With people. Xander brought me out of that…" His purple eyes slid to mine.

"I…I don't remember ever helping you. I was a kid." A tingle of unease spread over my skin like a second layer. Knowing I should have done more, I came to the realization it was never enough. No matter what I did.

"You being there helped me." He searched my face no doubt seeing the look of surprise written all over it. "You have no idea what you have done for me, do you?"

"Well…I…" I frowned. "No…I guess not."

"You introduced me to Lee. I know he's an asshole for what he did to Hope but through him, I met Erica."

"He saved me," Erica interjected. "I was in an abusive relationship. Caiden helped me see that I could be happy. I…yes…I'll marry you," she said softly.

Hope's breath caught. "Xander," she whispered in my ear.

I met her gaze and cupped her cheek.

"I told you," she placed her hand over mine and leaned into my palm. "I told you that you have helped him. That you have helped us. You're strong, baby. So strong. I love you. I love Caiden. I—"

Crushing my mouth to hers, I swallowed her breath like I needed it to live. Like I needed her air to survive. "I love you. God, I love you so damn much," I said, my voice low so only she could hear. "I don't deserve you. Any of you."

"We will get through this," Caiden said softly. "We have to."

I don't want to.

"I know."

My back stiffened, not realizing I had spoken out loud.

Caiden leaned his forehead against mine. "I know," he repeated.

"Erica, did you want to come get some drinks and snacks with me?" Hope offered.

Erica nodded, kissed Caiden on the cheek and whispered something in his ear.

He squeezed her hand and watched as they walked back into the house. A house where so many things had happened in a short amount of time. Revelations had been brought forth, some I didn't want to know and some I needed to know whether I liked it or not.

So many secrets between us. Lies. Feelings. As my best friend kept his forehead against mine, I couldn't help but wish he could transfer his strength into me from that small touch. So strong. Everything about Caiden Yeo was pure strength. He had lost more than a person should. But gained so much in return. And now that he was older, cancer would be the true destroyer.

At times, I had felt like God played tricks on us. My parents had taught me that he wouldn't give us any more than we could handle but sometimes I questioned that theory. At times he was like a little kid, looking down on the world. With his huge magnifying glass in hand, we were the ants, burning and screaming from pain.

"Tell me what you're thinking," Caiden demanded softly, picking at a few slivers of grass. He was worse than Hope, wanting to know my thoughts but I came to realize that talking opened up new possibilities. It filled the hole in my chest.

"I'm thinking how God is evil…"

"He's not. This is meant to be. It's not him taking my life from me."

"Then who is it, Caiden?" My heart jumped hard against my rib cage, my blood boiling at the possibility of losing my friend at any moment.

Caiden sighed. "Cancer. That is the ultimate evil."

"I'm also thinking how you are one of the strongest people I know," I said, my voice small. "Life won't be the same without you. That…" I swallowed hard. "A part of me will die with you."

He rose to his feet, pacing back and forth. "I'm not going to lie and say I'm not scared. Of course I am. I am beyond fucking scared. I'm terrified because I know once itgets to that point, I will suffer." He looked down at me.

"But you know what I'll hate most? What I absolutely can't stand about this shit? It's not leaving you because I know you'll be fine."

"Caiden."

"No." He held up his hand, stopping me. "Let me finish. It's not leaving this place because I know someone will live in it who deserves to. It's…it's giving up control. Of my life. Of…everything. I don't know if you know what type of relationship I have with Erica but I control her. She needs it and I need to give it. Having that type of power over another human being is exhilarating."

"But what about after? What happens then?" I tried to understand what Caiden was telling me. What he so desperately needed me to hear him say.

"Erica is strong. I know my relationship with her came as a bit of a shock. Especially after I told you how I felt and all."

I scoffed. No kidding. "It was a shock but I could never expect you to pine after me forever. I'm…"

"What?"

"I'm glad we're talking," I mumbled. "And not yelling and screaming like we have been doing."

"I think we're both tired. Of the fighting. The yelling. The addiction."

There was one addiction I couldn't kick. No matter how hard I tried, Hope Charming would always be a part of me. One that consumed my every waking thought. My dreams. Even my nightmares. She curbed my cravings for the liquid, the pits of the bottle that would eventually kill me. She helped me not want to inject shit into my body but replace it with her light instead. We both had darkness, shadows of ourselves that were shells of our reflections.

"So…marriage, huh?" I needed desperately to change the subject.

Caiden shrugged. Although the movement was small, it ignited a string of coughs to wrack through his body.

"Sorry," he wheezed when the coughing calmed down.

I didn't know if I could deal as I helped him to the patio couch. My eyes burned, my chest tightening. He let me walk him, guide him with each step. I had never

266

noticed but his clothes were looser, his bones practically poking out of the skin in his back. "Caiden." He shook his head. "Don't."

"Do you have any other appointments?"

"No." He coughed again. "The doctors said there is nothing more they can do. They offered to put me in a Hospice but I refused. I'd rather die here."

"Have you got everything in order? With your lawyer and...bank?"

Brushing a hand over his head, he let his arm fall to his lap. A chunk of black hair rested in his palm. "Yeah.

Everything is good to go." He stared straight ahead, his gaze taking on a faraway look. "I did chemo expecting it to do something. That was why you hadn't seen me for a while last summer."

"I wish you would have told me."

"I know. I should have told you but...I'm always in fucking control, I thought I could deal with this on my own." His shoulders slumped, admitting defeat.

"It's wrong to talk about your death like it's a normal thing." But it wasn't at all. I had known Caiden for most of my life. Meeting him when we were only kids, we had been best friends ever since. Then Hope came along and I fell in love. Or I thought I did. Now, it was intense, bordering on dangerous. But then? It was a teenaged boy's wet dream.

Slim. Tanned. Full-chested no matter what she said about her tits being small.

"Well unfortunately, it is a normal thing for us," Caiden said, pulling me from my thoughts.

"I don't want it to be. I want us to be able to fight this." "It's not your battle to fight."

Yeah. And that fucking sucked.

***

(Hope)

Standing at the patio door, I took a sip of my water and waited. For what, I wasn't exactly sure. I felt like I had been waiting my whole damn life. Even before meeting Xander. I was just a girl when I met Caiden, meeting Xander not long after. He was every girl's bad boy dream and I was the lucky one who ended up with him.

I smiled to myself, remembering the jealousy I had received from the other girls.

"How long have you known them?" Erica asked, coming up beside me.

"Years. But it's like I knew them, left, and then came back to get to know them all over again." Ten years. Ten long painful years. I never told Xander this but I wasn't able to keep a job because of my drinking. And then being sober for five years, I felt drawn to the needs of others. I wanted to help them help themselves. There were secrets Xander didn't know about me and I found myself wanting to give him every single dirty detail. I wanted to reveal all of the skeletons in my closet. I wanted to reveal me.

"But you kept in contact with Caiden...why?"

I opened my mouth to answer but nothing came out.

Not knowing why I kept in contact with him, I shrugged. "I was scared of the feelings I had towards Xander. It's no excuse. He was dark, dangerous but now," I took a deep breath. "He's intense. If they had AA meetings for Xander Brant, I would run them."

Erica grabbed hold of my hand, slipping her fingers between mine. "When I first met Caiden...something told me he would need me more than I needed him."

"Did you know about his cancer right away?"

She nodded slightly. "He was honest. It may sound weird and most probably wouldn't understand but I do love him and I will spend every waking breath with him until he passes."

The air was heavy and thick, surrounding us with sorrow and pain. So much darkness had clouded our lives over the past couple of days. Everything had happened so fast. Me coming back. Falling in love with Xander all over again. Caiden having cancer and that was it. Now he would marry Erica and wait out his days with her. I prayed that God allowed him a couple more years on this earth but the twinge of anxiety in my belly told me differently.

Xander and Caiden joined us in the house, the skies darkening as rain started tumbling down. It fit perfectly with our solemn moods.

Caiden got on the phone with a priest, demanding politely and saying he would pay whatever it cost for him to show up at the house to perform the wedding ceremony.

I was happy for Caiden and Erica but I wished it was under different circumstances. To marry someone, knowing you'll eventually lose them and become a widow, I couldn't do it. I couldn't marry Xander if I knew he was going to die at any time. It was selfish of me but I lost him once, I refused to lose him again. But

Xander wasn't the one dying. No. I wouldn't lose him. As much as our relationship had its problems, I would take the yelling and screaming. I glanced at Erica. Caiden was whispering softly to her. The look of warmth and love in her eyes took my breath away. Did I look at Xander like that? Did Xander see it? Did he know I loved him? I told him. God, I told him all of the time. But was it enough? Did he trust me again?

"Are you okay?" Xander stepped up behind me and wrapped his arms around my shoulders.

That question…such a simple question with an answer that usually was based on lies, made me break. I silently cried while Xander's hold on me tightened.

"Let it out, baby," he said, his voice thick.

I cried harder, the pain in my chest growing. It became extreme, to the point I couldn't breathe. I cried for Xander. For Caiden. For all of us. For the trust I felt was no longer there between Xander and me. I had only been back for a couple of weeks. Could that make things better in that short amount of time? Was it enough? God, so many questions I needed to know the answers to. Maybe Xander and I weren't meant to be. Bile rose to my throat, my stomach twisting with anxiety. So much anxiety. I had been anxious for years. Not knowing what the cause of the problem was, I had always assumed it was me.

"We'll get through this," Xander told me softly, his breath whispering against my hair.

The words left his lips and I heard them but I didn't feel them. Something had changed. Something was making me question everything I knew. My parents had called me, Embree called me, even my work called me but I ignored everyone. Focused solely on the man behind me, I put everything that was a part of me into helping him. I lived and breathed him. I woke up next to him and fell asleep in his arms. Every. Single. Day. Was there such a thing as spending too much time together? Oh God. What the hell was I thinking? I shook my head, trying to rid myself of these thoughts but the pros and cons to our toxic relationship kept playing over and over in my head.

"I love you," Xander said, kissing my neck.

"I love you, too. God, I love you with every inch of me. Every fiber of my being."

But we both knew it wasn't enough.

"Alright. The priest is on his way." Caiden let out a sigh of relief and slumped into the chair, pulling Erica onto his lap.

"You're going to do this?" I stepped out of Xander's embrace. "Are you sure it's a good idea?" I wasn't exactly sure why I was all of a sudden questioning Caiden's decision. The doctors didn't give him long to live, a week, a month. They said he would be lucky to live for another year. But what if God allowed him to live longer? What if it wasn't his time? Would he regret marrying Erica?

"Hope," Xander chastised. "Why are you questioning them now?"

"No," Caiden smiled softly. "It's fine. Come sit."

I moved to the couch across from him and folded my hands in my lap. Like a little kid who got in trouble by its parents, I sat still and waited.

"Look at me."

My eyes rose to Caiden's, glancing between Erica and him. "I'm sorry. I want you both happy but I don't want you to regret this."

"We won't," they answered at the same time.

"Listen," Caiden grabbed my hand. "After all of this…" He swallowed hard. "You and Xander need some time. You can't rush into anything. You've only been back for a couple of weeks. You can't expect everything to be perfect and fall into place."

"I love him," I said as Xander sat beside me. "But…" "But what, Hope?" Xander's voice lowered, laced with a hint of accusation.

This wasn't the time. Xander and I could talk later. "Nothing." I waited for the incessant badgering to start, demanding me to talk and lay everything out on the line. When that didn't happen, my heart sunk. As much as I didn't want to fight, Xander and I needed to talk.

Xander grabbed my hand, kissing my knuckles and fingertips.

That gentle touch brought tears to my eyes. It was a gesture that meant so much more than the actual act of it. He was telling me he was sorry. But did he even know what he was apologizing for?

TWENTY

FIVE

Xander

I KNEW SOMETHING HAD been off between us but I wasn't sure exactly what. There was no handbook at how to maintain a relationship. There was no how-to guide on how to keep it strong and whole. I loved Hope with everything in me. She filled the void in my chest since losing my parents so long ago. We reconnected on a physical level but mentally and emotionally? I couldn't feel her. She had closed herself off to me and I was too blind to see it before now. But when she started questioning Caiden's and Erica's decision to marry, I knew right then that if I didn't do something and fast, I would lose her. But I didn't know what to do.

A knock sounded on the front door, jarring me from my thoughts. While everyone remained talking softly amongst themselves, I answered it.

Pulling the door open, I was surprised for a moment to see who had showed up.

"Hey, grumpy," Shana greeted me.

"Hi." I closed the door behind me and joined her on the deck. "I am so sorry for…" My words trailed off when I saw a tear roll down her cheek. "What's wrong?"

She shrugged and sat on the patio swing.

The rain beat down around the house and that was when I noticed the blue van in the driveway. An older woman was sitting in the driver seat. She gave a small wave and I waved back. "Is that your mom?"

Shana sighed. "Yeah."

"This is good isn't it? They were travelling or something?" I joined her on the swing, stretching my legs out in front of me.

"It is. I'm happy they're back but…"

"What?"

"My parents are getting a divorce and I feel so guilty that it's bothering me as much as it is when you don't have your parents at all but…it fucking sucks." She let out a shaky breath.

My heart gave a start. I didn't know Shana for long but I grew to like her feisty attitude. This sad version of her was not normal and I knew it didn't happen often. "Your parents have to do what's best for them. Yeah, it sucks but would you rather them be unhappy? How would you feel if they only stayed together for you? You would feel guiltier than you already do," I pointed out. "Besides, you now have four homes."

"Four?" She looked up at me, wiping under her eyes. "Your grandparents. Your mom. Your dad. And here."

"Here?" Her eyes widened.

"You always have a place here. I expect you to visit me when you're staying with your grandparents."

She nodded. "I would like that."

"So would I." Never having a little sister before, Shana took over that role whether she knew it or not. "I'm sorry for not visiting you. I haven't been for a run in a couple of days."

"That's okay. How's everything here?"

Even though she was fourteen, I enjoyed talking to her.

I told her everything, within reason. Skipping the gritty details, I gave her the G-rated version.

"Wow. Sounds like it's been a rough couple of days."

I bit back a scoff and rubbed a hand over my buzzed head. Rough would be an understatement. But...I felt like it was needed. So many hurtful things had been said. Feelings had been revealed. If only Hope and I could tell each other exactly how we felt. But we didn't know, did we?

"Well I have to go. Summer break is over soon and I have to go home to get ready for school crap."

I nodded, not realizing summer had come and gone so quickly. "It was nice to meet you, Shana. You're like a little sister I've never been blessed with."

"Even though you're grumpy," she laughed. "I'd like to think of you as a big brother."

"Thanks." I chuckled. Pulling her in for a hug, I kissed

her hair. "Seriously. Thank you." "For what?" She sat back.

"I don't even know exactly. Not knowing you for long and talking to you has helped me. I still have some shit to work through but you've...helped me."

"I don't know what I did," she said, her cheeks reddening.

"I'm not exactly sure either."

She giggled and shook her head. "Well if you figure it out, let me know."

"I will."

At that point, a black car drove up the driveway. My heart raced hard against my rib cage knowing it was the priest.

Shana gave me her number, programmed mine into her phone and ran down the steps to her mom's van. She turned back, waved and slid into the vehicle before she got soaked by the rain.

I returned her wave and sat there, waiting. The cool wind whipped around me, brushing over my skin like a blanket.

The priest made his way up the steps and I vaguely remembered him asking me where Mr. Yeo was. I motioned for him to go inside but that was it. I didn't follow him. I didn't do anything. I sat there, staring out in the vast expanse of the front yard. Caiden had this place built, starting it years ago. The inside wasn't perfect yet but it was home. His home. And now mine. Right? Would he kick me out after Erica and he married? Where would I go? Move in with Hope? Could I even live with her? We had practically been living together for the past couple of weeks but we had Caiden with us to lessen the blow. Hope and I were like oil and water. We didn't mix but then on the other hand, she knew everything about me that a person could know about someone. But I didn't know everything about her. She had tried to tell me what she had been doing for the past ten years but I didn't want to hear it. God, I was such a selfish asshole.

My chest tightened, a flutter of unease twisted at my gut when a thought slid into my mind.

She'll cheat again. Once a cheater, always a cheater.

She was pregnant with another man's baby.

"Fuck," I growled, gripping my head.

Stop. Please stop. She loves me. She needs me.

But does she trust you?

I couldn't deal with this now. It was Caiden and Erica's night. They needed to get this over with before he took a turn for the worse. The not knowing was what hurt the most.

"Hope." I loved her. More than I loved myself. But was it enough? Could our love save us? Shit. These thoughts, these questions, they would eat at me until I was able to confront Hope. I knew already my temper would win out and I would lash into her. A tingle brewed, boiling with rage in the pit of my soul. Waiting. Always waiting.

The door opened, interrupting my questioning thoughts. "Zee," Caiden peeked his head out. "We're ready."

I nodded and followed him back into the house.

"Are you good?" He clapped a hand on my shoulder, giving it a light squeeze.

"I'm fine," I lied. "Xander."

His firm voice stopped me in my tracks and I turned back to him.

"Whatever happens, know it's for the best. With time comes great reward." He kissed my forehead. "Have patience."

I searched his face, allowing myself the reprieve of actually looking at him this time. His olive skin tone had paled in comparison to what it once was. His strong cheekbones were hollow due to him losing weight. His pink scars were more pronounced but his eyes remained the dark blue they had always been. You'd think after what he had been through, they would take on a sadness but not Caiden. He was a firm believer of everything happening for a reason when I was the type that wanted to give up.

"I don't have any patience," I heard myself say. "What if Hope and I aren't meant to be together?"

"Then it was never meant to be in the first place. But look at how far you both have come. Even if it doesn't work out, you have helped each other. But please, don't let it set you back."

I nodded, looking away. Hope had told me I was strong, that I had control over my addiction, when really, I had no control at all. Of anything. Not of my life. Certainly not of myself. A part of me gave into the craving because it silenced the demons. Another part gave in because it helped me forget.

"Let's do this," I said and stepped out of his embrace.

We walked into the living room and were greeted by Erica and Hope.

"Are you okay?" Hope brushed a hand down my chest, grazing her fingers lightly over my hard abs.

I pinched her chin and placed a soft peck on her mouth. "No."

She nodded and grabbed my hand.

Knowing we would talk later, I felt a sense of relief wash over me. Whatever happened would be because it was meant to be. God, I was starting to sound like Caiden.

"I love you. I hope you know that," she said softly.

"I do." Was it enough?

"I know this is an untimely circumstance and that this is unconventional but I am honored to be a part of this," the priest told us, standing by the fireplace. "I understand you don't have any rings, right?"

Caiden shook his head. "No. This wasn't exactly planned." He grimaced. Always being the type to organize and plan far in advance, I knew this was throwing him off. He shifted on his feet but when Erica stepped up to him and held both of his hands, he relaxed.

For the first time ever since he introduced us to Erica, I saw the love he had for her.

"That's completely fine." The priest pulled a folder out of his briefcase. "I think I already know the answer to this but did you apply for a marriage license?"

"We did. I know someone who works in that field so they pulled some strings and had it faxed over to me immediately."

"Perfect." The priest clapped his hands together. "Let's get you both married then."

***

(Hope)

Never would I have imagined that I'd be standing at Caiden's wedding. He told me he thought he wouldn't be here before he could get married, proving himself wrong. As he and Erica exchanged vows, Xander held tight onto my hand. I didn't know what he was thinking. I didn't know if he was hurt by all of this. Everything was moving so fast out of desperation. Caiden didn't have to say anything. I knew he was marrying Erica because he didn't want to die alone. It was heartbreaking. Life was cruel. It took from us everything that made us strong, expecting us to be fine and completely whole in the end.

My mom had called again while the priest was getting everything set up but I allowed it to go to voicemail. I wasn't in the mood for her judgment. I knew I would have to face them eventually but I prayed Xander would be with me. He was my strength and I didn't know if I could do it without him.

"I now pronounce you husband and wife."

Tears welled in my eyes at the priests words. Knowing I missed their vows, I gave Erica a hug and then Caiden. I wrapped my arms around his waist.

He kissed my hair. "Don't cry," he said, his voice thick.

I shook my head, unable to help it. Tears flowed down my cheeks of their own accord. I couldn't control them. It felt like a hot knife had ripped into my heart, twisting and turning before being pulled free from my aching body. Sobs wracked through me, shaking my shoulders to the point my muscles hurt. I ached everywhere.

"Hope, please." He cupped my cheeks, kissing my forehead. "Don't cry for me."

"I...I can't..." I said between sobs. Crying so hard I couldn't form a proper sentence, I broke. Sorrow crashed into me, washing over my body like a billowy cloud of darkness.

Heavy arms wrapped around me, holding against a hard body. "I'm here, Hope. Let it out. Don't let the sadness consume you," Xander whispered in my ear soothingly.

When had he become so strong? "Xander, I can't...I can't do this."

He lifted me, cradling me against his chest like a newborn babe. He said something softly to Caiden and Erica and carried me to his room.

"Xander, put me down. I'm fine," I insisted, struggling against him until he placed me on my feet.

"Are you? Are you fine?" He pinched my chin.

"What do you want from me? We're losing our best friend. I'm sorry I'm not happy and chipper about his wedding day. I can't help it."

He sighed and grabbed my hand, pulling me into the bathroom. Much to my dismay, he started undressing me.

"What are you doing? This is not the right time to have sex," I said, slapping his hands away.

Xander held my wrists, backing me against the door.

"As much as I love fucking the shit out of your beautiful body, right now, you need to relax. We both do. We have to be strong. For Caiden and Erica. She's going to lose her husband. We don't know when. It could be tonight.

Tomorrow. Next fucking year. But I can't do this alone. I need you to be strong with me, Hope. I can't do this...I can't...I need you."

All I could do was nod as the words poured from his mouth. Words I had wanted to hear in so long. How he felt. I wasn't that type of girl that demanded to know exactly what my man was thinking but our problem was that my man didn't talk at all about his feelings. He kept them bottled up inside until he exploded and I was always the brunt of that said explosion.

I pulled from his grasp and stripped until I was completely bare. Turning on the shower until it was too hot, I stepped under the scorching spray. Soaking my body from head to toe, I waited.

Xander stepped up behind me, running his hands over my body. Massaging, kneading, giving me what I needed. What we both needed.

"Talk to me," he said, brushing a soapy cloth over my skin.

I swallowed a couple of times, trying to find the words, trying to figure out exactly what I wanted to say. "I've had problems keeping a job," I blurted. Maybe that wasn't the thing to start off with but I felt the need to have Xander know every single dirty detail about the ten years I was away.

"Same here. I was able to save some money but I have it set up that I can't touch it until I'm thirty."

"Well that's good at least. My...my parents...or my dad I should say, set up a college fund for me when I was a baby but I haven't touched it. I never went back to school. I never amounted to anything but the thing I don't regret is coming back. To you." I turned in his arms. In all of his glorious nakedness, I couldn't help but let my eyes roam down his hard ripped body. Thick in all of the right places, my heart gave a start.

A slight smirk spread on his face. He placed a soft peck on my mouth. "I felt lost when you left. I'm a dick and wouldn't admit it to myself or to anyone but it's like a part of me left with you. And I didn't know how to deal with that. But I never should have tried to push you away.

I...wish I would have let you in. But I wish more that I would have fought for you in the beginning." "You were a boy."

"I knew right from wrong. I was a teenager. I knew I was in love with you but I was so mad, I wanted you to suffer."

"You've been holding that anger in for the past ten years, baby." I leaned my forehead against his chest, wrapping my arms around his hard waist.

"That's no excuse. I love you. That should have been reason enough to fight for you but yet I pushed you into another man's arms. And you were pregnant."

I grimaced, my throat becoming thick. "You don't trust me." I didn't like the taste of those words but we both knew they were true. He loved me. I knew he did but without trust, there was nothing. We were nothing.

He didn't say anything. He didn't have to.

Turning back around, I stepped under the water, wishing it could wash away our pain. Tears clouded my vision. Letting them fall freely, a sob escaped my lips when Xander wrapped himself around me.

I was gone for ten years and came back. I had no problems leaving the first time. As much as it hurt, it was needed. But this time would destroy me. This time it would take something from me I had so desperately been trying to get back. It would take away the part of me that belonged to Xander. My heart. But he really owned everything didn't he?

We finished washing each other, not saying anything.

No words. No sounds. Xander spoke to me through his body. He took me to bed, drying me off and kissed me. It was slow, tender.

A goodbye.

We made love out of a fit of need, trying to find that connection that had worked so well for us. It was there, bordering on the brink of destruction. My heart hurt. My everything ached.

"I love you, Hope Charming," he said softly, his words whispering over my skin as he brought us both to that place. That ultimate high that left me breathless and always wanting more. He swallowed my cries, our tears mixing as one.

This was it. The end.

Of us.

TWENTY
SIX

Xander

I WOKE THE NEXT morning. Alone. The scent of Hope wafted into my nostrils as her smell etched its way into my memory. The sheets and pillow gave off a scent of peaches and cream, the lingering sweet taste of her arousal still on my tongue. But I was alone.

Knowing it would happen, I shouldn't be too surprised but a part of me was. A part of me figured she would stay. Was it giving up? Did we love each other too much that we couldn't be together? So many questions ran through my mind but I didn't know how to find the answers. I didn't know how to get any of the information I needed. How did people survive with this hole in their chest? This undying pain that stayed there until it was too late. Until it consumed you completely, letting you know you were never really in control.

Rising from the bed, I bit back a groan. My muscles tightened, aching for a good stretch. I had spent the night wrapped in Hope, hoping somehow, someway, she would be there when I woke up. But I knew…for some unknown reason I knew this wouldn't last.

A soft knock sounded on the door.

After pulling on my black sweatpants, I answered the door, greeted by a smiling Caiden. He held two cups of coffee, handing me one before stepping to the side.

I took the steaming cup and followed him out into the hall. A moment of disappointment fluttered through me when I saw Erica seated at the kitchen table. Alone.

Caiden didn't say anything as he kissed his wife, standing at her side.

The silence was annoying, louder than the questions I knew they had but I didn't have any answers. Hope and my relationship was toxic. It would eventually destroy us. I knew it. She knew it. So it never mattered what anyone else thought. "How was your first night as a married couple?" I leaned against the counter, taking a sip of the much needed caffeine.

They glanced knowingly at each other before they both came up to me.

Raising an eyebrow, I asked what they were doing when they pulled me in for a group hug. They told me they were there for me, they would do anything to help and that they would be there.

I surprised myself when I didn't cry. I surprised myself when I didn't push them away. I returned their embrace but other than that, I didn't do anything else. I never responded to their words of sympathy. I never said Hope should have stayed, she should never have left me. But all of that wouldn't have been true. I tried telling her to leave me in the beginning but she didn't listen. She stayed and she helped me through my addiction. But would she come back and help me when Caiden passed? I didn't want to think about the inevitable. I only wished we knew so we could prepare.

"I assume you both talked to Hope?" I inquired even though I already knew the answer.

Erica pulled from the group hug. "Want some breakfast?"

My stomach rumbled at the thought. Knowing I needed the sustenance, I nodded. Not in the mood to eat or even chat, I wished I could have been alone. To wallow in my own misery. Dive inside of myself and disappear.

"Hope came to us earlier this morning," Caiden said, leaning against the counter beside me.

"What did she tell you?"

"You both accepted that your relationship is done." His eyes bored into mine and when I didn't respond, he continued. "She loves you and I know she'll wait."

I pushed off the counter and grabbed another cup of coffee. It wasn't the drug I craved but it would have to do. It would have to take the place of that high. The substance abuse I had inflicted on myself for years was nothing compared to the withdrawal I would have from not being with Hope. "I don't expect her to."

"I know but you two have been through so much. You can't expect things to end like that."

"Why not?" He was right but I felt the need to argue anyways. I would never want Hope to wait. As much as it would destroy me, I would let her go.

"The love you two have goes beyond anything I've ever seen."

Our love. It hurt. It broke what we had. Love…love sucked.

"It wasn't enough." Without trust, there was nothing and although deep down I knew Hope would never cheat on me again, a part of me didn't believe her. It was my fault. I pushed her to the other guy. That little voice inside of me told me to let her go and pray she would eventually come back to me. I just didn't know how long I should wait.

***

(Caiden)

A part of me felt like I was giving up. Like I had been battling a war for so many years that I became tired and useless, not wanting to fight anymore. I knew my time had come. I knew this was it. But I was terrified. Not of leaving Erica. But of leaving Xander. I tried so hard to make him see that he was worth it. That he was worth everything.

Everything happened for a reason. I was a firm believer of that.

Erica was strong. The strongest woman I had ever met. I loved her. My wife.

I surprised myself by asking her to marry me. Knowing I was still in love with Xander but couldn't do anything about it, she said yes anyways. Why would I put her through that? How dare I marry her and then leave. I was a horrible person. Broken in so many ways beyond my control. Those thoughts battled each other in my mind.

Forcing them to their knees. Demanding me that I crack.

I had been thinking about my life over the course of the past couple of hours. My parents. My little brother. I tried so hard to forget them because it hurt too much but the harder I tried to push those thoughts away, the more they consumed me.

If only I had someone to tell me that it wasn't my fault.

If only I had that one person to tell me that everything would be okay. I hadn't known Xander and Hope at the time of the fire. I was all alone. In the hospital. No family. It had always just been my parents, my brother and I. No more. No less. Just the four of us.

It was so hard to move on. To let go. Knowing I was leaving so much behind. But he was ready. Xander would be fine without me. Call me selfish, but I wanted to stay for myself.

So he could help me.

I just wanted to hear it once. That it wasn't my fault.

No wonder I was fucked up and in love with my best friend. He was broken. I was shattered.

My family leaving me at the mistake of my own hands about destroyed me but I pulled through. Me being thrown into foster care was another story. I left as soon as I turned sixteen. The cold ruthless eyes of those men, who were supposed to be caring and father figures wanted one thing and that was it.

I got out. And I thanked God every damn day I got away in time.

It had been a week since Hope left. Since her and Xander had broken up. I watched him suffer. I watched him disappear right before my very eyes. The strong man I knew turned into that of a boy being kicked while he was down. But he didn't give in to the addictions he had. I was proud of him. So fucking proud of my best friend.

A soft knock sounded on the door. "Caiden?" Hope peeked her head into the room, holding the door slightly ajar.

I sat on the edge of the bed, taking a couple deep breaths before rising to my full height. "Help me walk down to the basement?"

She nodded, coming up beside me. She never met my gaze but slipped her arm around my waist. "Where's Erica?" she asked, her voice thick.

"I told her to give us a few," I said, trying my hardest not to lean completely on Hope. Giving up this small ounce of control was enough to wear me out. By the time we got to the basement and I was back in bed, my muscles hurt. My chest ached. And my throat burned. But not because of the disease. It took everything in me not to cry.

"Does he know?" Hope knelt at my side, holding my hand tight in hers.

"Not yet. I needed to see you first."

"Why?" She looked up at me through tear soaked lashes.

"I know things are over between you two for the moment." She opened her mouth to argue but I continued. "But I know that everything will work itself out."

"How…" her voice cracked. "How can you possibly know that?"

"Because I have faith." And as pissed off as I was at God for taking me away so soon, I understood. I tried to blame him completely but I knew that it wasn't his fault.

The devil had a hand in this madness. Maybe I was losing it. Maybe I was finally gone. My body lying on this bed, empty and lifeless, while my brain went crazy.

"I love you," Hope whispered.

"And I love you." I let out a contented sigh. "Take care of our boy."

They say you see a white light when you're about to die. They also say that your soul goes to heaven. I didn't know what I believed. But I did believe that without faith, I would have died long ago. But I felt that I was meant to help Xander and Hope when really, they were the ones that had helped me.

I was ready. I was done. This was my time. And I embraced it with open arms.

***

(Xander)

I woke up in a cold sweat. A lingering nightmare pulled at my being, cold fingers of fear gripping my spine.

Hope.

It had been a week since she left. Seven days since I touched her. One hundred and sixty-eight hours since I felt her. Her warmth. The sweet taste of her breath on my tongue. The hint of desire. The dark look of lust in her eyes as I made love to her body. I would always remember the husky tones of her purrs of pleasure. Her moans as I forced the ecstasy from her.

Every time I went to call her or text her, I froze.

Caiden and Erica would eventually catch me and pull me from my inner battle of should I or shouldn't I. Depression had begun to set in, eating at my soul, destroying my personality. I didn't want to live without her. I didn't want to go from day to day wondering if I would ever see her again. I didn't want to move on. I didn't want anything.

Rising from the bed, I slid my legs over the edge, letting my head drop in my hands. "Hope," I croaked out. The hole in my chest grew, expanding until it would no doubt consume me.

In a zombie-like state, I pulled open the drawer in the end table and breathed a sigh of relief when my gaze landed on a rolled up joint. It was all I needed. Sticking one end in my mouth and lighting the other, I watched the glow of the ember as I sucked in a breath. Holding the air deep in my lungs, I waited a moment before exhaling. My skin buzzed, the hairs on my body vibrating.

Fuck me, that shit is good.

The drug took over my body, claiming the control it always had. This was where I deserved to be. Hope didn't want me. I was losing my best friend. I couldn't even keep a damn job. I was stuck. Drugs and alcohol. They would kill me in the end but at least they wouldn't leave me.

A soft knock sounded on the door interrupting my thoughts.

On shaky legs, I staggered to the door and opened it, revealing a disheveled Erica. "What's wrong?"

She chewed her bottom lip, her eyes welling over.

Swallowing a couple of times, she took a deep breath. "It's time."

My heart fell to my feet. The next couple of minutes were all a blur. It was like I was having an outer body experience, watching myself push past erica, run down the stairs to the basement and barge into Caiden's room.

He was lying in his bed, pale and thin. Ghostly. Every so often he would grimace as if he were in pain. And that was when it all hit me. Caiden was dying. I was losing my best friend. Who knew how long it would be now? A couple of minutes? Hours?

"Xander," he wheezed out, pulling himself higher up onto his pillow.

I rushed to his side and fell to my knees, grabbing his hand in mine. His skin felt clammy. I knew he hadn't been feeling well but I didn't think things were taking a turn for the worse already.

"Xander," he whispered, running his other hand over my head. "Look at me. Please."

Shaking my head, I refused to. It meant it was real if I looked at him.

"I'm sorry. I am so sorry."

"Why?" I sobbed. "Why the fuck are you sorry? For leaving me? Is that why?" I yelled, pushing away from him. "Yes," he said calmly. "That is why. That's always been why. But I know you're ready. You're ready to be by yourself. No more noise, Xander. You fought that battle from within. You're strong."

"I don't want to be strong. I don't want anything. I want Hope and I want my best friend." God, I sounded like a whiny child but the demands I had were the truth. Even though they were unreasonable, they were what I always wanted. The only things I needed.

"I will always be with you and Hope will come back to you. You have to be patient."

"I…" My throat became scratchy. The room started spinning around me and before I fell over, I sat on the edge of Caiden's bed.

"I don't want to leave you but I know you're ready," Caiden repeated softly, grabbing my hand and pulled me down beside him.

"I love you," he whispered.

Squeezing my eyes shut, I let the tears fall. I tried breathing past the pain, the emptiness in my chest but the harder I tried, the bigger the hole grew. The ache spread through me, tightening and twisting my bones. It hurt. It hurt so damn much.

Caiden's breathing became shallow. "I'm ready."

And that was the last thing he said before he died in my arms.

***

"Hi, Xander."

My heart jumped as Hope's voice washed over me through the phone. Allowing myself to let it soak in for a moment before I dampened the mood even more, I waited a beat.

But she knew. Didn't she? Her tone was casual, like she had been expecting my call. I guess in a way it made sense. We all knew it was coming. We knew the end was near but we had prayed it wouldn't happen so soon. But as Caiden said, it happened when the timing was right.

Whatever that meant.

I cleared my throat, swallowing a couple of times before giving her the news that was the reason for my phone call. It was the only reason I would call her.

"Xander," she whispered, her voice shaky. "He's gone."

TWENTY

SEVEN

Hope

"THE LORD TOOK ANOTHER soul, laying to rest a beautiful human being. Caiden Yeo had fought the evil monster that is cancer, for years, the disease finally winning in the end. It's heart-breaking and bone crushing…"

I couldn't hear any more of the priest's words as I knelt in front of Caiden's casket. Eyes were on me but the only pair I cared about belonged to Xander. He hadn't talked to me all morning. He nodded once and that was it. No hug.

No remorse or sympathy. Caiden may have been his best friend but he was mine too. God, I felt like I lost a piece of me. Leaving Xander the second time around was one of the hardest things I ever had to endure but burying a man that had stood by me throughout the years brought me to my knees. I surrendered to the domination of the sadness tearing through me. Sobs escaped my lips, my shoulders wracking with hard and powerful cries.

Warm arms wrapped around me, pulling me into a tight embrace. The spicy scent of cologne and man wafted into my nostrils. It was familiar.

Xander.

He was holding me like I wanted. Comforting me like I needed. But it stopped there. He told the priest to go on while he spoke to me quietly.

"Be strong, Hope. Please be strong. For me, but especially for you."

"I can't, Xander. I can't," I cried. "I miss him." And it had only been a couple of days. How would we get through a lifetime without him? Without his Yoda personality.

Without him. Bile rose to my throat and I swallowed past it, the acidity burning my tongue. "Take care of Erica," I said, jumping to my feet. I quickly headed back to my car when the nausea set in. My stomach bubbled. By the time I reached my vehicle, I was hunched over, spewing my breakfast onto the concrete. The bottle I had dove into earlier that morning, laughed at me as I continued spilling my guts at my feet. I broke. I caved into the addiction.

Jumping into the sea of self-inflicted abuse head first.

A white cloth surfaced in front of my vision.

I slowly rose to my full height, being met by a pair of beautiful grey eyes I had fallen in love with so many years before. "Thank you," I said, taking the cloth from Xander and wiped my mouth.

"You're welcome," he said, searching my face. His gaze darted to the car, his brows furrowing a second later before he met my gaze once again. "And thank you."

"For what?" I frowned.

"For helping me realize I'm not the only one who breaks."

TWENTY EIGHT

Xander

Sometime later…

I STARED AT THE paintings adorning the walls around me. Never in my whole entire life would I think I would make it this far. Always being accused of living off of Caiden and being a bum, I would never amount to anything. It got to the point I questioned whether those were right.

Voices sounded around me, flashes of cameras went off, taking picture after picture of the display. But all I could focus on was…her.

Hope Charming.

She was everywhere. In my heart. My mind. The blood flowing through my veins. She was in every painting I drew. Even the paintings of scenes. There would still be something in it reminding me of her. A time when I was with her. Sunlight. Darkness. Cracked walls. I drew and painted them all. Whatever mood I was in, whatever my soul called for, I would let my hands flow on the canvas.

A throat cleared behind me.

Turning around, I blinked, once, twice, before I finally focused on the beauty before me. "Hope."

Her perfect teeth grazed over her bottom lip. "It's been awhile."

"Yes," I nodded. "How long?"

"A year…" Her eyes sparkled in the bright lighting of the room.

"You…you look good." That familiar sense of pleasure raced down my spine.

Her blonde curly hair was cut short, the strands grazing her shoulders. She had filled out some like she had been working out but it left an ache deep in the pit of my gut.

God, she was beautiful. Still and always would be.

"You look good too." Her cheeks reddened. "I see you've done well for yourself."

"I guess." I glanced up at the painting beside me and sighed. "So," I turned back to her, putting on a fake smile. "How have you been?"

"Alright. I'm back in school and I work part-time, running AA meetings. I want to be a drug and alcohol abuse counselor." She stepped up beside me. "I…" She looked around her, her gaze darting over the paintings. "Xander."

The scent of peaches and cream filled my nostrils. My fingers itched to push the strand of hair off her shoulder and replace it with my lips. She was the only woman that could get this reaction from me. The only person in my existence that could bring me to my knees by a look.

"You're my muse, Hope," I told her. Reaching out to grab her hand, I hesitated and pulled back, crossing my arms under my chest.

"I...wow...these paintings are beautiful."

"Thank you but they're only beautiful because my model is," I said, sitting on the bench.

"Xander, we have some reporters who want to interview...Oh," Melanie Gomez, my personal assistant stopped in her tracks when she came into the room and saw Hope with me. "Hi." Mel held out her hand. "I'm Melanie, Xander's PA."

"It's nice to meet you." Hope returned her handshake. "I'm Hope."

"Oh I know." Mel's gaze darted between us, a huge grin spreading on her face.

I rolled my eyes.

"You know?" Hope frowned, a question of confusion written all over her face.

"All Xander does is talk about you."

"Alright, Mel. Why don't you go tell the reporters I will answer their questions in a bit?" I ushered her out of the room.

"Are you going to ask her out? It's been a year, Xander. Please tell me you're going to ask her out," Mel said, pushing her black rimmed glasses up the bridge of her nose.

"I don't know. It's been a year." Those were the key words.

"Well, good luck." She patted my arm. "Alright folks. Let's move to the other room," she yelled out to the large crowd forming in the gallery. She turned back to me, winked and closed the doors, leaving me alone with Hope.

"I'm glad your painting took off," Hope said as she moved around the room, checking out each picture. She would graze her hand through her hair every so often, a nervous flutter I had grown accustomed to. She was beautiful in the way she moved. Almost like she was gliding.

"I never expected it to. I paint and draw because it's freeing. It's therapy," I told her, leaning against the set of double doors.

She nodded. "How are things?"

"Erica keeps in touch but she hasn't been back to the house since Caiden died. It's too hard for her. I feel the same way but every time I go to move, guilt threatens to consume me since he left the house in my name." He built it for me. Not that I was forced to stay but I knew he wouldn't want me to move. I had to get over my own fear. Living in that big house by myself was exhausting.

"Erica and I meet for coffee at least once a month. She keeps me informed about you." Hope's gaze met mine. "That's how I knew about the showing tonight."

"How long did it take you to decide to come?"

She laughed. "She told me about the showing two months ago and I decided tonight I was going to come. Even when I stepped foot into this gallery, I was going to turn around and head back home."

"I figured." I knew how she felt. "How are your parents?" The conversation carried on for a good hour.

Each of us passing back and forth information about our lives for the past year. Her mom had died two months after Caiden did and her father was now living in a retirement home. The depression had set in and he couldn't fend for himself anymore but Hope had told me the place he was in was beautiful and well kept. My heart became heavy at her words. Too much death all at once. It was unfair but unfortunately we couldn't control it. We had to make do and move on, hopefully becoming stronger in the end.

"How have you been?" Her eyes twinkled in the dim lighting of the room. "Besides becoming a successful artist."

I shrugged, sitting on the bench against the far wall.

"Good." But lonely. I didn't date after her and I broke up. I didn't see the point.

"I haven't dated since leaving you," she said softly, joining me and folded her hands in her lap.

"Same here." I shouldn't get as much enjoyment out of those words as I did but knowing she's single made all of the pain go away. It helped the loneliness in my heart. The hole in my chest. It filled the void in my life since she walked away.

"Why haven't we, Xander?"

"Maybe it's not meant to be. Maybe we needed time apart before we found each other again." I didn't know. I prayed something good would come out of this. I was tired.

"Something told me to come tonight. As much as it scared me. I was worried you would shut me out."

I grabbed her hand, sliding my fingers between hers. "Never. It's been a year, Hope. I've had lots of time to think. I'm a painter so I'm alone often."

Hope leaned her head against my shoulder and sighed. "What are we going to do? Can we be together?"

"Do you want to be?" I brushed my thumb along the back of her hand, hoping, praying that we could make this work.

"Yes. I've missed you. I've missed you so damn much." Her breath hitched. "Why didn't you say anything the day of Caiden's funeral?"

"What do you mean?" I frowned.

"You saw the flask on the passenger seat of my car. That's why I was throwing up. I was expecting you to yell and scream at me, telling me you told me so or something. Why didn't you?"

"For helping me realize I'm not the only one who breaks." I remembered saying those words like it was only yesterday. I wanted to yell at her. When I saw the metal flask staring up at me, I wanted to demand for her to tell me why she judged me for so long. Why she finally succumbed to the addiction I knew we both craved. "Because Caiden wouldn't have wanted that." I shrugged. "I know what it's like to lose control. Hell, I made you lose control one and only time."

"Many times."

"Excuse me?"

Her cheeks reddened. "Many times. I wasn't lying when I said I couldn't control myself around you." She chewed her bottom lip. "But thank you. Thank you for not lashing out. Thank you for…for being you."

"Will you go on a date with me?" I blurted. She sat back, her brows narrowing.

Pinching her chin, I tilted her head. "I want to take things slow. I've missed you. I've thought about you. I've dreamt about you. I live and breathe you. Every day I wake up, praying I'll get to see you again. When I go to bed, I'm happiest because I know you'll come to me in my dreams. I know we had our issues. I know our relationship was toxic but I want to try. Again."

"Yes. Please. I would love to go on a date." Tears welled in her eyes. "And more."

Leaning down, my thumb brushed over her bottom lip before I replaced it with my mouth.

She sighed, relaxing into my touch.

A spark ignited between us, burning into a raging fire I hadn't felt in so long. Even when I was with her, the kisses were always needy, frantic. Our touches were desperate, like we had to engrain ourselves in each other's bodies for fear of losing the other.

Breaking the kiss, I placed a soft peck on her mouth before sitting back.

Hope wrapped her hands around my arm, leaning against me and let out a contented sigh.

We sat there for what could have been minutes, maybe even hours. No talking. No words. We listened to the smooth sounds of our breathing and that was it.

I looked up, my eyes landing on the painting across the room from us. My heart jumped against my rib cage. The image staring back at me were of three hands. Two hands holding with a third hand covering them. When I painted the picture, it was meant to portray a bond between three friends. But now I realized it was Hope's and my hand with Caiden's covering our joined ones. His was cast in a silhouette glow, wrapping around us, protecting us.

The day Caiden died, I refused to wallow.

I cried.

Yelled.

Screamed, going through the several steps of grief before I changed my life around. For him. For me. For us. Knowing he would always be everywhere. I pulled the strength he had taught me and moved on with my life, relishing in the fact he would forever be in my heart. That I now had Hope. We would take our relationship one day at a time. Building and molding it into what we wanted. What we needed. We would start at the bottom and work our way to the top.

Hope Charming was the angel in my heaven. The light in my darkness. She was the piece of me that had been missing my whole life.

We were bound together by the ropes of our love, finding that connection.

From. Within.

EPILOGUE

XANDER,

If you are reading this, then I am gone. But know it means nothing. I'm still here. Inside of you. Around you.

I'm the air you breathe into your lungs. I'm the sustenance feeding your soul.

I am.

Leaving you is one of the hardest things I have ever had to do. I know, it's not like I had much of a choice. We never have a choice do we? If we did, I would still be alive. But would I be with you? No. You want to know why?

Because of her. Hope Charming. My best friend. Your lover. God, I pray both of you have made it through your problems. You are strong-willed and stubborn. Put two people together with those qualities and you get an explosion.

You never had to tell me but I knew before I died you weren't sure it would last with Hope. I get that. But I hope, no I pray, even if you're not together, then you're at least civil. Friends.

I wish I could have said goodbye in a proper way. But what way is proper when I'm dying and suffering in my bed? I never wanted you to see me that way but I know if the roles were reversed, I'd be by your side every step of the way. As hard as it was for me to give up control, I thank you for being there. For me. For Erica. But you need to focus on you, whatever you decide to do, whoever you decide to be with. You need time for yourself. You're strong. You're tough. You will get through this. Please know that. Promise me you won't give up. Promise me you won't dive back into the hell alcohol provides. Stay away from Lee. He's a bad influence. You don't need the drugs. Keep running. Keep working out. Keep being you. But don't you dare give in.

The moment I found out the doctors couldn't do anything else for me, I wrote this letter. And then I ripped it up and tried again. I probably started this letter at least a hundred times. I didn't know what to say but I felt like I had to say something. I didn't even know if you would read this but knowing Hope, she would make you. So either way, if she's reading it to you or if you are reading this on your own, I hope you can hear my words. Hear what I have to say. Hear what I need you to know.

I also left you something. Know it is for you. It's for us. It's for all of you.

I love you, Xander.

Don't ever forget me.

Thank you. For making my twenty-eight years of living on this planet the best it could be. Thank you for helping me through some of the most difficult times a person should never have to endure. Thank you. For being you.

Caiden

I glanced up after the word left my lips, my gaze landing on Hope. Tears poured down her cheeks. It had been so long since Erica gave me the letter Caiden had written me. I could never find the courage to read it.

When I smoothed out the crumpled up piece of paper, Caiden's fancy script stared up at me. And although I read the words he had written so long ago, I felt he was speaking through me.

It had been two years since Caiden died. Since God took a hero. Since I was reborn.

As Hope greeted me when I left the pulpit, all I could think about was Caiden. How he would be standing back, arms crossed under his chest and a smug smile of I told you so on his face.

"He would be so proud of you," Hope said, pulling me from my thoughts.

Grabbing her hand, I walked with her to the back of the room, needing to be alone for a moment.

"Xander, are you—"

I cupped her cheeks and captured her mouth in a hard bruising kiss.

She sighed, relaxing against me, leaning into the passionate touch of my lips. "What was that for?" she asked when I released her.

"For being there for me and also…" I pulled out a small gold pin from my jacket pocket. "One year, baby."

Hope took the tiny item from me. "One year sober." She pulled out her own pin. "And one year for me." Five years and she was no longer addicted to the alcohol she craved. Bring me into the picture and she caved. I apologized every damn day and I would keep apologizing for almost setting her back permanently.

"I love you," I blurted, my cheeks heating. We had been together for a year, going to an AA meeting for our first date but we hadn't said those three words to each other again until…well…now.

Her eyes welled, her chin quivering. "I've been waiting…for so long to hear you say that."

"I'm sorry. I wanted it to be perfect. I wanted to say it to you when I knew I would be the last person that said it."

"What are you saying?"

"I'm saying I want to spend the rest of my life with you, Hope. We don't have to get married. We don't need to have any kids. I want you. That's it. Nothing more. Nothing less."

"I would like that. To be with you. To go to bed with you and wake up next to you."

"To spend every chance I can inside of you," I said, brushing my thumb over her bottom lip.

She shivered, her cheeks reddening. "I love you too, Xander."

***
(Hope)

My heart jumped when he pulled me in for a hug. Wrapping his arms around me, he held me against him, every inch of my soft body molding to his hard one.

At first, it had felt like I had a cup of water in the distance and I couldn't get to it. I had been so thirsty for him.

It had been a year. One. Year.

Looking in on the outside, nothing had changed.

Xander looked the same. I looked the same. We still fought occasionally but nothing like before. It usually resulted in what we wanted for supper or what we wanted to do for our evening. But it was definitely not like it was before Caiden died.

Xander trusted me. I could feel it. He didn't look at me with dark accusation. He didn't make snide remarks like he once did. He was…himself. He loved me. Completely. And I loved him in return. I had never loved him so much than right at that moment. The twinkle in his eye over being sober for a year proved right then this was it. This was meant to be. We were meant to be.

We would continue going to meetings together. He would continue to paint and I would continue to counsel people who gave into the sins of a bottle or a joint. Or worse.

Xander and I leaned against the back wall, holding hands and looking out into the small group of people. It was our home away from home. These people were our family now.

I glanced up at Xander.

His strong jaw ticked, his eyes taking on a faraway look. He was thinking about Caiden.

I knew I would never take Caiden's place in Xander's heart but I would like to join him. A flutter soared in my belly and I smiled. Placing my hand on my lower stomach, I nudged Xander.

"What's wrong, baby?"

"Nothing," I sighed contentedly. "Nothing at all."

ABOUT

J.M. Walker is an Amazon bestselling author who also hit USA Today with Wanted: An Outlaw Anthology. She loves all things books, pigs and lip gloss. She is happily married to the man who inspires all of her Heroes and continues to make her weak in the knees every single day.

"Above all, be the HEROINE of your own life..." ~ Nora Ephron

Website: http://www.aboutjmwalker.com/
Facebook: https://www.facebook.com/jm.walker.author
Reader
Group: https://www.facebook.com/groups/JMsJems/
Twitter: https://twitter.com/jmwlkr
Instagram: https://www.instagram.com/jmwlkr/
Goodreads: https://www.goodreads.com/author/show/51 32169.J_M_Walker
BookBub: https://www.bookbub.com/authors/j-m-walker
Amazon: https://tinyurl.com/y7dpjkud
Newsletter: https://tinyurl.com/ya9hycak

Want more? Head on over to my website for my complete backlist!
https://www.aboutjmwalker.com/books